OBEY ALL LAWS

OBEY ALL LAWS

A PROBATION CASE FILES MYSTERY

CINDY GOYETTE

LeVel
BEST BOOKS

First published by Level Best Books 2024

Author Photo Credit: Paul Hummel

First edition

ISBN: 978-1-68512-534-9

Cover art by Christian Storm

This book was professionally typeset on Reedsy.
Find out more at reedsy.com

For Craig, my first and toughest editor

Praise for Obey All Laws

"A hard-charging crime novel powered by combustible realism and driven by a fresh, new heroine—probation officer Casey Carson. Buckle up for a wild, white-knuckle ride."—Lee Goldberg, #1 *New York Times* bestselling author

"Goyette's *Obey All Laws* is an incredible debut shot with true-to-life details, making it an addictive page-turner. Casey Carson is a sharp, spunky series character, and I look forward to more."—James L'Etoile, award-winning author of *Dead Drop* and the Detective Emily Hunter series

"A dynamite start to an excellent new series. This is the kind of book that can grow legs and take off just by word of mouth. The character Casey Carson has grit, loyalty, and honor. *Obey All Laws* is a top-notch thriller, and I can't wait for the next one. Author Cindy Goyette is here to stay."—David Putnam, bestselling author of The Bruno Johnson series

"From the first page, *Obey All Laws* had me hooked! A propulsive debut, the novel is laced with realism, wit, and heart. And, of course, a crime worthy of Casey Carson's skills to solve! I can hardly wait to see what the author has in store next! Bravo!"—Mary Keliikoa, author of the award-winning *Hidden Pieces* and *Deadly Tides*

Chapter One

I realized I was in trouble when the door bounced open before my feet hit the front steps. "What the fuck do you want?" the man towering in the doorway said.

I recognized him as my new client from the mug shot in his file. I tried to disarm him with a smile but received a death glare back.

"I'm Casey, your new PO," I said in an upbeat voice.

Javier Ramirez was massive—at least six-foot-four. A grimy tank stretched across his puffed-out chest. Ropes of muscles running down bare arms were no doubt compliments of long hours on the weight bench during his recent stay at the Arizona Department of Corrections. The pitchfork tattoo on his bicep told me he was a member of one of Phoenix's more dangerous gangs. *Nice to know.*

Javier clenched his fists and bounced from one foot to the other. The vein on the side of his bald head pulsated. His eyes were crazy and popping.

All signs he was about to go apeshit.

My oh-crap meter tilted to the warning zone. I probably should have brought another officer or two with me, but I was used to working alone, and his gang involvement wasn't documented in the file I'd received.

"Look, Javier…" I backstepped off the front porch. "I just want to schedule an appointment. We can talk in the office tomorrow, okay?"

"I ain't going to no probation office, Lady. We can settle this here and now. Where's Hope?"

Good question. My cousin, Hope Carson, also a probation officer, had mentioned something about a conflict of interest when she gave me the case. She did not say the conflict might be my desire to live another day and Javier's plans to the contrary.

"Your case has been transferred to me." I struggled to keep panic from my voice, but I hit a high note that would surely bring a pack of stray dogs my way.

He spat on the dusty ground, continuing to flex his hands into fists. "She gave it to you. What did you do with it?"

I had no clue what he was talking about. "Do with what? We don't have a phone number for you…I just want to schedule an appointment."

Broad shoulders shifted as he moved down the steps. "I don't need no appointment. We both know we got bigger problems."

Like the fact that he was intent on assaulting me? So far in my career, my verbal de-escalation skills had gotten me out of some tight spots, but my charm was wasted on Javier. I moved my hand to the pepper spray clamped to my belt.

"Just call me," I tried. "We can set up an appointment on the phone." I was back-peddling now, moving across the yard, but he was gaining on me. I pulled out my pepper spray and aimed it at Javier's face.

Javier laughed. "You ain't gonna live long enough to use that."

I took another step back and pressed the lever. The spray hit him square in the eye. Javier didn't even blink.

I should have paid more attention to things like expiration dates. It was time for plan B—run like hell.

I turned to do exactly that, when my foot caught on a rock, and I fell flat on my ass. The hard dirt, like concrete after months without rain, sent shock waves through my body and reverberated in my molars.

Javier was over me before I could say ouch. I tried to hit the panic button on my police radio, but he ripped it out of my hand and tossed it across the yard.

Pepper spray dripped off his face onto mine. Not expired. The liquid burned my skin, my eyes watered, and it sent me into a coughing fit. Javier remained unfazed. Maybe because he was amped up on meth or maybe he was just mad enough to overcome the effects, but I had to find another way to stop him. Pulling a gun wasn't an option since I'd opted not to carry one, unlike some of my peers. Now I saw the gaping flaw in my thinking.

His hands wrapped around my shoulders before I could contemplate further, and he yanked me to my feet and latched onto my arm. I kicked his shin, but it had no effect as he pulled me toward the house.

It was in this moment—the one where my stupidity was staring me in the face—that I usually would have made a deal with the big guy upstairs. Get me out of this, and I'd be more careful next time. But the man upstairs and I weren't exactly on speaking terms since my mom died nine months ago. I couldn't let my family go through another loss so soon. I had to survive this.

Even if Javier had other ideas.

He held on tight and successfully dragged me closer and closer to the house.

"Fire!" I yelled, trying to get the attention of anyone nearby, as I used every ounce of strength I had to pull out of his grip.

But it was summer in the desert, and everyone was sealed up in their air-conditioned houses. No one could hear me.

Javier shook me like a wet rag. "Shut. Up."

My options dwindled. If he got me into the house, it would be a death sentence. I balled up my fist and swung, putting my weight behind it. My hand connected with the side of his head, and something flew out and landed on the ground. What the hell?

Javier's free hand shot up and covered his eye. I jerked out of his hold and stumbled back. Something crunched under my running shoe.

"My eye," Javier cried. "You stepped on my eye."

I looked down and saw a shattered eyeball under my shoe. "Ewe!"

"Bitch."

He lunged forward, and his empty eye socket zoomed toward my face. I felt for the keys in my pocket, yanked them out, and stabbed my three-inch long handcuff key into the gaping hollow where Javier's eye used to be. He stood dumbfounded and undoubtedly in a lot of pain. The key stuck into his head like a flagpole in the dirt. My other keys dangled, hitting him in the nose.

3

He growled. Foam sprayed out of his mouth like a rabid dog. Uh, oh. Now I'd really made him mad. No way was I winning a fight with this tank of a guy.

I did what I should have done right from the start—I ran.

Javier's heavy footsteps sounded on the sidewalk behind me. A vehicle approached, and I turned to wave them down, but the dark van didn't slow. It narrowly missed me as I made it to the sidewalk on the other side of the street. I heard the thunk before I saw Javier go airborne and land on his back like a turtle overturned in his shell.

The van was a blur as it continued on. Grateful for the help, I didn't bother to get the license plate number.

Javier lay still. I wondered if the impact had killed him but didn't intend to get close enough to find out. I ran to my Jeep, which I couldn't enter because my keys were stuck in Javier's head. But I felt comfortable with the distance between us. Well, that and the fact that he seemed unconscious. I pulled out my cell phone and dialed 911.

"Phoenix Police, what's your emergency?"

"Ah, this is Casey Carson with Adult Probation. I could use some help."

Chapter Two

The paramedics placed Javier on a gurney and loaded him into the ambulance.

"He's starting to come around," a freckled-face officer told me as I covered the speaker on my phone so my supervisor, Alma, couldn't hear. "The handcuff key in the eye socket was a nice touch."

I'd been trying not to think about that. I thanked the cop and got back on the phone with Alma, turning my attention to the gray Tahoe that pulled up behind my Wrangler. Betz, Detective Barry Betz, that is, got out and walked toward me, shaking his head.

He looked good.

Damn it.

He wore an ocean-blue shirt with the sleeves pushed up and Levi's that hugged body parts I'd long ago come to appreciate. His prematurely graying hair curled where it touched his collar. As he got closer, I noted lines around his sky-blue eyes I hadn't noticed at my mother's funeral. They certainly weren't there when we ended things almost three years earlier.

How the hell did he know I was even here?

I was so distracted, I forgot I had Alma on the line until I heard her say my name. "I'm fine," I told her. "Look, I gotta go." I disconnected as Betz came to stand before me.

He gave me the once over, a look of concern clouding his face. "Here I was, just monitoring the radio while having lunch, and I heard a call of a probation officer in trouble. I had a feeling it was you."

"She handled herself pretty well, Detective," Freckles said, joining us. "She

5

hit the guy so hard, his glass eye popped out."

"Whew," I said. "I thought that was his real eye. Probably why the pepper spray wasn't effective."

Betz shook his head and sighed. "You okay?"

I nodded. "Yep, fine." But the words caught in my throat and came out hoarse.

"You done with her?" Betz asked.

The cop nodded. "You should probably get checked out, Ms. Carson."

"I'm fine." I rubbed the finger imprints on my arm where Javier had grabbed me. "Just a few bruises."

Betz scratched the back of his neck— a sign I was getting to him. There'd been a lot of neck rubbing the last few months of our marriage. "You need a ride?" he asked.

Not sure how much longer I could hold it together, I held out my hand to the officer. "Just need my keys." Last thing I wanted was to fall apart in front of Betz, or anyone else for that matter.

"Ah, those will have to be surgically removed from Mr. Ramirez's skull, Ma'am."

Now that made me queasy.

Betz motioned toward his SUV. "Let's go."

Out of options, I followed and settled in the passenger seat.

"Where to?" he asked, starting the engine. "More specifically, which hospital?"

"No hospital. Just take me back to work. I have to talk to my boss."

Betz sighed, but he maneuvered the Tahoe toward my office. It almost seemed like old times. Betz was law and order down to his skivvies without all that macho stuff many cops were known for. I'd met him when he was investigating one of my charges a few years back, and he asked to ride along on a home visit. There was an instant connection, and by the end of the night, we were groping each other against the trunk of Betz's Chevy.

Unfortunately, mutual lust wasn't enough to keep a marriage going. Trouble was, Betz had the annoying habit of thinking he was right all the time. Impossible, since he often disagreed with me. It took us almost a year to agree on what color our new sofa should be. When we discussed bigger issues, like choosing a new car or, God forbid, having kids, we just about wore ourselves out. In the end, the only thing we could agree on was that we were better off as friends. Since the divorce, I tried to distract myself by dating other men, but no one made my heart flutter the way Betz had. So far, keeping my distance from him worked, but sometimes, I missed snuggling up to him after a long day.

I caught a glimpse of him with my peripheral vision. Hmm...

Betz glanced at me. "You sure you're okay?"

Back to the present. Not my favorite place right now.

I fought the urge to crawl onto his lap, wrap my arms around him, and let the emotions I choked back explode. "Fine," I said instead.

"I thought probation officers carried guns these days."

"It's optional." Although, after what happened to my mom, I had a strong aversion to them.

"Well, promise me you'll explore that option. These aren't puppies you're dealing with."

"I'm aware." I'd read the file when I'd received it the day before. Javier was a drug dealer, but he had no record of violence. Nothing to indicate he was more dangerous than the run-of-the-mill probationer. His gang affiliation had not been in the file, although I got the message the minute I saw his tats. Unfortunately, that was a little too late. Maybe he'd worn long sleeves when he met with Hope, and she hadn't seen the telltale markings.

"Why would you go there by yourself?"

"Doing fieldwork with another officer slows me down." Truth was that many POs worked alone unless there were red flags. Our caseloads were huge, and it took time to work with a partner. Even longer to find one I trusted.

"For the love of God," he said.

"Stop. We're not married anymore. You're not allowed to scold me."

"I just don't want to go to your funeral."

I crossed my arms. "Who says I'm inviting you?"

Betz laughed. "You don't give invitations to funerals." As quickly as his mood brightened, it darkened again. "I'm sorry I haven't checked on you since your mom—"

"It's okay," I said. He had come to the funeral, sat with me, rubbed my back while I sobbed. He'd text messaged me a few times afterward, but eventually he stopped. We were divorced. I understood.

He pulled up in front of my office and put the Tahoe in park.

"Thanks for the ride." I undid my seatbelt and opened the door. I had one foot on the ground.

"You sure you're okay, Case?"

I nodded, but as my adrenaline dump evaporated, nausea threatened to give me away. The concern in Betz's eyes only made it worse. I forced a smile, slid out of my seat, and walked into the building without looking back.

Chapter Three

Alma Martinez was on the phone when I walked in. She motioned for me to close the door and sit down. Files and papers littered her desk, and her inbox was stacked so high, the mountain of files overflowed onto the floor. She was usually a hands-off supervisor, which suited me just fine. But in a use-of-force situation, everything you did was scrutinized. There would be paperwork. Alma hated paperwork.

After I'd called Phoenix PD, I had reclaimed my radio from the bushes and informed dispatch I was waiting for police. After they questioned me, I called Alma and advised her of the situation. She'd offered to come and get me, but by then, Betz had pulled up. I wouldn't need a ride. Besides, I didn't feel up to being lectured by two people at once.

Alma finished her conversation and hung up the phone. "Casey, Casey..." She gathered her long black hair into a bun and held it there. "What the hell happened?"

"Hardly a scratch on me," I tried.

She let her hair fall, took off her glasses, and rubbed her eyes. "There is nothing funny about this. You could have been hurt."

I bent down and wiped an imaginary smudge off my running shoe. Betz always said tending to my shoes was my nervous tick. I hated people fussing over me.

"I looked up Ramirez," Alma continued. "Nothing jumped out at me. But the world is such a dangerous place these days. Many other officers only go out in pairs. It's not mandatory, but I'd feel better if you partnered up when you do fieldwork from now on."

"Everybody's so busy," I said. "Who has time to partner up anymore? Too much downtime when you're seeing another officer's people."

"I don't mind you getting a bit behind in your work if you're safe."

"It was on my way in."

Alma sighed. "I get it. You're a team player when you need to be, but you prefer to work alone. But sometimes—"

"I know, I know. Safety first."

"Is it because of Gina?" Alma asked.

Was it? Gina used to be a PO. We were hired at the same time and quickly became close. I trusted her. Until I found out she'd been lying on her timesheets, saying she was working when I knew she wasn't. When she got caught, she tried to get me to vouch for her. She wanted me to lie. My name was dragged through the mud even though I refused to back her claims. She got fired, and I hadn't heard from her in years. And I hadn't worked with a field partner unless absolutely necessary since then.

She looked like she wanted to say more, but thankfully moved on.

"You need to get checked out medically. And I want you to talk to our crisis intervention team as well. You've been through a lot this year, with your mom and all. You're probably numb right now, but this run-in with Ramirez is going to hit you hard eventually."

"Really, I'm good."

She put her glasses back on. "The doctor is not negotiable. Neither is the incident report I want on my desk in the next 24 hours. I take it PD will charge Ramirez with assault on an officer, but let's put a hold on him once he gets released from the hospital for probation violation as well."

"Will do."

"And I'll assign him to another officer, since you're now a victim."

Victim. Great. "Got it." My hand was on the door.

"Think about getting a field partner."

I nodded.

"Go to the doctor and then go home. You should take a few days off," she called as I limped out the door.

I appreciated Alma caring so much, but standing there listening to her list of concerns made me feel sick. I believed my coworkers respected me. We got along just fine, and many of them regularly came to me for advice on how to handle a case. But I only had a small circle of people I depended on. It pretty much consisted of my sister Kate and my mom. I had a friend from high school, but she moved away a few years ago, and we only talked once in a while. Betz had once been in that circle, but divorce changed that. I was like my mom in many ways, but I'd inherited my father's bullheadedness, and we often butted heads. People had to prove themselves for me to trust them. Even more so after what Gina did. Betz used to tell me that my life would be easier if I let more people in. I'd tried a few times, but look where that got me. My mother killed herself, Gina almost ruined my reputation, Betz and I split up, and my best friend moved away.

Back at my cubicle, I wrote an incident report. I had just emailed a copy to Alma and shut my computer down when my cousin Hope came to stand at the side of my cubicle.

"Got a minute?" she asked.

I wondered if she'd heard about Ramirez and had come to offer some information. She worked in a different office, so she wasn't usually in the building. "What are you doing here?" I asked.

"I'm in training downstairs."

"Glad you're here," I said. "That case you gave me…the conflict of interest—"

She held up her hand to stop me and nervously glanced over her shoulder. "Not here. Is there somewhere we can go to talk?"

I raised an eyebrow, but the frantic look on Hope's face made me comply. "Sure." I stood and led her down the stairs, through the break room, and outside to a courtyard area that we used to eat lunch during nice weather. It was empty today because it was one-hundred-and-eight degrees.

We stood in the shade, but sweat still dampened my T-shirt.

Hope's expensive clothes, shellacked nails, and highlighted hair were a testament to how much she cared about her appearance. Still attractive, but she looked like she hadn't slept in days, and she seemed preoccupied.

Other than family genes and both of us being POs, about the only thing we had in common was that we were both a bit man crazy. I was slowing down, but I had a history with men for sure, and the label stuck. Although Hope had never been married, she certainly had her fair share of relationships.

"I've been meaning to call you." She tapped a well-pedicured sandaled foot on the concrete. "We need to chat."

"I'd say. That client you gave me assaulted me today."

Her face clouded over. She ran a hand through her hair, and I caught sight of a bright emerald ring on her finger that was either a fantastic knock-off or cost more than my Jeep.

"Ramirez?" she said. "Oh my God, Casey. Are you okay?"

"Only because of dumb luck."

"You didn't go alone, did you?"

"I did."

"But I attached a note to the file warning you he was a dangerous gang member. Didn't you see it?"

I huffed. "No note made it to me."

Hope put her hand to her mouth. "I'm so sorry. It must have gotten lost when I transferred the file in interoffice mail. I should have called you and given you the low down instead of writing a note. Are you sure you're okay?"

I nodded. "Yes. You said there was a conflict of interest. What did you mean by that?"

Her eyes grew wide. "If he came after you, he must have found out. But how? I only told one person."

"Found out what?"

The door opened, and two POs walked out and over to the smoking area ten feet away. They nodded hello, then continued their conversation as they lit cigarettes.

"Not here," she whispered. "I have to get back to training, but stay away from Ramirez until we talk."

"Not a problem," I said. "He won't be in the community any time soon." I wanted to press her. My hands were still shaking after my encounter with her former client, and my tailbone screamed from my fall onto the dirt. But

Hope looked desperate, so I bit my tongue.

She glanced at her watch. "I have to get back. Can you meet me at Macayo's after work tomorrow?"

I would have said I had to check my schedule, but Thursday night, like all my nights, was free.

"How about sooner?" I asked. "Like tonight?"

"Can't. Look, I have to go."

As she turned, a shadow showed under her eye. I slid my sunglasses on top of my head so I could get a better look. She'd tried to cover the mark with makeup, but the darkness of a bruise was visible. I grabbed her by the arm to stop her from going inside. "Is that a black eye?"

She wrenched out of my hold and pulled her hair, so it covered the spot. "It's nothing."

Before I could press her, the door bounced open as another smoker exited. Hope took the opportunity to grab the door and hold it ajar. "Everything's fine." She let herself back inside and hurried down the hall.

But I knew by the pained look in her eyes that everything was not fine. Hope had a lot of explaining to do. I would call her later. My questions couldn't wait until dinner tomorrow night.

Chapter Four

Per Alma's instructions, my sister, Kate, met me out front in her SUV to take me to the county clinic. There were two empty car seats in the back for my niece and nephew. Her husband, Kevin, was home with the kids.

I slid into the passenger's seat, and she reached over and hugged me. "Okay, what happened?"

Kate hated my job, and I didn't want to give her more ammunition for when she often pleaded with me to find something less dangerous. "Just a little incident in the field. I'm fine, but it's policy that I get checked out, and I don't have my Jeep."

Kate slid her sunglasses in place and put the SUV into drive. "Bullshit. I know there's more to the story. Where's this place we're going?"

I gave her the cross streets of the clinic the county used for workplace injuries, and she started driving. Her blonde bob was perfect, as were her tan Capri pants and plain white shirt. Kate, who was two years older than me and my only sibling, always looked pulled together. I was pretty sure taking care of two people under five would have me tearing my hair out.

"So, you're not going to give me details?" she said, navigating through heavy traffic.

"Just an uncooperative probationer," I said. "You'll never guess who showed up at the scene."

Kate glanced my way. "Betz?"

I nodded.

She went wide-eyed. "And?"

"He looked great."

"Of course he did. He got a girlfriend?"

I shrugged. "Didn't come up."

"Not that it matters," Kate said. "You would never put yourself through that again."

"It wasn't so bad."

"Please." Kate turned into the clinic parking lot. "You were a complete mess when it ended. Knowing you're better off apart doesn't mean the split was easy. I was right there with you, remember? I always liked Betz; you know that. I just don't like to see you hurt."

"Splitting up was my idea," I reminded her. "Sometimes I wonder if it was a good idea, is all."

"Maybe, maybe not," Kate said. "I don't think anyone will be a good fit for you until you learn to trust people."

I didn't like the way the conversation was headed, picking at my personality flaws and all. I opted to change the subject. "You see Hope lately?"

Kate shook her head. "Not for a few weeks. Why?"

"Something's going on with her. Have you seen the rock on her finger?"

"An engagement ring?"

"I don't think so. It's not a diamond, but it looks expensive."

"They have some pretty good replicas these days," she said.

"I guess it could have been fake. She also had a black eye."

"Oh, no," Kate said. "Did she explain it?" She found a space and pulled in.

"Not really. We're having dinner tomorrow. I'll find out then."

Kate put the car in park. "Hopefully, she has a good explanation. I'd hate to think she was in a violent relationship. Do you want me to come inside?"

"Not necessary."

"I'm going to run an errand then," she said. "Text me when you're done."

The doctor who examined me found only a few bruises and a scrape on my knee. My tailbone, that ached every time I sat down, would heal on its own. I had no idea how the cut on my knee, or the tear to my jeans, occurred because I only remembered falling flat on my ass and being dragged across the yard. When I explained what happened, the doctor declared me lucky as hell and suggested I find a desk job. Although that sounded tempting, I'd be bored to death if I didn't get out of the office as much as I did. Today was an exception, but otherwise, fieldwork was my favorite part of the job.

After the doctor, Kate brought me to my place to retrieve the spare house key I'd hidden under a planter in my yard. Since my everyday keys were stuck in Ramirez's skull, they were dead to me—I had no plans to reclaim them. I let myself inside the house and grabbed my spare key to my Wrangler from the kitchen junk drawer.

Kate then drove me back to Ramirez's house to get my Jeep. All that running around pretty much used up the day, and it was after six when I returned home.

My place, a beige stucco bungalow, only stood apart from the houses flanking it because we all had different landscaping. One neighbor had rocks and cactus, the other grass, a palm tree, and a for-rent sign. Mine had grass and pine trees, compliments of the last owner.

Not much about the house spoke of me. My garage was nothing more than an empty room to park my Jeep, bicycle, and lawn mower. Just bare concrete and unpainted walls. No tools or junk from my life.

I let myself in through the door that led to the kitchen and flipped on the wall switch since the overcast sky had left the room dark. I tried not to think about the silence and emptiness of the place. My last boyfriend, Vincent, got the four-bedroom house we'd shared, along with almost everything in it. Occasionally, I thought about retrieving my share of furniture, kitchen stuff, and other doodads that make a house a home. But stuff comes with memories. And memories of yet another failed relationship were something I didn't need.

The inside of my new little two-bedroom, coined "cozy" by the realtor, looked more like the showroom at a thrift store than a home. When I first bought the place, Kate regularly rousted me out of bed at dawn on Saturdays to hunt for garage sale bargains. The result was a household of mismatched finds that reflected other people's lives. Better than being slapped in the face with my past every time I walked into the room, I supposed.

I sat on the sage green velvet sofa Kate found at an estate sale, kicked off my running shoes, and pulled off my socks. The sofa sagged just enough to be comfortable, a smidgen shy of being deep enough to swallow me whole. I leaned back, sank into the cushions, and watched the ceiling fan go round.

Rubbing the sore spot on my upper arm, I reviewed the day's events. Despite the obvious reason that we deal with criminals, I never thought of my job as particularly dangerous. Sure, there were instances around the country where probation officers got hurt, and we even had a few shooting incidents in our department, but most people didn't pose a threat. Most of my clients were decent people who had made a mistake or two due to drug use, toxic relationships, and just plain poor choices. Still, one could never predict human behavior.

Although a field partner was more a luxury than a practicality, I probably should have brought another officer with me since I'd never met Ramirez before. If I'd gotten Hope's note, I would have had back up.

If I were honest, I'd admit that I didn't form the easy relationships most people did. I didn't have a lot of patience and mostly enjoyed spending time puttering around the house or hiking at my own pace on the numerous trails around the valley. But now that I saw that Alma viewed my lack of friends as a weakness, it really depressed me.

I knew there would be many questions about the Ramirez thing from management, and I had some of my own. I still didn't know why Hope had asked me to take the case in the first place. What was the whole conflict of interest thing about? I assumed he'd hit on her, or she knew someone close to him. Those were common reasons to switch cases. But Ramirez's bizarre statements and Hope's refusal to talk about it at the office had me wondering if something more sinister was at play.

I slid my phone out of my pocket and scrolled through my contacts for Hope. I pushed send and waited while the call went to voicemail. I left a message asking her to call as soon as possible. Tomorrow night's dinner was too far away.

I felt like talking but couldn't think of anyone else to call. My dad would be three drinks to drunk by now. Ever since my mom died, he'd been as out of reach as if he'd died with her. I missed my mom every day, but at times like this, the ache in my heart was almost unbearable.

A framed photograph Kate had given me shortly after our mother's death sat on the table beside me. I reached for it and held it on my lap. It wasn't my favorite picture, but it was the last photo we'd taken before she died. We were on vacation in Coronado, my mom's favorite spot. I squinted into the sun and had a stain on my shirt. Kate looked perfect, as usual. But my mom looked distant. Like she was already fading from our lives. I probably wouldn't have even noticed if we hadn't held a service for her just a week later. When the medical examiner ruled her death a suicide, the look on her face in that photo became even more haunting. No matter how unhappy she looked in the picture, I still couldn't come to grips with her taking her own life. Kate reminded me of how distracted our mom was in the weeks before her death. I'd been in the midst of leaving Vincent and was a bit preoccupied, sure, but I still thought I would have known if my mom, my closest confidant, was so miserable the only way out was a gun to her head.

In the beginning, I questioned the suicide ruling. I asked a lot of questions of family members, her friends, and her coworkers at the county attorney's office. Everyone told me I was in denial. It was natural, they said. Something like this was always hard to accept. There were no signs of foul play. Still, it nagged at me. Mostly in the middle of the night, when I stared at the ceiling fan, wide awake, my thoughts running wild.

Holding the photo to my chest, I let the tears come. They didn't come often, and I felt guilty for that. And when they came, I usually stopped them. Suck it up. Take a deep breath. What did a good cry get anyone other than a red, puffy face and a runny nose?

I put the photo back in its place, shuffled into my bedroom, changed into my running clothes, and headed out for the three-mile loop I tried to do a few times a week. The heat of the day made my steps sluggish, but I felt like I deserved to feel uncomfortable, although I wasn't sure why. If the run didn't clear my head, there was always plan B—the bottle of Chardonnay in the refrigerator.

Chapter Five

At the sound of my alarm, I instantly regretted the several glasses of wine I'd downed after my run the night before. My head pounded, and my mouth tasted like last week's garbage. I slid out of bed and padded to the bathroom. The bright overhead light was a bad idea, so I brushed my teeth and showered in near darkness.

In my world, Diet Coke can solve a lot of problems, and by the time I swallowed half a can, I felt marginally better. My cell on the kitchen counter buzzed with an incoming text message. I couldn't fathom who would bother me so early, and I was hoping it was my cousin returning my call. When I saw an old photo of Betz pop on the screen, I picked up the phone. *Call me.*

I wondered if he had some information on Ramirez as I made the call.

"Hey," he said on the first ring.

'Hey," was my brilliant reply.

"Just wanted to check on you. You doing okay?"

"Fine," I said, but I was too tired to make it convincing. "Any news on Ramirez?"

"He'll survive. Your key didn't cause any damage. He lost his eye in a prison fight a few years ago. Most of his injuries are from being hit by the van. You know this guy's history, don't you, Case?"

I twirled my Diet Coke on the counter. "I know he's a drug dealer."

"He's Diablo," Betz said.

Diablo was a local motorcycle gang that made the Hell's Angels look like Boy Scouts. The reports I had access to didn't show Ramirez was a member. I had, however, figured it out when I saw the telltale pitchfork tattoo on his bicep. By then, it was a bit too late for the information to do me much good.

"He joined while in prison last time," Betz added. "I talked to the guys in the gang unit, and Diablo has been active lately. Dealing heroin has always been their thing, now they've expanded to human trafficking. Nasty stuff."

"Cripes. I've been reliving what happened. Ramirez seemed to think I had something on him."

"Any idea what that could be?"

"I just got the case," I said. "I didn't notice anything in the case notes other than a dirty UA for meth." Oftentimes, we got tips from the community that our people were running amuck, but there were no such notes on Ramirez. I wanted to talk to Hope before I brought her name into this, so I didn't share her connection with Betz. "Maybe there isn't anything," I said. "Maybe he was just meth paranoid."

"Maybe. I'm worried about you, Case. Don't think Diablo will let what you did to Ramirez go."

"I'll be careful."

"I think this deserves more than keeping on your toes. Can you stay with your sister for a while?"

"And drag her family into this? No."

"A friend?"

Betz knew I wasn't exactly rich in the close friend department. "Can't think of any. Look, I know you mean well, but I can take care of myself. I'll be careful. Promise."

"Case…"

"I gotta go." I hung up, my hand shaking as I reached for my Diet Coke.

My phone immediately buzzed again. Thinking it was Betz calling back, I was about to ignore it, but then I saw it was a text from Hope. *Sorry I haven't returned your call. I have a lot to tell you, but I think it's best to wait until dinner and do it in person. I'll see you at five.*

Not ideal. Something was going on with my cousin, who had a connection to a very dangerous man who was in a very dangerous gang. My thoughts roamed to all kinds of wild ideas as to why she didn't want to supervise him but felt it was okay to send him my way, but I tried to quiet them and wait for Hope to explain herself. So much easier said than done.

Chapter Six

The best way to take my mind off Ramirez and his thug buddies was to get back to work. Back on the horse and all that crap. At least I could add my baton to my limited arsenal if anyone came after me. I'd lost confidence in pepper spray after Ramirez. Then again, what were the chances I'd have to fight another guy with a glass eye?

I made it to the office before my coworkers, allowing me to dodge the gossip and questions I didn't feel up to answering. I rifled through three file cabinets before I located my baton. Since it was optional that we carry a firearm, my chemical spray and baton were the only weapons I had to defend myself. And we weren't required to carry our baton. I dusted my nightstick off and stuffed it into my messenger bag, then slipped a new canister of pepper spray into my pocket. After attaching my client address list to a clipboard, I returned to my Jeep.

Logging onto the radio per procedure, I started driving toward South Mountain. It was a cloudless summer day and already ninety degrees at eight in the morning. Usually, I stopped checking the weather forecast in May, as for the next six months, it would be pretty much the same: hot and sunny, with the occasional monsoon storm that would blast through the valley in minutes, leaving everything covered in dust.

I heard Hope clear an address on the radio. Dinner was hours away. Maybe I could convince her to meet me earlier after I finished a few home visits.

A Harley pulled up beside me as I waited at a red light. My pulse quickened, hoping the rider wasn't associated with Diablo and looking for me. The old man sitting on the bike smiled a toothless grin and sped off as the light turned green. Deep breaths, I told myself. Not everyone on a motorcycle was a gang member.

I continued through South Phoenix until I reached Clyde McKinley's house at the base of South Mountain. Clyde was on probation for exposing himself at a bingo game at the senior center. Some things still surprised me.

One car sat in the driveway. Everything was quiet. No signs of vicious dogs or one-eyed gangsters waiting to jump out and get me. I needed to relax but called in the address and did all the required safety checks just the same.

At the front door, I knocked and waited. Clyde jerked the door open and smiled. "Why hello, Officer Carson." He wore a cowboy hat and nothing more.

"Jesus, Clyde!" I fixed my gaze on his face. "Put some pants on."

He shrugged thick, freckled shoulders. "I live an alternative lifestyle." A tilt of his hat in my direction, and he turned, padding down the hall.

I tried to shield my eyes from the sight of his broad, white ass, but before I could look away, the image stained my brain.

"Cripes," I mumbled. And I thought yesterday was a bad day.

A few moments later, Clyde returned wearing gym shorts. I took a brief tour of his house to make sure there was no pornography or evidence he had contact with children, or, in Clyde's case, the elderly, which were conditions of his probation. We briefly talked about how treatment was going. I reminded him to report to the probation office next Wednesday, discussed the appropriateness of wearing pants when opening the door, and returned to my Jeep.

Sometimes, I couldn't help but roll my eyes.

The rest of the morning was routine. As the hours passed, I started to relax. Ramirez and the threat Diablo posed never left my mind, but I was able to keep it near the back and not dwell on it. It had been a while since I heard Hope's voice on the radio, and I wondered if I'd missed her going out of service.

I had started back to the office to document my home visits when the dispatcher came over the radio. "X-Ray Young 203."

Hearing Hope's call sign, I turned up the volume. There was only static as the operator waited for Hope's response.

"X-Ray Young 203?"

Sometimes, officers forgot to go out of service and were later found safely back at their desks, oblivious to the fact that people were looking for them. Because I was already on edge, I didn't take comfort in that thought. I grabbed my cell, scrolled down to Hope's personal number, and pressed the call button. It rang four times before going to voicemail.

Ending the call, I tried to remember the last address Hope had called in, but all I could recall was that it was in central Phoenix. If the dispatcher followed procedure, she'd try to reach Hope at her work and personal phones before she called Hope's supervisor and sent police to her last known location.

I wasn't about to wait. I phoned dispatch. "This is Bravo Adam 145. You hear from X-Ray Young 203 yet?"

"No," the dispatcher said. "Do you have any information that might help us locate her?"

"I don't. Can you give me her last twenty? I'm her cousin, and I want to make sure everything's okay."

The dispatcher hesitated. "I've informed her supervisor and police."

"Please. I'm in the field and can get there quicker than her supervisor. I can meet the police."

She gave me the address. "Let me know what you find."

"Will do." I dropped my phone onto the passenger seat, flipped a U-turn, and headed uptown.

After violating a few unimportant traffic laws and one semi-important one, I turned onto Mountain View Street. Hope's Jetta was parked on the curb at a house west of her client's house. Maybe she was having radio trouble, but my heart beat faster in anticipation of finding something worse.

I drove slowly past her car. Empty. The house was a single-story bungalow with crumbling stucco walls and a yard full of overgrown weeds. I turned around in a driveway three doors down and parked my Jeep two houses away.

After calling in my location to the dispatcher, I got out and surveyed my surroundings. Spider webs attached to a car on blocks in the driveway had me deducing it had been there a while. A fresh oil stain on the concrete behind it told me a working vehicle was parked there not long ago. I took my pepper spray out of my pocket, which I admit is not the preferred carrying method, and kept it in my left hand, my radio in my right.

I walked to the front door, my heart pounding, taking note of two folding chairs and a rusted coffee can overflowing with cigarette butts. A heavy metal screen door, the kind you can't see through, was ajar. Hooking it with the toe of my Converse, I pulled it toward me. I rapped on the almost-closed wooden door with my radio and pushed it open a few inches.

"Hello? Probation. Anybody home?"

Radio traffic transmitted, and I turned the volume down. Yet the traffic continued to broadcast loud and clear. The sound directed my gaze to the filthy carpeted floor about five feet away. An identical radio lay among dirty laundry and discarded food wrappers.

"Hope?" I broke into a cold sweat. Stepping a foot inside, my eyes took a moment to adjust from the bright afternoon sun to the darkened living room. The place looked like a car crash. Empty pizza boxes, soiled rags, and crushed beer cans littered the carpet. Cigarette butts erupted from various makeshift containers. Pill bottles sat on a coffee table that was crooked because one of the legs was broken. A once white, now grimy sofa had red spatter on one of the cushions.

While I wrestled with the idea of going further inside, which was a major safety no-no, a patrol car came to rest in front of the house.

I backed my way out and hurried over to the cruiser as a pudgy gray-haired cop grunted his way out of the car. He adjusted his gun belt under his substantial gut. "You Hope Carson?"

"Casey Carson," I said, relying on the presence of my police radio to help me look legit. My identification was in my pocket, but I hadn't seen my badge since I switched purses several months before and hoped he wouldn't ask to see it. "Hope's my cousin. This is the last contact she called in. Her car's out front, and her radio is on the floor in the living room."

He scratched the beard on his puffy face. "So, her stuff's here, but she's not."

"Exactly." Sherlock.

"You go inside?"

"Not really. I saw her radio from the doorway. And it looks like there's blood on the couch."

Another patrol car pulled up, and a petite red-headed officer with a pixie cut exited and walked over to us. Peter Pan without the tights. The first officer explained what we knew so far. I wanted to scream at them for their lack of urgency, but that wouldn't get me anywhere.

"Wait here," Sherlock said.

Both officers walked toward the front door, where they announced their presence. When no response came, they disappeared inside, guns drawn.

Time seemed to stand still. I paced the driveway, chewing my already ragged nails. Questions rushed through my head faster than I could answer them. Was that blood on the sofa? Where was Hope? Did this have anything to do with the conflict-of-interest thing she wanted to tell me about?

The cops emerged and conferred out of my earshot. Peter Pan walked to her car, cell phone to her ear. Sherlock came my way. "She's calling our sergeant. Don't like the looks of things, what with her car and radio being here and no sign of her. And it looks like blood on the couch."

My own blood seemed to drain from my head, and I swayed, dizzy. It sounded so much worse coming from the cop and not my over-active imagination.

"Do you need to sit down?" Peter Pan said as she joined us. "You don't look so good."

I lowered myself onto the three-foot high block wall that separated the yards. I tried to think clearly, but a rush of bad thoughts continued to jam my brain. I shook my head clear, tried to concentrate. My family had been through enough. This couldn't be happening.

The best chance of finding Hope was to know who she'd been here to see. I took out my phone and called dispatch.

After updating the operator, I asked for Hope's supervisor's number, jotted it on my palm, and quickly made the call.

"Probation, this is Ian."

"Ian, it's Casey Carson. I'm out at Hope's last twenty, and things don't look good." I gave him the rundown. "PD is here."

"I know," Ian said. "Dispatch called me. I was just looking at Hope's caseload to see who lives there."

"That's what I need," I said, grateful for some useful information. "The defendant's name and info so I can give it to police."

"Hold on," Ian said, keyboard clacking. "Here it is. Harlen Jones. On for delivery of a controlled substance. Glancing at Hope's last notes, he's been reporting and going to treatment. No red flags, but I'm not taking time to read everything. I've got to call my boss, then I'm on my way."

"Okay." I disconnected and called Betz. No way was I going to trust Sherlock and Peter Pan with my cousin's safety.

Chapter Seven

Betz was at Harlen Jones' house in twenty minutes. The squad lieutenant pulled up behind him, followed by several patrol cars and a Channel 6 news van. I inwardly rolled my eyes when I saw Suzy Vega jump out of the vehicle. Suzy had it in for law enforcement, and if she was covering the story, she would find whatever angle she could to make the cops, or the probation department, look bad.

Betz and Lieutenant Jasmine Faulk stood in front of me, their backs to Suzy. Jasmine was Betz's older half-sister. She was nearing forty and had a muscled body that spoke to the countless hours she spent at the gym. She gave everything one-hundred-and-ten percent. Her hair, short and wild, worked with her high cheekbones and purposeful gaze. She was no-nonsense on the job and protective of Betz, like a mama bear with its cub, since they were the only family each other had. Their parents were unreliable drug addicts, and at a young age, she'd pretty much taken over raising Betz. She was fiercely proud of how they had risen above their troubled upbringing, and Betz was indebted to her for guiding him through his otherwise messed-up childhood.

I was terrified of her.

I hadn't seen her since the divorce, although she did send a card when my mother died. "Don't talk to the press," Jasmine said. "She'll find some way to make us look like buffoons." Then she looked at Betz. "What are you doing here, Bro?"

Betz cleared his throat and nodded in my direction. "I heard Casey on the radio. What do you expect me to do?"

"Ah," Jasmine said, nodding. I could see her weigh her response. She once considered me family, and I felt like I could depend on her if needed. On the other hand, she thought I broke her brother's heart.

"If I told you to stay out of this, you wouldn't listen, would you?" she said to Betz.

He shrugged. "Don't see how I could."

Jasmine ran a hand through her hair. "You're on special assignment right now, right?"

He nodded.

"I'll talk to your commander to see if you can help us with this, but everything runs through me, got it?"

"Got it." Betz turned to me. "Any more updates since you filled me in on the phone?"

"Nothing."

While I brought Jasmine up to speed, Betz pulled Harlan Jones' mugshot up on his iPad, then got on his radio and put out descriptions of both Hope and Harlan. He then called the Department of Motor Vehicles, learning that a red Ford pickup truck was registered to Harlan. He also relayed that information. Minutes later, all police officers on duty in the state were looking for Hope, Harlan, and his red pickup. Other officers blocked off Harlan's house with yellow crime scene tape, and detectives and a forensic team swarmed the property.

Suzy Vega stood on the street, talking to the Phoenix Police Information Officer, who was doing a good job keeping her away from us.

With the swarm of activity unfolding around us, I continued to focus on breathing. I took deep breaths, hoping they would keep me from passing out or throwing up from the nerves that choked me.

My phone buzzed in my pocket. A text message from Kate. *Saw the story on the news about a missing PO. Just making sure you're okay.*

Not me, I messaged back. I didn't want to tell her about Hope over a text message, but Suzy Vega would put the information out soon, so I had no choice. *It's Hope. Not many details yet, but I'll call you as soon as I know something.*

29

My God, came her response. *Keep me posted*

Betz finished talking to another detective and then walked over to me. "How you holding up?"

I grimaced, knowing if he were too nice to me, or if he touched me, I'd be reduced to a pile of hysteria.

"What can I do?" I asked. "I feel so useless. Dispatch doesn't start looking for you until they haven't heard from you for an hour. She could be far from here by now."

"Not much we can do at the moment."

Not good enough. "This may not be related," I said. "But something was going on with Hope and Javier Ramirez. She asked me to take over his case due to a conflict of interest, but she never told me what that was. We were supposed to meet for dinner tonight, and she said she'd give me the details then."

He took notes and nodded a lot. "You've had a rough couple of days. I'd tell you to go home, but I know you wouldn't do it."

"I can't. I have to help."

Betz rubbed the back of his neck and sighed. He knew better than to argue with me, but I could see him struggle with the idea. "You feel up to driving?"

I nodded eagerly.

"You could go to her office and review the file on Jones. Maybe there's something in there we can use. Some associate info, employment, that kind of thing."

"You'll let me know the minute you learn anything?"

"Of course."

He walked me to my Jeep. My legs felt like noodles, and I mentally questioned my ability to drive a stick shift out to Hope's office in Mesa. At my car, Betz gave me a long, tight hug. "We'll find her."

Suzy Vega waved me over, looking concerned, like she actually cared about anything but a story. But I wasn't that stupid.

"Get out of here," Betz said. "We got this."

I lingered in his embrace a second longer, then cleared my throat and pulled away. "Talk to you later." I climbed in my Jeep. Without looking back at Betz or the crime scene, I drove away.

The Mesa office was at least thirty minutes away in late afternoon traffic. I spent most of the trip wondering what Hope had gotten herself into. Was her disappearance connected to Ramirez? If only I'd pursued a closer relationship with my cousin when I had the chance. I scolded myself then for thinking I wouldn't get another opportunity. It was best to remain positive.

When we were kids, we lived next door for a few years before our parents decided they didn't want to live that close, and my family moved across town. There were four cousins. All girls. Me and Kate. Hope and her younger sister, Joy. We were each a year apart – Kate, then Hope, then me, followed by Joy. We played with the other children in the neighborhood, hung out at the school bus stop in the mornings, and walked home together in the afternoon. I tried to align myself with the older two, but often got left behind with Joy. It was enough of a battle for me not to be seen as the pesky little sister, but with Joy in tow, it was impossible.

As we got older, Kate and Hope frequently gave us the slip, and I was stuck with the often-disagreeable Joy. That was probably when I got comfortable with my own company, because it beat hanging with my younger cousin, who whined and tattled whenever she didn't get her way. By fifth grade, she'd packed on enough pounds that she was almost twice my scrawny size. She sat on me more than once, held my arms over my head, and threatened to spit in my face unless I gave her my dessert. I never forgave her for that.

The four of us drifted apart over the years. By the time Hope graduated high school, I barely knew her. We pretty much lost touch during college, only hearing about each other through our mothers and meeting briefly on holidays. We followed each other on social media, but that was superficial information. When my aunt and uncle died in a car accident shortly after college, the connection weakened even more. Hope moved to Seattle but returned to Phoenix when a relationship ended badly. When the probation department was hiring, I forwarded her the job announcement. Once she landed the job and was assigned to a different office, we rarely saw each other.

But last I saw her, she wanted to talk. To share whatever the hell was going on. Did what she wanted to tell me about Ramirez have something to do with her disappearance? Ramirez was temporarily out of the picture, but gang members always had backup. I should have pressed her for more information when I had the chance.

I brought up Hope's Facebook and Instagram accounts, only to find they'd been dormant the last few months. That was unlike her.

I hadn't accepted Joy's friend request when she sent it a few years back, because her drama-filled life sucked my energy dry. But last I'd heard, she was happily married and living in Boston. She called when my mom died but didn't come out for the memorial service because she was battling the flu. I hadn't had a real conversation with her in years, and I wasn't looking forward to reconnecting over such bad news. I would wait to call her, I decided, until I had something concrete from Betz.

By the time I fought afternoon traffic to Mesa, it was after five. The office was closed, and I was unable to get inside, since my ID access only worked at my downtown Phoenix office. I scrolled down the list of contacts in my phone, hoping I knew someone who might be working upstairs that could let me inside. It was then I realized Ian hadn't made it to Harlan Jones' house before I left. I redialed his cell.

"I just got here," he said. "Traffic was a bitch. I just spoke to Detective Betz. Neighbors didn't hear anything."

"Figures," I said. "Everybody's sealed in their houses with the air blasting, it's so damn hot."

"Gotta love Phoenix in the summertime."

Enough with the chitchat. "Ian, I'm at the Mesa office. I want to review Jones' file. Know how I can get in?"

"Pete Pajerski should still be there." Ian gave me Pete's number, and I wrote it on the back of my hand. Ian promised to keep me posted if he learned anything new, and I did the same.

I dialed Pete's number.

"Yello?" was the greeting.

"Pete, Hi. I don't think we've met, but I'm Hope's cousin, Casey."

"Casey Carson," he said. "You're that leggy blonde with those intense blue eyes. We met at Alex Smart's retirement party. I tried to buy you a drink, but you turned me down. I'm crushed you don't remember me."

I remembered him now. He had an overdeveloped torso, skinny legs, and breath that smelled like wet dog. Everybody called him Jerski, just not to his face. "Well, Pete, I'm standing out front and need to get inside. Can you let me in?"

"Sure thing."

He must have run down the steps; the door flew open so quickly. Face-to-face, I found myself wishing he'd taken a minute for a breath mint. He still had the wet dog thing going on.

"Step inside, gorgeous," he said with a wink.

Somebody needed a sexual harassment refresher. I ducked under his arm, then followed him upstairs to the office he shared with Hope. While Jerski's desk was orderly, Hope's was covered with files and papers.

Sometimes, I wondered why anyone wanted to be a PO. The work was endless, and it was impossible to get everything done as new crises popped up without warning. I hoped Jerski would back off so I could concentrate. "I'm going to look for a file."

He pushed some papers aside and sat on the corner of Hope's desk. "Ian told me about Hope. What do you think happened?"

"Wish I knew." I opened a file drawer and found a thin file for Harlan Jones. Most of the file contents were electronic, but the monthly reporting slip that clients filled out whenever they came into the office were kept as a hard copy. I plopped the file on the desk and smiled at Jerski. "Look, Pete, I need some space. Do you think you could give me a moment?"

Jerski hopped off the desk, bowed, and backed toward his own desk just three feet away. "Whatever my lady wants."

Oh, brother.

I ignored him as I pulled up Harlan's information on Hope's computer. He was on supervision for three years for delivery of methamphetamine. He had a lengthy criminal history, which made his sentence to probation odd. He had mostly drug cases on his record, some identity thefts. The sentencing minute entry showed the assigned attorney was Matthew Peterson, a private attorney, who would be pricey, but he clearly delivered. Maybe a family member had helped him out. I could tell by Harlan's house that he wasn't flush with cash. However he managed it, he got his money's worth. Most of our clients used the Public Defender's Office, or as I'd heard them called, the public pretenders. There were good ones, no doubt, but most of them were so overworked they barely learned their client's names, never mind knowing the cases well enough to offer a good defense. But most people in the system simply didn't have the means to pay for a private attorney like Matthew Peterson.

I flipped the hard file open. Harlan listed himself as unemployed, living alone, and the only associate he wrote down was his girlfriend, Mary McDonnell.

I grabbed the receiver off Hope's desk phone and dialed the number Harlan had provided for Mary. I got a cheery voicemail message and left my name and cell number, asking Mary to get back to me as soon as possible. I also tried the number Harlan listed for himself, but his phone was turned off.

Frustrated, I closed Harlan's file and glanced up at Jerski, who watched me like a dog waiting for table scraps.

Focusing on the mess of papers on Hope's desk, I shuffled through them, finding the typical stuff a probation officer deals with. Evaluations from treatment providers, progress reports, urinalysis test results, and court orders. Hope was old school, and her day planner was open to today. She'd written "field" in the morning slot, and "dinner with Casey" was circled in the 5 pm space. I checked my watch, five-thirty. Neither of us kept that appointment.

I quickly scanned the planner for anything out of the ordinary, but nothing jumped out at me. I shoved the calendar and Harlan's file in my messenger bag and turned my attention to Jerski. "Before I go, anything about Hope I should know? Was she dating anyone?"

"She turned me down, just like you did." Jerski followed me to the door. "She doesn't talk to me much, but I know she's seeing someone. Always texting with a lovesick look on her face. She's gotten flowers twice this month."

I adjusted the strap on my shoulder bag. "You know anything about the guy?"

"No," Jerski said. "But if you let me buy you dinner, I'll see what I can remember."

"You'll do that anyway, Pete, like any decent person would." I handed him my card. "Use this to contact me about Hope, and only about Hope," I warned.

I had the feeling Jerski had more dog-like qualities; he seemed like the kind of guy who would follow you home, and that was the last thing I needed. I hurried down the stairs and into the stifling summer night.

Chapter Eight

In my Jeep, I unzipped the window and blasted the air conditioning to blow the blistering air out of the car. The steering wheel was too hot to touch. Retrieving a hair tie from the center console, I pulled my damp hair to the base of my neck and tied it back before sending a message to Betz.

Any news?

I didn't know what to do next. I pictured roadblocks across the state looking for a red pickup truck. Of course, they'd had time to leave the state, maybe even make it to Mexico.

Satisfied with the airflow, I zipped the window shut and put the Jeep in reverse.

In my rear-view mirror, I caught sight of Jerski flying out of the building, arms waving madly as he ran toward me.

Good Lord. I put my car in neutral and unzipped the window. "What?"

He came to a stop, breathless. "I found a set of keys in Hope's duty bag. Thought maybe you'd want to swing by her place. See if we find anything."

We? I held out my hand for the keys. "Thanks, Jer...I mean Pete. That's actually a good idea."

Jerski clutched the keys to his chest. "I'm not letting you go alone. I'm coming with you."

I searched my brain for an argument but only managed an eye roll as Jerski ran around to the passenger side and hopped in.

"I need to get that lock fixed," I said under my breath as Jerski fastened his seatbelt. All I could do to make the trip bearable was fish in my purse for a pack of gum. "Want a piece?" I'd shove it down his throat if he didn't accept it.

As we drove toward the suburb of Ahwatukee, an upscale part of Phoenix at the base of South Mountain, Jerski talked nonstop. Most of it I could ignore, but then he mentioned Betz.

"What?"

"Your ex-husband. I hear he's a cop."

That was creepy. I barely remembered meeting Jerski, yet he knew about Betz. "So?"

"I'd like to meet him. I've applied to Phoenix PD four times and can't get an interview. I have PO experience for goodness' sake; you'd think they'd beg me to join the force."

Maybe the psychological testing held him up. But Jerski had another idea. "It's the minorities. They take all the jobs."

I glared at him. "Like women?"

He opened his mouth to respond but then seemed to think better of it and stared out the window.

I was sure it had nothing to do with his buzz-cut hair, camouflage army pants, and the badge that unnecessarily hung around his neck, making him look like he was about to conduct a raid. "Betz doesn't have anything to do with the hiring process. He's a detective."

Reminded of Betz, at the next red light, I grabbed my cell and checked to see if he'd answered my text. He hadn't.

"Do you know how dangerous that is?" Jerski said. "Do you know how many crashes occur because of distracted drivers?"

Crashing might be preferable to continuing this conversation, but I dropped my cell into the cup holder and continued on.

We exited onto Ray Road. I'd never been to Hope's new house, but she'd given me the address a few months ago. For once, I didn't procrastinate and stored it in my phone. As I drove, Jerski programmed the address into the GPS application on his phone, and an annoying computer-animated voice dictated our route.

Leaving strip malls behind, we entered true suburbia. Neighborhood after neighborhood of stucco houses with red tile roofs. My house could fit into most garages.

"Please turn right," the GPS directed.

I hung a right, dead ending at the gate that protected the upscale community from riffraff such as us. Hope hadn't given me the access code. I pulled to the side and put the Jeep in park. "This can't be right. Hope's a PO like us. She can't possibly afford this neighborhood."

"She's always on the phone about the house," Jerski said. "Interior decorators, landscape artists, flooring companies."

"It doesn't make sense." As far as I knew, Hope's parents didn't leave her much when they died, and I couldn't think of anyone else who would leave her an inheritance. What was Hope up to?

From the rear-view mirror, I saw a car pull in, and the gate swung open. Not intending to miss the opportunity, I tailgated through.

The GPS guided us past rambling houses with meticulous front yards to a two-story that backed up to the mountain preserve. As I climbed out of the Jeep, I had a nagging feeling. The house easily cost half a million dollars, and that was in a bad economy.

We walked up the walkway and rang the doorbell. When no one answered, Jerski tried the keys he'd lifted from Hope's desk drawer. None of those worked. While he pounded on the door, I got personal with the oleander bush under the living room window.

The blinds were open just enough to give me a view of a room that resembled something from a glossy, overpriced magazine—expensive sofas, rich mahogany furniture, and exquisite fabrics. I was almost convinced that we were in the wrong place, but then I spotted my grandmother's hutch in the corner.

I straightened and exited the bushes. "I'm going around back."

Unlatching the gate, I traipsed through a lush, well-manicured backyard to the sliding glass door that led to the family room. Jerski was on my heels.

We stood, our noses pressed against the glass. Before us was yet another beautifully decorated room with rich, heavy furniture and expensive accents.

"Nice place," Jerski remarked.

Uneasiness dried my throat. "Yeah."

I checked the patio slider. Locked. I took a few steps back and spotted a second-story window. It was closed, normal in the summer heat. But maybe since it was hard to access, it would be unlocked. "See if there's a ladder in that shed over there, would you?" I asked.

Jerski stared at me. "What? You gonna break in?"

"It's not breaking in. She's my cousin." Okay, so it was a gray area. But I knew Hope wouldn't mind if I went inside. The cops would do that soon anyway. And each moment that passed could equal Hope's life in greater danger. I'd take my chances.

Jerski sighed and started toward the shed on the other side of the pool, mumbling under his breath the entire time. He returned shortly with a ladder. "I'm not climbing up there," he said. "This doesn't feel legal."

"I didn't ask you to." I leaned the ladder against the house, so it lined up under the window. "Just make sure you hold it steady."

Jerski put his hands on his hips. "No kidding."

I climbed several rungs before I remembered I wasn't fond of heights. Ignoring the constriction in my chest, I reached the window.

Squinting through the screen, I could see the room was a mess. Bedding was on the floor, and drawers and their contents were strewn about. I tried to wedge my fingernails under the frame of the screen and wished I didn't have the habit of chewing them to stubs.

"Can you get me a screwdriver or something I can use to pry this damn thing off?" I called down to Jerski.

"Uh, oh," Jerski said. "This is getting ugly. This is against the law."

"Just get me something."

Jerski pulled a Swiss Army knife from his pocket and climbed two steps so he could hand it to me. "If we get busted, I'm telling them you made me do this."

In my head, I mimicked his words like a snotty five-year-old as he handed me the knife. "I didn't ask you to come."

A few moments of work, and the screen popped off easily. Okay, so I bent the frame and ripped the mesh a little before letting it fall within a few inches of Jerski, but Hope wouldn't mind.

Sure enough, the window was unlocked, and I slid it up enough to go in headfirst, snagging my Levi's on something as I pulled my body through the opening. I landed on a pile of clothes.

"What's going on up there?" Jerski yelled.

I hung my head out the window. "Room's been ransacked. Put the ladder away, and I'll come down and open the back door."

Stepping over the mess in the room, I hurried down the hall to check the other bedrooms, careful not to touch anything since it was now looking like a crime scene. Since Hope had disappeared from her client's place, it was doubtful she would be in the house, but I looked for her just the same. I prayed I wouldn't find anything I couldn't handle. A guestroom was torn apart, as was the office. What the hell?

I backed out of the last room and took the stairs two at a time to the first floor. I slid the back door open, but before Jerski could come inside, I stepped out and closed the door behind me.

"I don't like the looks of this," I said. This was looking less like a kidnapping because Hope was in the wrong place at the wrong time and more like she'd become involved in some serious shit. I felt protective of Hope and wished Jerski wasn't here to witness whatever this was.

I woke my phone and called Betz. When he answered, I said, "If you're not busy, I could use your help."

"Again?" Betz said.

Chapter Nine

"I told you to go to Hope's office," Betz said when we met him in the driveway. "Not initiate a full-fledged investigation. This is police business."

"Yeah, well... You guys move too slow."

"I had a patrol officer come by earlier. He saw nothing alarming. Things like warrants are needed before you barge into somebody's house."

I looked at my shoe. Jerski lurched forward and pumped Betz's hand. "It's nice to meet you, Detective. If you don't mind, I have a few questions about my application to Phoenix PD."

"Easy, Pete," I said. "Let's deal with my cousin before we plan your career."

Jerski slid his hands into his pockets and lowered his gaze like a chastised child.

"So?" Betz asked. "What did you find?"

"Upstairs has been ransacked."

"You have a key to your cousin's house?" he said. "I didn't think you were that close."

Jerski cleared his throat and made a show of being fascinated with the hair on his arm.

"Not exactly," I said.

"Then how did you get in?" Betz asked with a sigh.

"I sort of climbed in a window," I said softly.

Betz raised an eyebrow. "You break or just enter?"

"The window was unlocked."

"Yeah," Jerski said. "She only needed to climb a ladder and pry the screen off to get in."

I shot Jerski my best death glare. And people wondered why I liked to work alone.

Betz rubbed the back of his neck. "Is there a door open now?"

"The back one."

"Let me call this in," Betz said. "There are procedures to follow."

"I don't think she cares much about procedures," Jerski said.

"Maybe you should call a cab, Pete. I don't want to take up any more of your time."

"No way. This was my idea, remember?"

Betz shook his head and made a miserable attempt to suppress a grin. "Let's get started. Why don't you show me the office first."

Jerski had a knack for pushing my buttons, and Betz, like a peeping Tom, seemed to enjoy the show.

I led Betz to the back door with Jerski in tow.

"Nice pool," Betz said.

I gave the yard a second look. There were queen palm trees, fronds twisting in the breeze behind a kidney-shaped pool with a waterfall. The patio was complete with a misting system, over-stuffed patio furniture, and a bar. It looked more like a resort than a backyard. The only thing missing was a cabana boy with a tray of margaritas.

Betz and Jerski followed me inside.

"Don't touch anything," Betz warned. "This could be a crime scene."

We walked through the kitchen. Two wine glasses were set to dry in the dish rack. "Looks like she had company last night," I remarked.

"She dating anyone?" Betz asked

"Think so, but no idea who," I said.

"I saw her being dropped off at work the other day," Jerski said. "She got out of a sweet BMW."

"Can you describe the driver?" Betz asked.

"The windows were tinted," Jerski said. "I couldn't see inside."

I led Betz and Jerski upstairs to the office. Betz surveyed the mess from the doorway. "I'm going to get a team out here. Hopefully, whoever did this left something behind." We toured the rest of the second floor and headed for the stairs.

As I walked back by the office, I spotted a worn leather briefcase on Hope's chair. I beelined straight for it, running my hand over the soft, cracked leather. I would have recognized it even if it hadn't been monogrammed with my mom's initials. CLC. Carissa Lynn Carson. My dad gave my mom the briefcase when she landed the job at the district attorney's office when I was a teenager. She carried it to and from work every day. Why in the world did Hope have it?

Sure, I'd been slow to go through my mom's things, even when Kate begged me to. It was just too hard. Had Kate given Hope the briefcase? No, she would know better than to give away something of such meaning without checking with me first.

Despite Betz's instructions not to touch anything, I lifted the flap and looked inside. It was empty.

"Let's go," Betz called from downstairs.

I would return for it once police had done their thing.

I found Betz and Jerski in the kitchen. "Strange that downstairs wasn't touched," Jerski said.

"Looks like they either got interrupted or found what they were looking for," Betz offered.

His cell rang, and he brought it to his ear. "Betz," he said. His expression was grim, and he nodded a lot. My heart constricted, wondering if there was bad news about Hope. He hung up and turned to me. "Ramirez is fully conscious. I better get over there. I'll have a team finish up here."

Chapter Ten

One benefit of being in law enforcement is the ability to have personal information redacted. I hoped that would stop Ramirez and the rest of Diablo from tracking me down at home. But with today's technology, I didn't feel very protected.

Betz went to the hospital to question Ramirez, first making me promise I would go home and leave the investigation to the police. Jerski had gotten on my last nerve by the time I dropped him back at his office. He offered to buy me dinner, but I passed, claiming I had no appetite, which was mostly true.

Driving home, I realized I couldn't put off alerting the family about Hope's disappearance any longer.

At my house, I poured myself a glass of Pinot and settled on my sofa with my phone. I couldn't face calling Joy, so I started with Hope's coworker Elise, who also worked at the Mesa office. Rumor had it they were close. I was sure she'd heard of Hope's disappearance, with the news coverage and all, but I wanted to see if Hope had shared anything useful with her before she disappeared. POs were on call twenty-four-seven, and I was counting on that, but her voicemail said she was on vacation for the next two days. I left a message but hoped this would be over with Hope home safe and sound before she ever called back.

I moved on to Kate. When she answered, I heard the television in the background as well as my nephew Kyle, who was wailing. "I've been going crazy waiting for your call," my sister said. I pictured her stirring spaghetti sauce while soothing Kyle with one hand and hanging wallpaper with the other. Okay, she probably wasn't hanging wallpaper.

I gave her the Cliff Notes version of Hope's disappearance, fighting to be heard over the crying.

"Jesus," Kate said. "No hope of a reasonable explanation?"

"If there was, wouldn't she come forward?"

"I left her a message yesterday," Kate said. "I was thinking we should get together after what you told me about her black eye, but she never called back."

"Do you know who she was dating?"

"Gosh," Kate said. "She dated a lot of guys. It was hard to keep them straight."

"Anyone who stood out, maybe?"

"Not at the moment." My four-year-old niece, Ashley, begged for a cookie. "No treats before dinner," my sister said. "Did you call Joy?"

"I'll give you seven million dollars if you do it."

Kate laughed. "Nice try, but I have a bit going on."

No arguing with that. I promised to keep her posted and ended the call.

After taking a moment to enjoy the tranquility of my house, I called Joy. I took a big gulp of wine while I waited for her to pick up, half-hoping her voicemail would say she was unavailable for the next six months.

"Son of a bitch!" came the voice at the other end. "I told you to never call me again, you roly-poly mother fucker."

I sprayed my mouthful of wine across the coffee table. "Joy?"

She took a quick breath. "Who is this?"

"Casey. Who did you think it was?"

"Oh, God, Casey. I thought you were Harry, the son-of-a-bitch. I kicked him out two weeks ago, and he keeps begging to come back. I just hung up on his no-good ass for the second time tonight. I thought he still didn't get the message that I'm done talking to him. 'Cause I am. I'm through with him…" She fell silent for a heartbeat, then started sobbing.

Talk about timing. I wished my news was something I could put off. "I can see this isn't a good time," I said. "But I do have something important to discuss."

"I'm glad you called." The sobbing stopped as instantly as it had started. Hate and bitterness returned like a second personality. "I need to get out of here. I was thinking of coming your way. I'm through with this place. Yes, that's what I need, a little distance between me and that heartless mother—"

"I know the rest," I interrupted. "Sorry to hear you're having marital problems, but we've got problems here."

"Marital problems!" Her voice rose so high, wild dogs were probably making their way to her door. "Is that what you call it when someone you've loved...Someone you've wasted the best years of your life on... Someone who prefers our interior decorator to his wife... And I'm left with a living room that's painted a God-awful burnt orange... Oh, God, I'm having chest pains."

Oh, boy.

"I'm putting my head between my knees. If I pass out, call 911."

I grabbed my wineglass and sucked the whole thing down.

"Okay," she said. "It's passing. Where was I?"

Ah, an opening. "Have you heard from Hope lately?"

"She's no help. She'd just say I told you so. She'd say I never should have married that lumpy lowlife in the first place. She'd say—"

"Joy!" I yelled so loudly, I startled myself. "I think something may have happened to your sister."

"Well, why didn't you say so?"

I grabbed my wineglass and headed to the kitchen, where I refilled it with one hand while holding the phone with the other. "When was the last time you spoke to her?"

"Last week, maybe. Why, what happened?"

I gave her the most succinct version of events I could manage, trying to keep the possibility that Hope was okay and that this was a big misunderstanding open, so Joy didn't start hyperventilating again.

"Is it her blood on the sofa?" Joy asked.

"I don't know. Investigations take time, and the police haven't gotten that far."

"Can't you get them to move faster? Can't Barry do something?"

Her use of Betz's first name felt wrong. Too familiar. "He's doing something. He's one of the detectives on the case. He put a rush on the blood, but the lab is backed up."

"I'm coming out. I'll be on the first plane out in the morning."

Oh, boy.

"And I'll stay with you."

I'd need a lot more wine. "I don't think it's necessary for you to come out just yet," I said with a silent prayer. "I mean, what can you do?"

"I can help, that's what. I'm not sitting here by the phone when I can be there looking into things."

I couldn't blame her. If the shoe were on the other foot, I'd already be driving to the airport. My phone beeped, signaling a low battery. I reached for the charger and stood leaning over my counter so I could plug it in and keep talking.

"Can you tell me anything about the guy she was dating?"

"I remember her talking about some guy. Quinn, I think. It reminded me of that actor, Aidan Quinn. He has the most incredible eyes, don't you think?"

"Focus, Joy, focus. Do you know anything about their relationship?"

"Seemed like he was just a filler boyfriend."

"Filler?"

"You know, a guy to tide you over until the right one comes along. She's had so many boyfriends. Kind of like you."

I let that one pass. She did have a point. In high school and college, I had a string of boyfriends, but nothing serious until I met Betz. I had one relationship after our divorce and almost married Vincent, but came to my senses before I could walk down the aisle. Anyway, that wasn't the point. "Let me know when your plane is due, and I'll pick you up at the airport."

"Do you have a pool?" Joy asked. "It's done nothing but rain here, and I could really use some sun."

"No, I don't have a pool. See you soon." I ended the call and finished my wine.

I stopped myself from pouring another glass. Two was my limit, and I wanted to stay semi-sharp in case I got a call about Hope.

Grabbing my messenger bag, I pulled out Hope's day planner and the file on Harlan Jones and laid them on the counter. I flipped through the planner. The pages were full of client appointments, court appearances, hair, and doctor appointments. The usual stuff. I thumbed to the back page, where she'd listed several names and phone numbers, including my own. One name jumped out at me. Joel Quinn. Could this be the filler boyfriend Joy talked about?

It wasn't much, but I thought Betz should know about Mr. Quinn, so I phoned him and left a message. He called back within five minutes, the sound of paper rustling and crunching noises in the background.

"What's for dinner?" I asked.

"Dinner, hell, this is lunch. I've hardly taken a bathroom break. It's been homicide city tonight. What started out as a home invasion turned into a carjacking and assault on a police officer. Three people dead. Four, if you count the suspect who jumped off an overpass on I-10. Add that to all the calls we've been getting about Hope sightings since her story hit the news."

"Any of those pan out?"

"Unfortunately, no."

I leaned back against my kitchen counter. "What did Ramirez have to say?"

"He lawyered up. We're keeping him under guard, so we're hoping he won't be able to get word to Diablo to go after you."

I swallowed the ginormous lump in my throat. Best not to think about that. "Look, I got a possible name of a guy Hope may have been dating. Got the info from Joy, and she's not the most reliable source. Don't know where Hope got the black eye or if that has anything to do with her disappearance. Maybe the boyfriend angle won't get us anywhere."

"Give me the name," he said. "Until we find her, all details are important. I'll have somebody look into it."

I gave him the name.

"So, you spoke to Joy?"

"Remind me to tell you about that when you have a few hours."

"How'd she take it?"

"She's catching a flight out tomorrow."

"You up for that? I remember you two having a complicated relationship."

"I have no choice."

"Look, Case, I gotta go. Be careful and remember your limitations. Call me before things turn to crap, not after."

"Funny," I said.

I hung up and looked around my quiet kitchen. I still felt the warmth of Betz's voice, so why did I feel so alone?

Chapter Eleven

I settled at the kitchen table with a sandwich I threw together and my tablet in front of me. At my home page, I typed in Joel Quinn. I got a few hits, but nothing that jumped out at me. I grabbed Hope's planner again and opened it to the page with Joel's number. As long as I didn't ask any questions that could mess up the investigation, it wouldn't hurt to see how he knew her and just what their relationship was.

But when I called, the phone just rang like it was turned off.

Back on my tablet, I found an online phone book and one listing in Tempe for Joel Quinn. Some people still had landlines these days. I tried that number.

A woman answered, sounding groggy. A glance at the clock over my fireplace told me it was just after ten, a little late to be calling people, but the evening had gotten away from me. The deed was done, so I asked for Joel.

"Who wants him?"

"My name's Casey. It's important I speak with him."

She let out a barking laugh. "You and every other ho in town. I got better things to do than take his messages."

Boy, people were grumpy tonight. "Look, I never even met the guy. I need to speak to him about my cousin."

"What about your cousin."

"It involves a police investigation."

"You didn't identify yourself as a cop."

Be vague, Case. Let her infer what she wants. "May I speak with him?"

"He's not here. Claims he's working, though I doubt that's true."

"Where does he work?"

She hesitated, then sighed. "Don't see why I should protect his cheating ass. It's a place called Technerds. It's a computer repair shop in Tempe. Down off Mill on 5ᵗʰ. He says they have some big project, and he's been working a lot of overtime. My guess is the only thing working overtime is his pecker."

"Well, thanks for the info." Too much of it maybe, but I appreciated her ratting out the bastard. "Could I have his cell number?" Although that was probably the number in Hope's planner, and the phone was turned off.

She hesitated. "I don't feel comfortable giving that out."

"I understand. If you hear from him before I can track him down, can you have him give me a call?"

Silence. I pictured her contemplating taking the message versus packing her bags and leaving his no-good ass. For her sake, I hoped she was looking for her suitcase.

"Give me a second to find a pen," she said. "Okay, go ahead."

I gave her my information, thanked her for her time, and disconnected. Another Internet search told me Technerds was exactly where she said it was. I dialed the listed number. A recording told me to call back during business hours.

A dead end for the moment. I slipped on my running shoes and headed for the door. I'd never be able to sleep anyway.

Technerds was about two blocks from Arizona State University off Mill Avenue in Tempe. Crowds spilled out of noisy bars and trendy restaurants. Young women in super short shorts clung to guys in board shorts and flip-flops. For a minute, I wished I was twenty again. Then I remembered the bring-it-on attitude that came when I'd recently turned thirty. Failed relationships had plagued my twenties. I hoped maturity would bring stability to my life. Problem was, I didn't feel very mature.

I parked my Jeep in a space reserved for visitors behind Technerds. Being so late, there was only one other car in the lot. An old Toyota Camry, I assumed belonged to Joel, occupied the spot closest to the back door of the business. I walked over and, using the limited light my phone provided, peered through the windows. It looked like a fast-food restaurant had exploded inside. Wrappers, drink cups, and French fries covered the seats and floorboards. I couldn't imagine Hope being attracted to a guy who lived like that.

I turned my attention to the no-frills single-story red brick structure as I made my way through the parking lot and around the side to the front entrance. A white sign, complete with a cartoonish nerdy-looking guy with a crew cut and thick, black-rimmed glasses, his hands on a keyboard, hung over the door.

The double glass door was locked. A sign in the window indicated they'd open at ten in the morning. Enough light spilled from the back room for me to make out two plastic chairs and a laminate counter. Pretty low-tech for a tech place if you asked me. I pounded on the glass door, hoping that if someone was in back, they would hear me. My knocking met with zero results. I returned to the back of the building where I'd left my Jeep. One knock and the back door popped open.

A lanky guy with bushy brown hair and a goatee looked me up and down. He seemed disappointed, like he expected somebody else. "We're closed," he barked. He tucked his polo shirt into his pants and checked the zipper of his fly.

Looked like Joel's wife might be right about the overtime thing. I tried to see past him, thinking I'd get a glimpse of some floozy buttoning her blouse. Hoping that floozy would be my cousin. But Joel moved to block my view.

"Hey, Joel," I said, guessing he was the guy. "You got a minute?"

He eyed me suspiciously. "And who are you?"

"I'm the cousin of a friend of yours."

"Which friend?"

"Hope Carson. I understand you two were dating."

Joel cringed, turned to see if anyone was behind him, and stepped outside, closing the door. "I don't know where you heard that. I barely know her."

I'd dealt with enough liars to know he was at least omitting part of the truth, but I didn't feel comfortable confronting him about it in the dark

52

parking lot. My encounter with Ramirez had at least taught me that much. "Have you heard from her in the last few days?"

"No." He pushed his hands into the pockets of his Dockers.

"She find out you were married?"

He laughed. "You've got it all wrong. Hope wasn't interested in me like that. Why are you asking all these questions anyway?"

"She's missing. You have any idea where she could be?"

He frowned. "Yeah, saw that on the news. How did you get my name?"

"She'd written it down, which means you must have a connection to her."

He didn't answer.

"Look, I'm really worried about her, or I wouldn't be here." I could think of a million places I'd rather be than in a sketchy parking lot in the middle of the night.

He glanced over his shoulder toward the back door, checked his watch, and looked past me into the parking lot. Maybe he was expecting someone else. "You should go."

"But…"

He turned to go back in the building. "My advice," he said, hand on door, "is to mind your own business. If Hope had, you wouldn't be looking for her." He ducked inside and pulled the door shut, clicking the lock into place.

What the hell did he mean by that? I pounded on the door, but he didn't come back.

It was quiet, the noise of the main street, about a block away, had died down. Joel's warning raised the hairs on the back of my neck. My oh-crap meter was practically screaming at me to leave. I hadn't given it the respect it deserved at Ramirez's place, but not this time. I had my key in the lock of my Jeep when another car pulled into the lot; its headlights illuminated me like I was on stage.

I shielded my eyes from the light, my heart hammering, and strained to make out the occupants. But I couldn't see a thing.

I expected the car to park. Or honk. But it idled in front of me for a moment, then did a K-turn, barely missing me in the process. As the lights moved away, my vision came back, and I could just make out a male driver and a female passenger. The woman was young, maybe not quite a woman at all. She gave me a look of hopelessness just before the car left the lot.

A chill raced down my spine, and blood roared in my ears. Something wasn't right. I jumped inside my car, shoved the key in the ignition, and shot out of the parking space, and sped across the lot. Traffic forced me to stop before entering the street. By then, the car with the girl was gone.

Was it someone just turning around in the Technerds parking lot or a friend of Joel's who didn't want a chance meeting with me? I couldn't get the haunted look on the girl's face out of my head.

When traffic broke, I pulled onto the street and forced myself to breathe. Slightly calmer, I let the uneasy feeling guide me. I would send Betz a text when I got home. I'd had enough excitement for one night. Joy was arriving tomorrow, and I saw a sleepless night ahead of me.

Chapter Twelve

Eight-thirty the next morning, my cell phone rang, jarring me from thoughts about Hope and what could have happened to her. I sat in bumper-to-bumper traffic on Interstate 10, and I wasn't going anywhere any time soon. Checking the number before answering, the prefix told me it was someone from work. "Probation, this is Casey."

"Hi, Casey. It's Nancy Rivera from Court Liaison. Afraid I have some bad news for you."

Like Court Liaison ever had good news. "Go ahead."

"Judge Dorfman's requesting your presence in court at nine."

Nine was impossible unless my Jeep could fly.

"What for?"

"The Michael Crowne case."

"I have no idea who that is."

Nancy chuckled. "He's on Andy Bell's caseload. You're covering while he's on vacation, right?"

I sighed and looked down at my Levi's and T-shirt with a spot of Diet Coke above my right breast. "Right. Any chance you can get a continuance? I'm not dressed for court, and there is no way I can get there in time." Not to mention, I had no idea who Michael Crowne was, what he was on supervision for, or why he was presently before the court.

Nancy cleared her throat and spoke in a whisper. "This is Dorfman we're talking about. Difficult Dorfman."

"I don't know anything about the case."

"I have the petition Andy filed. You can read the allegations when you get

55

here."

I looked at the jammed freeway in front of me. "Okay, but I won't make it by nine."

"I'll stall him best I can. Just get here as soon as possible."

Like I had a choice. I put my blinker on and got off at the next exit. Hopefully, side streets would get me there faster. Either way, I had a feeling this was going to suck.

I snuck into Judge Dorfman's courtroom twenty minutes late. Probation violation court usually had a pretty casual atmosphere. Attorneys ran in and out, conferring with inmates on the chain and out-of-custody defendants, as well as witnesses, while other matters were heard. Not in Dorfman's courtroom. He demanded silence. One person talking at a time. My blood pressure spiked just entering the room.

Luckily, the judge was not at the bench to notice how late I was. Nancy, who was seated at a small desk next to the judicial assistant, saw me walk in and motioned me over.

I pressed through the swinging gates that separated spectators from the heart of the courtroom and walked to Nancy's side.

She handed me the petition Andy Bell had written to revoke Michael Crowne's probation. I scanned it. Crowne hadn't reported, hadn't lived at an approved address, had tested dirty for meth a zillion times, and had not paid his court fees. In other words, he hadn't done squat. The attached report had a recommendation to revoke his probation. Court Liaison could have easily handled this. What did Dorfman need me for?

"All rise," the bailiff said, jumping to his feet.

Everyone stood as Dorfman glided into the room. At well over six feet tall, he looked quite impressive in his black robe. His jet-black hair was streaked with gray. Although too distinguished for my taste, he was handsome.

"You may be seated." Dorfman settled at the bench. He perched bifocals on his regal nose and looked at the file before him.

After calling the case, the defense and county attorneys gave their names for the record. I never heard of the county attorney, but Matthew Peterson represented the defendant. I remembered Peterson's name from Harlan Jones' file. He was private, which meant he needed to give Crowne his money's worth. Michael Crowne was taken off the chain by the deputy and, still shackled, was seated next to his attorney.

"Has the probation officer managed to show up?" Dorfman asked as every word was recorded.

I cleared my throat. "Andy Bell is on vacation, your honor. Casey Carson here on his behalf."

The judge looked over his glasses and gave me the once over. "And dressed like a lumberjack."

I smoothed my hands over my jeans. "Sorry, Your Honor. I was given short notice of the proceedings today."

I felt myself shrink as he stared at me.

"There are several mistakes in this petition before me, Ms. Carson."

I bit my tongue, assuming a snappy comeback would not win him over.

"Do you have a copy?" he asked.

"It was just handed to me."

"And?"

"I haven't had a chance to review it carefully."

Dorfman leaned back in his chair. "By all means, take your time. The court has nothing better to do."

He drummed his fingers on his desk. The county attorney turned from the prosecutor's table and stared at me, as did counsel for the defense. In fact, every eye in the courtroom was on me except Nancy, who seemed overly interested in the files before her. I looked down at the paper in my hands and couldn't concentrate on a damn thing.

"I believe I will need the file to detect any errors," I said.

Dorfman sighed. "Let me guess, you didn't bring it."

I kept eye contact with him and tried to look composed even though I felt like jumping over the bench and strangling him. "No."

"Which further proves my point. I've called you here today because I'm sick of reviewing shoddy work. Motions from attorneys with typos, bad grammar in reports, dates that don't match on this petition."

I crossed my arms.

"Am I making you angry, Ms. Carson?"

He was calling me out for the mistakes of others. Angry didn't begin to cover how pissed off I was, but admitting it would not only be career suicide, but it could also earn me a contempt charge. "No."

"Well, I'm angry," he said. "I want you to go back to your office and tell your coworkers what happened today. Spread the word that incompetence will not be tolerated in my courtroom. And you better pray the next paper that crosses my desk with your name on it is in order. Professional. And with merit. I am a judge. Do you know what that means?"

The courtroom was so quiet; I was afraid Dorfman could hear my blood boil. "I don't know how to answer that."

He sighed, took off his glasses, and rubbed his eyes as if dealing with an idiot like me was incredibly tiresome. "Respect. For me and the job I do. Do you understand?"

"Yes." Got it. You are God because you have a robe.

He turned to the inmate. "Please stand, Mr. Crowne."

Crowne jumped to his feet.

Ass kisser.

"It's your lucky day, Mr. Crowne. Although I'm sure your behavior on supervision has been deplorable, I am dismissing the petition to revoke your probation. I simply cannot find you in violation with this piece of crap I've been given. You are to report to Ms. Carson by day's end. Don't let me see you back here again." He closed the file and slid it toward his judicial assistant. "Next case."

I was shaking when I walked over to Nancy and handed her back the petition. I marched out of the courtroom, feeling Dorfman's purposeful stare on my back. I wished Andy Bell a second-degree sunburn as he sat his butt on the Beach in Mexico. He owed me big.

I waited in the hall, trying to calm down while watching for Matthew Peterson at the same time. A few minutes after the hearing I was still wound tight when Peterson came out the door, stuffing a file into his briefcase while keeping a brisk stride. I hurried beside him. "Mr. Peterson, can I have a minute?"

He never missed a step. "I've got a trial that started ten minutes ago."

"I'll be quick." I struggled to keep up with him. "What can you tell me about Harlan Jones?"

He stopped at the elevator and repeatedly pushed the up button. "Off the top of my head, not much, other than the name's familiar."

"That's understandable. You represented him about eight months ago. But I'm a bit desperate. My cousin went missing from his house yesterday."

He stopped and faced me, running a hand over his sparsely haired head. "I don't know anything about that."

"I'm not saying you do. I'm just trying to find anything that might help locate her."

The elevator opened, and he scurried inside. "Look, I'm sorry about your cousin. But I don't see how I can help you."

The door started to close, and I stopped it with my hand. "If you think of anything..." I held out my card. "Please."

He took my card, and I allowed the door to close. Peterson watched me, like he wanted to say something after all, but then the door shut.

On my way out, I opted for the stairs. On the first floor, I hurried down the long corridor and out the side door onto 3rd Avenue. The County Attorney's Office loomed ahead, and the sight stopped me as memories of my mother flooded back.

It used to be the most natural thing in the world to wait on the front steps for her to exit the glass door, hand held high to block the sun, as she scanned the area for me. We'd typically walk to the Greek restaurant two blocks away. The restaurant was often frequented by court staff. If we had something personal to discuss, we'd walk a few blocks more where the walls didn't have ears.

She always asked me about my day and listened like my answer was the most important thing in the world. No one really asked anymore. Sometimes Kate did, but she had so much going on in her life with her kids.

My chest tightened. I missed my mom so much; it was sometimes hard to breathe. I waited for the anger I felt toward her for selfishly taking her life, but today, it didn't come. I just felt sad. I turned away from the building and headed for the parking garage.

Chapter Thirteen

T
he Violent Crimes Bureau, and thus Betz's cubicle, was located at the main police station in downtown Phoenix. A squat, four-story building, the seventies architectural marvel took up most of a city block. On the west edge of the hustle and bustle of the city's business district, it stood off to the side with a couple of crappy hotels and seedy bars.

I found a spot behind the building and went in through the public entrance. The uniformed cop stuck behind the front desk yawned as I showed him my badge that I had dug out of an old backpack that morning. Best to carry it if I was going to be running around looking for Hope.

He pointed to a sign that told me as long as I displayed my identification, I didn't need a visitor's tag. I folded my badge case over the waistband of my jeans, making the shield clearly visible. He nodded in approval, and I was free to go about my business.

On the third floor, I made my way down the clinical hallway to a door labeled Criminal Investigations and stopped at the reception desk protected by bulletproof glass.

Marge Hewson swiveled in her chair and met me with a welcoming smile. She'd been the receptionist ever since I'd known Betz, probably before. She carried herself with more confidence and grace than a supermodel. The detectives in the bureau once had a bet going regarding Marge's true hair color, as it was never the same for more than a month, and it was often dyed to match her outrageous outfits. Nobody ever won that wager, as Marge claimed she no longer remembered the natural color of her hair. Today, it was as bright as the nectarine-colored muumuu she wore. "Long time, girlfriend."

"Yeah, well… Divorce has a way of changing one's routine. How've you been?"

"Riding the wave to retirement," she grinned. "Sixty-two more days."

"The place will go to hell without you."

Marge laughed. "Betz is in back. I'll buzz you in. Don't know how the poor guy's holding it together, half the detectives are in training in Tucson, and we've got cases up the yin-yang. I'm sorry about your cousin."

"Thanks." The door squawked, and I pushed it open, entering a large room with row after row of cubicles. Industrial gray carpet met slate blue partitions. Each workspace was equipped with a built-in desk and file cabinet. Several desks were messy, some anally clean, but most lay in between. Some were occupied, but many were vacant while detectives were in training or working in the field. Insults flew between occupied cubicles like fighter planes. I walked down the aisle until I came to Betz's desk at the end of the row. If he craned his neck, he might have a view of the building across the street and South Mountain in the distance.

He sat, leaned back in his chair, tennis shoes propped up on his desk as he spoke on the phone. His desk definitely fell under the messy category. Jumbled piles of papers were six inches deep. I knew Betz well enough to know that despite appearances, he could put his finger on whatever he needed in seconds. Organized chaos.

I waited for him to finish. He raised an eyebrow when he saw me and spoke like he was wrapping things up.

I leaned against the side of his cubicle, eyeing a mug shot of Harlan Jones on his computer monitor. There were no personal touches at his desk. At one time, my picture hung on the bulletin board above his computer. I averted my eyes, so he didn't see that it bothered me that I'd lost that place in his life.

Betz hung up, crossed his arms over his chest, and gave me the once-over. "You doing okay?"

"Working on it. Any news about Hope?"

"Afraid not."

I sighed. "You have a chance to run Joel Quinn yet?"

On cue, Rick Johnson walked up, scratching his ass. I'd forgotten how endearing a room full of testosterone could be. "Oh, hey, Case." He smiled at me, then focused his attention on the paper in his hand. "Mr. Quinn has a few arrests. Trespassing, DUI, a couple of domestic assaults. Nothing to be ashamed of if you're white trash."

"Any warrants?" Betz asked.

"Well, yeah. He's got one for failure to appear."

"So, you'd have reason to pay him a visit," I said.

Betz reached out and took the printout from Rick. "You know where he is?"

"I do," I said. "Technerds."

"Technerds?" Rick said.

"It grows on you." I filled them in on my visit to Joel. "I got a feeling they are up to something shady. And he made a weird comment about Hope not minding her own business. He definitely knows something."

Betz rubbed the back of his neck. "You didn't question him, did you?"

"No. I was just trying to find people in Hope's life who might know what she's been up to lately. Don't worry, I'll leave the questioning to you."

Betz checked his phone. "I gotta take care of something, but I'll send a patrol officer over to see if he's there. We got a home address?" he asked Rick.

"We do."

"Send them there as well. We'll see if Mr. Quinn has anything interesting to say."

"That works," I said.

At the probation office, I fielded inquiries about Hope's disappearance as I walked through the support staff area, signed in, and collected my mail. Upstairs, I dumped my stuff on the floor of my cubicle. My coworker, Claire, sat at her desk across from me, her feet elevated on a rolling cart of files she would bring home so she could telework.

She held her cell phone to her ear and rolled her eyes, making her fingers flap to indicate the caller was long-winded. "Stop right there, Amanda." She sounded bored. "I don't want to hear any more excuses. Drop a UA today or you can explain why you didn't to the judge." She made a dramatic show of pushing the end button on her phone and dropped it on her desk. "Honestly, I'm so tired of whining. Any news on Hope?"

"Not really."

"You holding up okay?"

I gave her a half-hearted smile and settled at my desk. Claire was okay, but once you got her talking, she never stopped. I put my earphones on and cranked up the music on my phone, so I could avoid further conversation.

Booting up my laptop, I checked my email. The next hour was spent returning calls, signing off on paperwork, and sending them all on their merry way to court. I hesitated when I came across one petition that would end up on Dorfman's desk. My heart raced at thoughts of him perusing it for errors, looking for any reason to call me back for another tongue-lashing. I reviewed it three times, making sure T's were crossed and I's dotted and that my facts were straight.

I had a headache the size of Dorfman's ego and realized I hadn't eaten. It was after two, and I had to pick Joy up from the airport at four. I packed my stuff, powered off my laptop, and prepared to leave for the day when I heard myself summoned over the intercom.

I called the front desk to see what they wanted.

"Michael Crowne is here to see you," Tracy, our snotty receptionist, informed me.

I groaned. "I'll be down in a minute."

I didn't want to see anybody. I should be looking for Hope. I tried to remind myself the police were handling things and that just because I didn't know what they were doing didn't mean they weren't making progress. And I trusted Betz. At least seeing a client would occupy my mind until I had to pick up Joy.

I printed Crowne's conditions of probation and a directive with reporting instructions and brought them down to the interview rooms. They were all empty. It was two o'clock on a Friday, and officers were usually scarce.

Since we had such a flexible schedule, most POs had enough sense to get an early start on the weekend.

Still a little shell-shocked from my run-in with Ramirez, I picked a room closest to the exit so security could hear me if I needed them. I dropped Crowne's papers on the desk and went to the lobby to retrieve him.

Crown was a walking advertisement for an anti-methamphetamine campaign. About six feet tall, maybe one hundred and thirty pounds, with sores dotting blotchy skin that I figured were the result of picking at imaginary things in meth-induced anxiety. He was fidgety, wired. He must have stopped to see his dealer on the way to the office.

"Down the hall to the left," I said.

He leered at me, then walked ahead. His jeans sagged where his butt should have been. I followed him into the interview room and took a seat opposite him at the table.

"We're going to go over the conditions of your probation," I told him. "Make sure you remember what's expected of you."

Crowne gave a rotten-toothed grin. "Go ahead, pretty lady."

"It's Casey," I said. "First one is to obey all laws." I figured he'd already broken that one when he scored some meth on the way over, but I continued through the terms of his probation grant, not giving him a chance to comment. When I was done, I wrote a directive for him to drop a UA by close of business on Monday.

"And what if I don't?"

I shrugged. "It's your choice. You just got out of jail, so you know what the consequences are."

"Seemed like the judge was madder at you than me."

Tell me about it. I circled the instructions for him to report to Andy on his first day back from vacation and slid the paper across the desk for Crowne to sign.

"Why do I have to go back to Andy?" he asked. "You're a lot nicer to look at."

"Andy is your PO. He'll be back in a week. You'll report to him then."

"Can't I request a transfer to you? You could ask your supervisor."

"No." I tapped the table. "Sign the form."

"It was hot seeing you chewed out by that judge." A smirk broke his face. "I'm getting excited just thinking about it."

I grabbed the directive and tore off his copy. I didn't care if he signed it. I would document it as a refusal. Crowne took it and looked at it carefully. "Casey Carson," he said. "Are you related to that PO who went missing? The one who's on the news?"

He didn't seem the type to watch the news, but stories about her disappearance were everywhere. I stood up and pointed to the exit. "Goodbye, Mr. Crowne."

He slowly got to his feet, slithering his lizard-like ass down the corridor. "Good day, Ms. Carson. I'll see you soon."

"No, you won't." I pulled the door shut behind him.

I hadn't touched him, yet I still felt like I needed a shower.

Chapter Fourteen

I parked on the fifth floor of Terminal 4's garage five minutes before Joy's plane was due to arrive. I left the car on for a minute to let the news finish. The story of Hope's disappearance had been short and, at the end, not the top story it had been the day before. The reporter said anyone who spotted her should call police and not approach her. It made her sound like the dangerous one. I'd ask Betz if that was necessary after I picked up Joy.

An elevator, escalator, and quarter-mile hike got me the closest non-passengers could get to the gate. Panting, I scanned the flow of people passing by for my cousin.

I searched the face of each passerby, but I didn't recognize anyone. When the crowd dwindled to a few stragglers, I wondered if I had the right terminal. I hurried back to the arrival screen and scanned the list. Her flight had arrived thirty minutes ago. They'd been ahead of schedule. So where was she?

I tapped out a text to Joy and almost hit send when my name was broadcasted over the intercom system. "Casey Carson, please pick up a white paging phone. Casey Carson..."

I spotted a white phone on the wall about ten feet away. After adjusting my messenger bag, I walked over.

"This is Casey Carson," I told the operator.

"Your party is waiting for you in the cocktail lounge located near the entrance to gate C."

I thanked her as I noticed a pub across from the security checkpoint.

The television over the bar was tuned to a Diamondbacks game. Weary travelers watched with mugs of beer in hand. Tables were full of people sucking down drinks, killing time before their plane took off. I scanned the room but didn't see Joy.

"Casey!" A knockout Barbie-doll-figured woman called from a stool across the room. She motioned for me to join her. "Over here."

I didn't recognize her, but I'd supervised so many people over the years, I sometimes forgot faces. I really didn't have time for this. But the woman was insistent, waving her arms over her head like she was trying to land a plane. I shrugged and walked over, still scanning the other patrons for my cousin.

At the table, the woman jumped off her stool and wobbled on sky-high heels. She tugged at the hem of her tight pink skirt. It moved south about an inch, but still barely covered anything. Before I could duck out of reach, she pulled me into an embrace. Rock-hard breasts stabbed me in the chest. "Oh, Casey," she gushed. "You look amazing. The extra weight you've put on looks good on you. You look, you know…healthy."

I hadn't gained any weight, but I sucked my stomach in anyway.

The voice belonged to my cousin. I pulled back and looked at her carefully. Her eyes were familiar, and the face was, too, in a deflated sort of way. My God, could this be Joy? She must have dropped more than one hundred pounds, had a boob job, and highlighted her previously drab brown hair. It was an improvement in some ways, but there's such a thing as going overboard.

"Joy?" I asked. Her figure was impressive, but her outfit made her look like she rented motel rooms by the hour. "Wow," was all I could muster.

"I've lost a few pounds." She giggled whiskey breath into my face.

"I'll say."

"This is Tim." Joy motioned to a good-looking man in a thousand-dollar suit who shared the table with her.

He rose from his seat and offered his hand. "Tom, my name is Tom."

"Tom." Joy laughed. "I'm so bad with names. We met on the flight. Tom is here on business."

"Have a seat," Tom said, settling back on his stool. "Join us for a drink."

Hope was missing, Ramirez was mad at me, I hadn't eaten all day, and my watch read five o'clock. "Thanks, but we should get going."

"She's always been uptight," Joy said.

"I'm not uptight," I said through clenched teeth. "Did you forget why you're here?"

"Of course not. But, Casey, I've been thinking." She lowered her voice and leaned closer to me. "I just know Hope's okay. I'm psychic. I'd feel it if something bad happened to her."

Wish it worked that way. "Let's go, Joy."

Joy sighed, picked up her glass, and sucked down the remainder of her drink. Turning to Tom, she said. "Do you have a pen?"

Tom produced a silver one from his jacket pocket.

Joy scribbled down my number on a cocktail napkin and handed it to him. "Call me."

"You bet," he said with a wink.

Joy giggled, gathered her things, and followed me to the exit.

"Why did you give him MY number?" I asked.

"Harry gets the cell phone bills. I don't want him to see I'm talking to men. He could use it against me in the divorce."

"Don't do that again," I said when we were in the corridor. "He's a stranger. He could be a pervert."

Joy waved my words away. "He's not a pervert. Seriously, Casey, you need to relax."

"I mean it."

"Okay, okay," she said, jutting out her chest as she caught the eye of the next guy walking by.

Joy's monster suitcase barely fit in my Jeep. Settled in the passenger seat, Joy pulled a compact mirror from an enormous purse. "It's so hot here. My makeup is sliding right off my face." She hauled a cosmetic bag the size of a toaster out of her bag and spent the next ten minutes applying makeup as thick as frosting on a layer cake. I didn't see it as an improvement, but she seemed so pleased, I half-expected her to kiss her image in the mirror.

I told Joy about my meeting with Joel Quinn. "He said they weren't dating. And from what I could tell, he didn't seem to be Hope's type. Plus, he's married."

"Maybe she was just talking about him hitting on her. I don't really remember," Joy admitted. "My mind wandered when I started thinking about that actor with the incredible eyes."

"Can't you remember anything about the conversation?"

"Quiet!" Joy shrieked. She placed her index fingers against her temples. Eyes closed, she started humming.

"What are you doing?"

"Shush," she said between hums. "If you want me to help, I'll need silence."

The stoplight changed, and I slipped into first gear, trying to do so as gently as possible so I wouldn't interfere with Joy's psychic trance. What was wrong with me?

A block later, she spoke. "Hope's definitely okay."

"Then explain her disappearance."

She turned in her seat to face me. "Look, Casey, I find it insulting that you don't believe me. I truly have powers. My psychic abilities are what led me to know my shit-head husband was cheating on me."

"You had a vision of him cheating on you?"

"I had a vision of hot pink nail polish, which led me to return home to paint my nails. That's when I found him humping Oscar De La motherfucker."

I rolled my eyes.

"I saw that."

I prayed we would find Hope quickly so Joy could go back to Boston. I wished I'd taken Tom up on his offer of a drink. I was going to need something to help me calm down, or my hands would soon be around Joy's tiny neck.

We arrived at my home at nearly six o'clock, and my stomach was growling. Before I could remedy the situation, I set to work trying to dislodge Joy's eighty-pound suitcase from the back of my Jeep. I loved my little Wrangler, but at times like this, I sure missed a trunk. Come to think of it, the suitcase probably wouldn't fit in most trunks. Just how long was she planning to stay?

I'd gotten the thing half out before I had to stop and catch my breath. "I could use a little help here."

"Oh, my." Joy elbowed me in the ribs. "Would you look at that."

I followed her gaze to the house next door. A beautiful man, shirtless and in jeans slung low on slim hips, stood in the doorway. A cigarette bobbed on sensual lips. For once, I had to agree with Joy. Oh, my.

Joy patted her heaving chest. "Who. Is. That?"

"No idea. Last time I checked, the house was vacant and for rent."

"Well, property values just went up."

Wasn't that the truth?

The man gave a wicked grin, tossed his cigarette on the driveway, and ground it out with the heel of his work boot. Then he crossed the space between our houses. "Need a hand, ladies?"

My gaze dropped to his belly button. Navel, I corrected myself. Belly button insinuated he had a belly. His stomach was as flat as a can crushed by a tank.

A hot flash left me wondering two things: could I be going through menopause at thirty and was there smoke coming out of my ears? If I was on fire, Joy looked as if she were ready to explode. She waffled with so much excitement I feared her boobs would pop out of her minuscule top.

"Excuse me." He squeezed between us. In seconds, he had pulled Joy's suitcase from the back, heaved it onto his shoulder, and carried it through the garage to the kitchen door.

We watched him go. The rear view, well that was something to watch as well.

At the door, he turned. "Can you get the door?"

"Hurry up," Joy said. "Don't let him get away."

"Yeah, sure." I rushed ahead of him and opened the door to the kitchen.

He followed me inside. Joy came in quickly behind us.

"Where do you want it?" he asked.

"The guestroom." I pointed down the short hallway. "On your left."

"That'll be MY room," Joy said, scurrying along behind him. "Keep that in mind."

He lowered the suitcase onto the floor and turned to face us. "I'm Marcus." He offered me his hand.

I shook it. Firm handshake. Slightly callused hand. He didn't let go quickly, which was fine by me.

Before I could become too mesmerized, Joy shoved me aside and took his hand. "I'm Joy. Can you stay for a drink? I know I'd love a drink. I'm just parched after that long flight." She took his arm and led him to the kitchen like it was her place.

I followed.

We stood awkwardly in the kitchen as Joy rummaged through my refrigerator. Bent at the waist, she gave us a startling view of leopard print panties. At least she wore underwear.

Marcus took in the view, grinned, and shook his head. I was pleased to see he could break his gaze away and focus on me. "I didn't get your name."

"Casey."

"Casey," he repeated. "I like that."

Joy pulled three bottles of Corona from the refrigerator. "Grab some glasses, would you, Case?"

"Bottle's fine." Marcus took one from her and leaned against the counter. He ran his hand through brown hair that was a bit too long, but perfect in a disheveled sort of way. Personally, I rather liked the scruffy look.

Joy pushed a bottle toward me and then fished around the kitchen drawers for a bottle opener. I didn't help her. After all, she was psychic. She found one in the third drawer, opened her bottle, and passed the opener to Marcus.

"So, what do you do, Marcus?" Joy asked.

He popped the caps off both our bottles, took a tug of beer, and shrugged. "This and that. I just got into town."

"Me too," Joy shrieked. "Where are you from?"

"Jersey."

"Really? I'm from Boston."

"Wow," I said. "What a coincidence."

Joy shot me a look that said, back off. I'm working here.

I wasn't accustomed to handing off gorgeous guys to anybody, and I didn't want to start with Joy, but I knew she was going through a rough time after her husband cheated on her, and she probably needed the validation. Aside from that, I hadn't heard from Betz in a few hours, and I started to feel like I might miss something. I hated to leave these two alone. I just hoped they wouldn't have sex on my couch. I really liked my couch.

"I gotta go," I said. "I'll pick something up for dinner on my way home."

"But I just got here," Joy said. "Aren't we going to look for Hope?"

"Ah, Joy, you don't want to go. You should let the police handle it."

"You're not the police," she said.

"I know. I'm staying out of it. I just want to ask Betz how the investigation's going."

"Police investigation?" Marcus asked.

"It's just terrible," Joy cooed. "My big sister is missing. I'm just devastated."

That was obvious. I was sure she'd be willing to let Marcus help her feel better. As much as I didn't want that to happen, I didn't want Joy tagging along on my jaunt to Betz's office. She was already wearing on my nerves. "Why don't you rest? I won't be long."

Joy guzzled her beer, threw her purse over her shoulder, and joggled after me. "I'm coming," she said. "I have as much right to know what's going on as you do. More even."

Marcus followed us out the door, taking his beer with him. "It's gonna be fun living next to you too." He waved goodbye over his shoulder as he walked back to his house.

"Likewise," Joy said, settling into the Jeep and buckling her seatbelt. "Oh, baby, I can see us having all kinds of fun."

Chapter Fifteen

At Betz's office, Joy and I signed in like regular folks, displayed our visitor's badges, and waited in the lobby for Betz to come down and get us. I wished he'd hurry. Joy so obviously ogled the men in blue around us, I wondered if she could be arrested for such an outward display of horniness.

When Betz stepped off the elevator, she waved him over as if he could possibly miss us.

"Wow," he said, blowing out a long breath. "You've done some changing, Joy."

She giggled, ran over to him, and playfully tapped him on the chest before wrapping him in a bear hug. Betz seemed to be taken off guard as he stumbled backward a few steps. Joy, as attached as a dog humping your leg, went along for the ride. "Oh, Barry," she cooed. "It's good to see you." She let go, struck a pose, and spun around. "I've lost weight. You like?"

Betz scratched his head and gave her the once over. I knew him well enough to know he was biting back a string of puns related to her transformation.

Joy seemed to take his devilish grin the wrong way. "Oh, Barry, stop that. You're practically family."

"Good thing you reminded me." He grinned.

"Don't encourage her," I said. Joy bounced her attention from man to man so quickly, I had whiplash. "We stopped by to see how the investigation's going."

"Let's go upstairs." Betz pushed the button for the elevator.

On the third floor, we followed him to his office. Joy lagged behind, her heels click-clacking all the way. "Vice is that way," Betz whispered so Joy couldn't hear. "Don't let your cousin wander down there, or they'll think she's one of theirs."

At Betz's cubicle, he pulled up a chair for Joy, offered me his, and leaned back against his desk, his arms crossed loosely at his chest. "We found Harlan Jones and his truck. Two gunshot wounds to the chest. Good news is the blood on the couch in the house was his, not Hope's. She armed?"

I nodded.

"Glock 22?" Betz asked.

"That's what the department issues to those who choose to be armed."

"Well, that's what killed him."

"That's good news, right?" Joy asked. "Even if he kidnapped her, she must have been able to get away after he died."

"Time of death was around the time Hope went missing. She would have had plenty of time to come forward if that were the case," Betz said. "Either others are involved, or..."

"Or what?" Joy's expression hardened. "What are you insinuating, Barry? This is my sister we're talking about."

For once, I agreed with Joy. Hope wasn't a killer. If her gun had killed Harlan, there had to be a good reason.

"Just exploring all the possibilities," Betz said. "We're conducting a search in the area where the truck and Jones were found." He turned to Joy. "What can you tell me about Hope's relationships?"

"I told Casey everything I know," Joy said. "Hope wasn't much of a talker."

Probably couldn't get a word in edgewise. Heavy or thin, Joy always took up all the space in the room.

"What about her cell phone records?" I asked.

"We've requested them," Betz said. "Unfortunately, the cell company gets countless requests from law enforcement daily, and we are in a long line to get a response. We tried to ping her phone, but it's turned off."

Betz turned to Joy. "When was the last time you spoke to her?"

"About a week ago," Joy said. "She was going to have dinner with Uncle

Albert."

My father? Hope had dinner with my father? I hardly ever had dinner with him. When I did, it was mostly out of family obligation. My father just wasn't emotionally present anymore, and I found it hard to be around him much. He and his house reminded me of everything we'd lost. He'd always had a drink or two at the end of the day, but now he drank all the time. "I didn't know Hope had contact with my father."

"Well, she did," Joy said. "Quite often, I think."

"Seems like I should pay him a visit," Betz said.

"You and me both," I said. "You have dinner yet? We can get something and bring it over there."

"I could eat," Betz said.

The good news was the blood in Harlan's house didn't belong to Hope. The bad news, Hope was still missing, and her gun might have been involved in Harlan's death. If she used it in self-defense, I couldn't imagine why she hadn't come forward. I remembered the only true lead we had so far. "I thought you were going to arrest Joel Quinn on his warrant and question him while in custody."

Betz rubbed his jaw. "I've had patrol keeping an eye on Technerds and his apartment. No one's been at either place all day. When he shows, we'll get him. In the meantime, let's visit your dad. I've got a few things to finish up here, but I should be able to meet you there after you stop for food."

"Sounds like a plan." I rose and motioned for Joy to follow. "Let's go."

"Okey dokey." She stood and planted a loud kiss on Betz, just west of his lips. "See you soon, Barry."

Jaws dropped at each cubicle as Joy sashayed ahead of me toward the exit. Her hips swung with such vigor, I worried she'd put her back out. I thought about taking the stairs and trying to lose her, but I was afraid to leave her alone in a building that housed so many men. Armed or not, they'd be defenseless against my cousin. Call it my civic duty, but I was stuck with her for the duration of the evening.

Chapter Sixteen

J oy was hungry for Chinese food, so we stopped for takeout on the way to my father's house.

It was after eight when we pulled into the driveway of his three-bedroom bungalow that was built in the fifties and hadn't changed much since we moved in when I was in high school. Over the years, my father had tried to talk my mom into upgrading to a bigger, more modern house, but my mother loved the neighborhood and the garden she had in the backyard, and she refused to move. Now, I don't think my dad had the heart or interest in making any changes. I never understood how my mother managed to grow anything in the desert heat, but she'd kept one of the most beautiful yards I'd ever seen.

As we parked, I was struck with guilt at the state of the place. Brown grass was overgrown, bushes unruly, and the trim around the brick was in dire need of a paint job. It had been a good two months since I'd spent a Saturday afternoon at my dad's with a weed whacker. I'd have to make time for it soon.

A bag of food in one hand, I rapped on the door.

"Hold your horses," my father bellowed from the other side.

He opened the door, and I stepped around him with Joy behind me. "Hi, Dad."

My dad gave Joy the once over. "Who's the tart?"

"Why Uncle Albert," Joy giggled. "You're such a stinker."

My father leaned toward me, and I gave him the obligatory kiss on his stubble-bearded cheek. He barely stood still long enough for me to finish the act before he moved toward the living room, whiskey sloshing out of the tumbler in his hand. By the tilt in his stocking-footed walk, I surmised this wasn't his first drink of the day.

When my mom was alive, there had been little need to induce happiness. She had the gift of the gab, and there weren't many silent moments. Sometimes, I could still hear her laughter echoing in the halls. My dad was always the more serious one. Sometimes, I wondered how they managed a marriage for so long. It was a mystery to me how sometimes people who were total opposites got along best.

When my mom died, my dad replaced her with two things: the bottle and the TV. It was like I'd lost both my parents at once.

We followed him into the living room. Typical of my dad, the A\C was turned up so high, outside might be cooler. He settled on the recliner, his attention on *Wheel of Fortune*. "Some things are better left unsaid," he read the puzzle. "I knew it."

My father, a wealth of useless information.

I held up the bag of food. "We brought dinner."

My dad broke his gaze away from the TV and stared at me like he'd forgotten we were there. "Dinner? It's only four o'clock."

"It's after eight, silly," Joy said. "I'm so hungry I could eat the Styrofoam box."

"What is it?" my dad asked.

"Chinese," Joy said. "We have almond chicken and shrimp with vegetables."

"Chinese gives me heartburn." He upped the volume on the TV.

"Everything gives you heartburn." I motioned for Joy to follow me into the kitchen, a room seldom used since my mother passed away. I took four plates down from the cupboard and set them on the counter. Joy shoveled equal heaps of food onto them, popping pieces of chicken into her mouth as she worked.

I opened the refrigerator. Tomato juice for Bloody Mary's, cherries for Manhattan's, and olives for martinis. My dad had one rule when it came to stocking his kitchen: if it didn't go with booze, it wasn't fit for consumption. He probably put rum on his morning cereal. Yet somehow, with all the liquor he soaked up, he never appeared drunk, just ornery.

I pulled two cans of ginger ale from the refrigerator, popped the tops, and handed one to Joy.

"Your father's changed quite a bit." Joy smacked a piece of shrimp between her lips.

He'd always been a bit of a homebody, but now he almost never left the house. "He's pushing seventy," I said. "He doesn't do much to keep young."

"Nothing? Not even golf?"

I shook my head.

"He's wearing golf pants."

"He's not exactly into fashion. I think he got them at a garage sale."

"He needs a date," Joy said. "It's not natural to go without companionship. I'll see what I can do."

I'd have begged her to stay out of it, and if I thought there was a chance my dad would be the least bit interested, I might have done just that. My mom had been gone less than a year, after all. But my dad and Joy were bound to butt heads, and it might be fun to sit back and watch, so I kept my mouth shut.

I left Betz's plate on the counter and carried mine, and my dad's to the living room, Joy following. My dad's gaze had never left the television.

"Guess who's coming to dinner?" he said.

"Who?" I asked.

"What do you mean, who? I'm solving the puzzle. Can't you keep up?"

I placed one plate on the snack tray next to the recliner. My dad ignored it, reaching for the bottle on the floor beside him. He added a splash of whiskey to his glass, took a sip and let out a satisfied sigh.

Before I could sit down, a knock came from the door. I opened it and let Betz inside. A smile lit my father's face when he saw his former son-in-law. He stood and walked over to shake Betz's hand. Sometimes, I thought he preferred Betz to me.

"Nice to see you, Detective," he said. My father always called Betz detective, no matter how many times Betz asked him not to.

"You too, Albert. How've you been?"

"Keeping busy," my father lied. He reached for the remote and turned off the TV. I went back to the kitchen and got the last plate of food.

When I returned, my father had gone back to his seat, and Betz had settled in an armchair. I handed Betz his plate and plopped on the sofa next to Joy. She had already scarfed her dinner down so quickly, for a moment, I feared she'd eaten her fork.

I followed her lead and stopped just short of licking my plate clean.

"So, Dad, I understand Hope was here for dinner the other night."

My dad shrugged. "So?"

My dad never watched the news. Game shows and reruns of seventies TV sitcoms were his source of entertainment. I didn't see the point of riling him, so I tried to downplay the news of Hope's disappearance. "She hasn't checked in for a few days, and we were wondering if she told you anything that would help us track her down."

"Hasn't checked in for a few days!" Joy screeched. "She's missing. Tell him about the dead guy and the blood."

"Blood?" my father asked. "What do you mean, blood?"

"It's not Hope's blood," I said.

"I knew that all along," Joy said. "I'm psychic."

"Who the hell are you?" my dad snapped.

"Oh, Uncle Albert, stop kidding around."

"I don't think he's kidding," I said. "Dad, this is Joy. Your niece."

He scratched his mostly bald head. "The fat one?"

I sighed. These two were wearing me out. I looked to Betz for help, but he seemed to be trying not to burst out laughing. "She lost some weight," I said.

"One hundred and twenty-two pounds," she boasted. "I lost one hundred and twenty-five, but then I got my breasts. They weigh about a pound-and-a-half each."

I smacked my palm against my forehead and took a deep breath.

"So, Albert," Betz said. "Anything you can think of about your recent contacts with Hope could be useful. What kinds of things did you talk about?"

My father straightened. "After Carissa died, she started coming by quite a bit. At first, I was touched. It's not like anyone else took the time."

The jab connected, and it hurt. In the beginning, I'd invited him over a lot. He always declined. Yes, I should have come over more, but I was grieving, too, and coming here was too painful. Even now. That was why I hadn't yet cleaned out my mother's closet or emptied her dresser drawers. Getting rid of her things would make it all too final. That didn't mean I didn't feel tremendous guilt for staying away.

"Anyway," my dad continued. "She seemed interested in what Carissa might have told me in the weeks leading up to, you know, what happened to her."

"What did you tell her?" Betz asked.

"The truth. I didn't notice anything going on with Carissa that was different than any other time in our marriage. She worked a lot, but that happened from time to time."

"Was it out of the ordinary for Hope to be so inquisitive? Was she close to Carissa?"

No, I wanted to say, but my dad said it for me. "Not really. I know Carissa tried to reach out to both girls after their parents died, but life got busy, and that lessened over time."

"Did Hope mention dating anyone?" I asked.

"God," he said. "Probably. I wish I would have paid better attention." My dad rubbed his temples. "Something about a lawyer."

"An attorney?" I asked. "Are you sure she talked about dating him? We work for the court, which means we deal with attorneys all the time. Could she have been talking about work and not her social life?"

I could see my dad struggling. "I wish I could recall. I'm sorry." He topped off his drink with shaking hands. "I can't believe she's missing."

"Did you give her mom's briefcase?" I asked.

"She asked for it. Not like you or Kate ever came by for anything."

"I'm sorry about that. We will," I said. "Please don't give away anything else."

Betz cleared his throat and stood. "Was there anything in the briefcase?" My dad raised his bony shoulders. "I'm not sure."

It was empty last I saw it. Since my mom's death happened at work, her employer would have removed whatever work files were inside before releasing the briefcase and her other personal belongings to my dad.

Betz handed my father his business card. "If you think of anything, Albert, give me a call, okay?"

"Of course," my dad said.

I saw Betz to the door. "Why would Hope ask my dad questions about my mom?" I said quietly.

Betz sighed. "I'm not sure. Could be she just wanted to reach out to family after losing her only aunt. Could be she was looking for something. Do you know what cases your mom was working on before her death?"

"My mom respected the confidentially thing that came with her job," I said. "I have no clue what she was working on. After she died, I asked if there could have been any connection to her work, and her coworkers assured me there wasn't."

Betz's phone buzzed in his hand, and he checked it. "I gotta go, Case. Thanks for the food."

"You're welcome."

I gathered the plates from the living room and took them into the kitchen. After cleaning up, I wrapped my dad's untouched food and left it in the refrigerator.

Saying goodbye, I kissed the top of my dad's head before joining Joy on the front stoop. A warm breeze rustled the trees, and I imagined it blowing this whole horrible situation away. In the Jeep, I unzipped the window and let the wind whip the hair around my face.

"Not to worry." Joy patted my hand. "I'll work on him."

I gave her a blank stare.

"It's your people skills," she said. "You have a habit of rubbing people the wrong way."

"Me?" I squeaked.

"I know how to talk to men," she said. "I kept quiet today because I was trying to get a read on your dad's aura."

She kept quiet because she was too busy ogling Betz.

"I'll take him to lunch tomorrow," she said. "I'll call you when I find out more about the attorney."

I rolled my eyes.

"I saw that," Joy said. "Exactly what I mean about your people skills. And would you please close the window? You're ruining my hair."

Chapter Seventeen

J oy wanted to see her sister's house, claiming her psychic powers might be stronger amongst Hope's belongings. When we pulled into the driveway, Joy let out a gasp. When I let us in with the key I'd lifted the day before, she was flabbergasted.

"This can't be Hope's house. How can she afford this? Look at this furniture. The hardwood floors." Hands on hips, she strutted about the room like a peacock. "It figures. Perfect Hope has a perfect house. Always perfect because she's beautiful and a size 6. Well, now I'm a size six, and where is she so I can show her?"

Way to make this about you, I almost said, but quickly checked myself as I didn't know if Joy's denial could be a coping mechanism. I hoped she wasn't that clueless.

"Calm down," I said. "You'll pop something."

"You, of all people, should understand how I feel," Joy said, still marching around the room, running her fingers through the fingerprint powder left on the glass table. "You've always been pretty and thin, sure, but your life is a mess. Don't you get sick of Kate being the good child? The successful one?"

That stung. "My life is not a mess."

"You know what I mean. You can't hold onto a man."

If Joy kept pushing my buttons, I might be forced to push her back. Maybe down the stairs.

Let it go. "Do you have any idea where Hope got the money for this stuff?"

Joy bit her lip. "By the looks of your place, I take it parole officers don't

84

make that much."

"It's probation, not parole."

"Same difference." Joy waved me away and wandered into the kitchen.

Not even, but I didn't see much point in educating Joy about the criminal justice system. It wasn't her world. "Don't touch anything," I said when she started opening cabinets. The police had processed the house, but I still felt a need to preserve it.

Joy closed the cabinet door. "I get a better reading if I touch things. Don't you watch psychics on TV? Police use them all the time. You're wasting a golden opportunity. I—"

The sound of a toilet flushing came from upstairs. We both looked toward the ceiling. I motioned for Joy to be silent and started for the stairs. With any luck, it was Hope, but my cell phone was in my hand, ready to dial 911 if necessary.

Joy followed so closely on my heels, she stepped on them a few times.

From above, footsteps moved down the hall toward Hope's bedroom at the back of the house.

I took the stairs slowly, careful to avoid the center of the steps where they would be most likely to creak. Unfortunately, Joy did not follow my lead. I'd made it to the top of the staircase when she stepped on a board that let out a tired moan.

We froze.

I didn't even breathe.

A moment of silence and then the thumping of feet as someone took an all-out run down the hallway.

A girl stopped several feet from me. Late teens at most, given the white crop top and skinny jeans slung low on narrow hips. Stringy, wet blond hair hung in her face. Hands gripping opposite walls, she stared us down, breathing heavily.

"Hi," I said, opting for nonchalance.

The girl's eyes narrowed, and then, bam, she charged me like a bull. A head-butt to my stomach knocked the wind from my lungs before I lost my footing and stumbled backward, ass over teacups, down the hardwood stairs. My cell phone flew out of my hand and skidded across the floor. Joy shrieked as she stepped aside to let me pass. I came to rest on my back on the slate foyer floor.

The girl ran over me, her flip-flop landing on my thigh as she passed overhead and out the front door.

"Casey?" Joy leaned over me, and I got an eyeful of cleavage. "Are you alright? Can you move?"

I took a moment to catch my breath. Rolling over, I got on my hands and knees and staggered to my feet. My chest hurt from trying to get air, and I was having trouble operating my left leg. I limped to the front door, still standing open since the girl's departure. It was too dark to see much. I flipped on the outside light and hurried out to the street, looking left and right. No sign of the girl.

Joy came to stand beside me. "We should call Barry. Something isn't right."

"You think?" I cracked my neck and hobbled back to the house. The girl had been young and too street-worn to be Hope's friend. Was she a squatter? Or was she involved in Hope's disappearance? I collected my cell and started up the stairs.

"Do you think you should go up there?" Joy called from behind me. "Don't you think you should wait for police?"

"I want to see what she was doing," I said over my shoulder.

I went to the bathroom first. If the girl was looking for prescription drugs, this would be the place to start. The mirror was coated with condensation from steam. Water still dripped from the shower nozzle, and a damp towel hung on the rack.

I moved down the hall to Hope's bedroom. The bedspread had been pulled down, and the sheets were mussed. A soiled, light-blue backpack lay at the foot of the bed. The girl's belongings? If so, she'd likely want them back at some point.

It took a lot of self-control to call Betz instead of going through her stuff.

"Stay put," he said. "I'm in the middle of something, but I'm sending an officer over to check things out and get a description."

I hung up and turned to go back downstairs to wait for the cop when a card on the floor caught my eye. Picking it up, I saw it was Hope's business card. A series of numbers were scribbled on the back. Underneath the numbers, in Hope's neat handwriting, it said: For Casey. Tell her not to share with police.

My heartbeat quickened. Was this girl sent to give me a message? For a moment, I debated following Hope's orders versus turning the card over to police. I needed to think for a bit on this one. Stuffing the card in my pocket, I hobbled back down the stairs.

Joy waited, holding a brass lamp like a baseball bat. "Let's get out of here," she said. "I'm getting bad vibes."

I peeled her white fingers off the lamp and placed it back on the table. Bad vibes didn't begin to cover it. I led Joy outside, where we waited on the front step for the police to arrive.

Chapter Eighteen

Saturday morning, I stumbled out of bed and made my way to the kitchen to retrieve a Diet Coke. It would take at least one before I acknowledged being awake. Muscles I didn't know existed screamed at me with each movement, reminding me of my tumble down the stairs the night before.

A bright light illuminated my kitchen. Joy had baking supplies spread across the counter, and she whipped batter in a bowl.

I groaned.

"Good morning," she sang, obnoxiously perky.

I struggled with the urge to punch her in the face.

Reaching into the refrigerator to grab a Diet Coke, I found it stuffed with food. "Where'd all this come from?" I panicked for a minute, but then spotted a six-pack of Diet Coke behind a giant bag of green grapes. Clutching a can in my hand, I turned to face her.

"The store, silly." She wiped her brow with the back of her hand. "You'd think a bachelor lived here; your cupboards were so bare."

"How did you get to the store?"

"Your Jeep. The cutie next door came with me since I had no idea where to go. He'll be back in a few minutes. I promised him pancakes." She looked me up and down, stopping mid-whip. "You should at least put a bra on. You don't want him to get the wrong idea."

Joy's cleavage spilled over her scoop-necked shirt. Braless or not, I couldn't compete with her.

I popped open the soda, took a satisfying gulp, and shuffled back to my bedroom, where I showered and did my best to look presentable. Wearing jeans and a navy T-shirt, I pulled my hair back in a ponytail and sat on the edge of my bed, holding Hope's business card in my hand. I had stayed up half the night staring at the card. The series of numbers looked like a phone number, but when I called, it was out of service. All night, I lay awake trying to figure out what the numbers meant and why Hope wanted me to keep them from the police. But just like the night before, no answers came to me. I stuffed the card into the novel I'd been reading to keep it safe and returned to the kitchen.

Marcus sat on a stool at my counter while Joy slid pancakes onto a plate in front of him.

"Good morning," he said.

I smiled at him. He looked as hunky as yesterday in a black shirt and jeans. He shoveled a forkful of pancake into his mouth.

Joy put half a pancake on her plate, squirted it with a drop of syrup, and sat on the stool beside him.

She made no offer of food my way. I grabbed an apple out of the basket on the counter.

"Any news on your cousin?" Marcus asked.

"No," I said.

Feeling like an intruder, I wandered into the living room and picked up my cell phone. There were three messages for Joy from the airport guy that I deleted. The fourth message was from Betz. "Can you come out and play?"

My pulse quickened. "Sure," I text messaged back.

"Good. I'm two minutes away."

I slid on my Nikes and passed through the kitchen on my way outside. Joy rubbed Marcus' arm while leaning forward and softly telling him something about a Swedish massage technique she was dying to try on him.

I might as well fold. I had no idea what a Swedish massage was, but it sounded like it would earn her big points.

Betz waited at the curb in his Tahoe. He handed me Joel Quinn's warrant once I buckled in. "Quinn finally returned to Technerds. Thought you might want to watch."

I filled him in on what happened at Hope's house the night before, leaving out the business card I'd left on my nightstand on the drive over.

He pulled into a 7-Eleven parking lot a few blocks from our destination. He grabbed his phone and went to the back of his SUV. I joined him and watched as he slipped a tactical vest over his shirt. Making sure his holstered gun was positioned properly on his belt, he started to close the door, then stopped. "You should wear a vest."

At one-hundred-and-two degrees, not enticing, but neither was getting shot, so I nodded. He rummaged through the back of the Tahoe, moving a duffel bag and first aid kit before he came across flattened body armor. He wiped off some dirt and handed it to me. "It's a large. Sorry, it's all I got."

I slid it over my head. It was so big and stiff, I felt like a turtle whose head was stuck in its shell. Oh well, if bullets started flying, I could fold myself inside and have head-to-toe protection. Betz loaned me an extra-large T-shirt to put over the vest. It said, Cops Have Big Guns. Yeah, that would make me less conspicuous.

Since Technerds was in the next town over, Betz called his buddies at Tempe PD to assist. They pulled up next to us in a decked-out Police Interceptor. Staying in the air-conditioned vehicle, the driver put the window down so they could talk to us. Betz showed them the photo of Joel Quinn he'd pulled from booking records.

"Can you describe the couple you saw in the car the night you went over there?" Betz asked me.

I gave the best description of the girl I could. It had been too dark to identify the man. Everyone except Betz looked bored. Although, as a PO, I was a sworn officer, some cops looked down at us. Others loved having us around because we didn't need warrants to search our charges or their homes or vehicles. Sometimes that came in handy.

Confident they had a plan, I got in the Tahoe with Betz and blasted the vent at my head. The vest rose up, swallowing the bottom half of my face.

Betz looked over at me and laughed. "You look like a linebacker."

"Ha ha." The high temperature made me cranky. Sometimes I worried the heat would make me self-combust.

We drove the short distance to Technerds in silence. The patrol officer who'd been watching for Joel's return went to the back of the building. Betz and the Interceptor, carrying two Tempe SAU members, parked on either side of the front entrance.

"Stay behind us," Betz said.

"No problem." I rolled out of the car.

As I waddled up the sidewalk behind Betz, I checked the area around us. The business to the left was vacant, as was the dilapidated gas station to the right. No neighbors. Nice setup if you had something to hide.

While the cops approached the front door, I waited beside a waist-high block wall. Betz and one of the SAU guys entered the building. The other one stayed at the door. I wished they'd hurry. I was drenched in sweat, and my Kevlar-encased torso itched like I had a bad rash. A reminder why I tried not to play cop in the summertime.

Without warning, the SAU guy keeping watch at the door ran inside. Suddenly on my own, I tried my best to blend into the wall I hid behind. As much as I wanted to know what was happening, I didn't dare move, or I'd be nothing but a big fat target.

I checked my surroundings for the best escape route in case things went bad. Betz once told me never to run to the car if there were gunshots. In such situations, people often shoot at cars.

Loud commands came from inside. "Put the gun down."

Then, a single gunshot.

My brain screamed stay put, but I was up and running for the building before I could talk myself out of it. If something happened to Betz, to any of them, I couldn't live with myself. Images of Betz dying on the floor stuck in my head. The panic, the sickness, I'd felt when I lost my mother engulfed my emotions.

I burst through the door, coming behind three cops with their guns out. On the floor in front of them lay a lifeless body. His head was turned away from me, but the man was dressed in civilian clothes. Not Betz. Not a cop.

I stopped short, taking ragged breaths.

"You shouldn't be in here," Betz said.

He lowered his gun and crossed over to me. "Case," he said. "Don't look."

Holstering his gun with one hand, his other arm went around my shoulders, and he guided me around the corner into Quinn's office so I could no longer see the body on the floor. The lifeless body.

"Was it?"

"Joel Quinn," Betz finished. "He shot himself."

"Is he…"

"Dead," Betz said. "Yeah."

"Oh, Jesus." I followed Betz's gaze around the room.

Aside from the desk, the space was empty except for a few traces of trash on the floor, some pretty disturbing dust balls, a mattress, and a tripod.

Not the typical things you'd expect.

The apple and Diet Coke I'd had for breakfast swirled like a tornado in my stomach.

"Well, look at this." Betz motioned to the messy desk against the wall.

An open laptop, the monitor on. I walked over to the desk and looked at the screen. It was open to a website called Private Room, a forum for johns to set up dates with working girls. Sort of like a dating website, only the date lasted an hour and cost about a hundred bucks, depending on the services provided. I'd arrested some of my probationers for using it before.

A photo of a teenage girl wearing a frilly pink negligee and blowing a kiss stared back at us. The girl was more put together than the one I'd seen the night before at Hope's place, but it sure looked like the bull I'd encountered.

"That's the girl who knocked me down the stairs," I said.

Betz sighed. "I'll get forensics to search the laptop ASAP. The setup here makes me think Mr. Quinn was managing the website versus looking for a date."

"Joel Quinn was a pimp?" I thought of the body in the other room and grimaced.

Betz grasped my elbow and steered me away. "You should get out of here. You're turning green. I'll have one of the patrol guys take you home."

"He shot himself?" I asked, taking one last look at Joel on the way out, thinking of his wife.

Betz rubbed the back of his neck. "When we came in, when he saw us, he put the gun to his head."

We walked outside. I could see this was weighing heavy on him. He'd been involved in shootings before, and I knew it wasn't something he took lightly, even if he didn't pull the trigger.

"Look," he said. "There's going to be lots of red tape. Hours of interviews when a shooting happens. I'll be tied up for the rest of the day. I don't know why Hope's involved with these characters, but I want you to be careful."

"No argument here."

Betz gave my arm a squeeze. "I hope you mean that." He flashed me a look that said he had more to say, but then he turned and went back inside.

I tried to collect myself while another patrol officer kept an eye on me. How was Hope connected to Joel Quinn? He wasn't on supervision, I'd checked. Did she somehow find out he was a pimp, and that led to her disappearance? For a computer nerd with a misdemeanor record to put an end to his own life, there had to be something big enough going on that he was willing to die for it.

With the officer looking on, I busied myself with taking off the vest Betz had loaned me and left it in the back of the vehicle. When I felt like I had a smidgen of composure, I slid into the passenger's seat of the patrol car. I smiled at the cop and tried to act cool – like I saw a guy just after he shot himself every day. But I couldn't help but think of my mother, and my shaking hands no doubt gave me away.

Chapter Nineteen

The cop dropped me off at my house. The moment I cleared the front door, I pulled off my sweat-drenched T-shirt, headed to the laundry room, and tossed it into the basket of dirty clothes. Turning around, I walked smack into Marcus.

I let out a scream.

"Good afternoon," he said.

"What are you doing here?"

"Joy asked me to stay and wait for her call." He lowered his gaze to my chest. "Nice bra."

My face burned hot, and I crossed my arms over my chest, covering my Jockey bra as best I could. "What call?"

"Something about her uncle."

"I'm not following you, Marcus."

"Joy was hysterical when she gave me the details, so they might be a bit off. But the gist of it was she went out to lunch with her uncle and lost him."

"Lost him?"

"Didn't make sense to me either."

"Where is Joy now?"

"Looking for him, I guess."

I sighed and walked around Marcus to my bedroom, where I found a clean shirt. So, Joy lost my father. With everything else going on, I didn't like the sound of it. Still in my bedroom, I called Joy's cell, but it went straight to voicemail. I rejoined Marcus in the kitchen, where he was leaning against the counter. I couldn't let Joy hunt a town she didn't know alone. I went to grab my keys off the hook by the garage door, but they were gone.

"Joy took your Jeep," Marcus said.

"Of course she did. Do you have a car?"

"My motorcycle."

I pictured myself on the back of his Harley, my arms around his waist. My face leaning against his back. Hmm…

"Casey?"

I snapped back to reality. "You mind giving me a ride?"

Marcus handed me a helmet, straddled the Harley, put his sunglasses on, and grinned. Damn, this would be perfect if I hadn't just seen a dead body and members of my family weren't missing.

I slid the straps of my backpack-style purse on my shoulders and put on the helmet. "I really appreciate this."

He nodded. "Where to?"

"I don't suppose Joy mentioned where she lost my dad."

"Nope."

I straddled the seat and let my legs mold around Marcus. "Then I guess we should start with his house. Head to the freeway."

Marcus revved the engine, and with a jerk, we sped off. My hands automatically wrapped around his waist. Aside from the slight fear I felt for my life, I liked this. I'd never been on a motorcycle before. If I didn't think about being skipped across the asphalt like a stone across a pristine lake, I could almost enjoy the sensation of darting through traffic with nothing but Marcus' driving skills between me and six months in traction.

Traffic was Saturday afternoon light. I resisted the urge to rest my head against Marcus' back or let my hands wander to his chest and focused on my father's disappearance. Until now, it hadn't occurred to me that it could have something to do with Hope being gone. Although it was more likely he wandered off, my stomach knotted. It was almost as if the earth was swallowing my family, one member at a time.

Within fifteen minutes, we were coasting down my father's street. My Jeep and Kate's minivan were parked out front.

Joy, my sister, and my brother-in-law, Kevin, stood in the driveway.

"Don't panic," Joy said when Marcus turned off the engine.

I reluctantly slid off the seat and handed Marcus my helmet. "What happened?"

"Well…" She made a pouty face. "I sort of lost your father."

"I don't understand how you lost him," Kevin said. "He's a grown man."

Joy shrugged. "I didn't actually lose him. He just, you know, disappeared."

Kate sighed heavily. "You don't just lose someone. Where did you see him last?"

My sister, the poster child for suburbia, looked totally put together in her black capris and crisp white shirt. I couldn't imagine having small children and wearing white. I couldn't even do that without children.

Joy, in contrast, would stand out at Mardi Gras—a blur of raspberry spandex pacing the driveway. "We were on our way to dinner. He wanted to go early enough to get some senior discount," Joy said. "I was telling Uncle Albert about my visit so far, and he was such a grouchy old thing. He didn't seem the least bit interested in anything I had to say."

"Sounds like Albert," Kevin said.

"Get to the part where you lost him," I said.

She stopped and stomped her high-heeled shoe. "I am!" Throwing her hands up, she resumed pacing. "Anyway, I stopped for gas at Circle K, and he just vanished."

"Vanished?" I said.

"Poof," Marcus said. "Up in smoke."

Joy giggled and batted her eyes at him. "No, silly, I'm not saying aliens beamed him up or anything."

That was a relief.

"What were you doing when you noticed he was gone?" Kevin said.

Joy tore her gaze off Marcus and sighed. "I was going to pump gas."

Kate crossed her arms. "Go on."

"Well… There was this guy…"

Oh boy, here we go.

"He was so handsome. He drove a red sports car. I may have talked to him for a while with my back to the Jeep. I guess Uncle Albert could have gotten out then."

"Just got out and left?" Marcus said. "That doesn't make sense."

"You must not know their father," Kevin said. "It makes perfect sense."

Kate stared at the ground. Everybody else looked at me.

"He's pretty impatient," I said. "Just how long did you talk to this guy, Joy?"

She shrugged. "I don't know. Could have been half an hour."

"You left an old man closed up in a car in one-hundred-and-ten degrees for half an hour?" Marcus said. "Maybe he did disappear. Maybe he melted."

"Uh oh." Joy resumed pacing. "I did turn the engine off. I forgot about it being so hot."

"Maybe he went to a friend's," Kevin said.

"He doesn't have any friends," I pointed out, trying to ignore the similarity that slapped me in the face. I held out my hand to Joy. "Keys, please. I'm going to look for him."

"I'll ride with you," Marcus said. "Since I wouldn't know him if I saw him."

"We'll try the lodge," Kevin said, taking Kate by the arm and steering her toward the van. "I know he sometimes hangs out there."

"What about me?" Joy asked, pouting like the last kid in gym class not chosen for the team.

"Stay here in case he comes home," I said. "And I don't care if Jason Momoa, Chris Hemsworth, and Captain America call. Do not leave until we've found my father."

Marcus drove my Jeep down Rural Road while I kept my eyes peeled for my father, a bow-legged man in plaid golf pants and white shoes.

"It's awesome," Marcus said. "How your family pulls together in a time of crisis."

He caught me off guard. "I never thought of it that way."

"Nice to have people you can depend on, is all," he said wistfully.

"And you don't?"

"I do alright without," he said. "Just saying some people don't have what you do. Some have to give up on their own hopes and dreams to take care of those around them."

I studied his profile. His Adam's apple moved as he swallowed hard. His grip was tight on the steering wheel. I had questions, but Marcus cleared his throat. "Your dad, he drink?" We were on the third sweep of a two-mile radius from the gas station where Joy had last seen my dad.

"Like a frat boy, why?"

"I don't know about your dad, but after a dose of Joy, I usually need a drink."

And I'd been worried they had hooked up. "Good point."

"I saw a bar about a block from the gas station."

"Let's give it a try."

The bar was a squat, perfectly square building with no windows across the front and a neon sign that flashed "Cocktails." We parked next to a truck with an "I love country" bumper sticker and headed inside.

Marcus opened the worn, graffiti-filled wooden door and held it for me as we stepped inside. It took a few seconds for my eyes to adjust to the dimly lit room. The air was so thick with smoke, it looked like ghosts floated by. Guess the patrons didn't adhere to Arizona's no-smoking rules. I squinted at the four men sitting at the bar. They glared back at me like it was a private club and I had just crashed the party.

A song about a broken heart and a Chevy played on the jukebox. Two straggly-haired guys with potbellies hanging over Wrangler jeans used the pool table, mugs of beer clenched in their hands. I guessed the truck outside belonged to them.

"What's he look like?" Marcus asked.

"A mole."

"That narrows it down."

It was weird. The few men perched on bar stools all resembled hairless nocturnal creatures. The hair on the back of my neck rose.

A toilet flushed. Seconds later, the door to the men's room swung open, almost knocking into Marcus, but he caught it with the toe of his boot. My dad waddled out and scowled at me, then continued to the bar, where he climbed onto a stool and gulped whiskey.

"What the hell are you doing here?" he asked.

"Looking for you. Joy said you disappeared."

"The woman's a tart."

Marcus laughed.

"Come on, Dad. Let us take you home."

"All right, already. Let me finish my drink."

After alerting Kate and Joy to call off the search, I drove to my father's house, my dad grumbling nonstop complaints all the way. "A man can't even have a drink without you calling out the National Guard."

"You shouldn't have left like that. We were worried."

"I was embarrassed to be seen with her," he said. "People would think I picked up a hooker."

Marcus snickered from the back seat. Guess I didn't have to worry about him and Joy soiling my sofa. He obviously had her number.

"Did you remember which attorney Hope mentioned to you?" I asked, intent on changing the subject.

"If I had, don't you think I would have told you? I know how important it is we find her." He crossed his arms like a sulking teenager and stared out the window. We drove the rest of the way in silence.

When we arrived at my father's house, Joy met us in the driveway. "Thank goodness you found him." She pulled the door open and attempted to help my father out, but he swatted her hand away. Marcus and I got out as well. But he stayed by his motorcycle and lit a cigarette. Nobody's perfect.

Joy and I followed my dad inside, where he headed straight for the liquor cabinet.

"You two going to stand there gawking at me all night?" My father settled on his recliner and shuffled through the pile of papers on the tray table next to him, probably looking for the remote.

"Actually, I have a date," Joy said. "Don't tell Marcus, though. I don't want him to get the impression I'm unavailable."

"All right, Dad," I said. "I'll come by and do some yard work soon."

My dad picked up a card from the jumble of papers beside him. "Hope's friend," he said. "She gave me his card because my neighbor keeps threatening to sue me over my tree that landed in his yard."

"A friend.... as in attorney?"

"What else would I mean?"

I crossed the room and took the card from him. Matthew Peterson, Attorney at Law. Harlan Jones' lawyer and he had represented Michael Crowne as well. He sure was turning up a lot.

I bent down and kissed my father's bald head. "Love you, Dad."

I texted Kate, assuring her our father was home safe and as ornery as ever, and joined Joy at my Jeep. Matthew Peterson would be my first call when his office opened in the morning, but I also sent Betz a text with the information in case he had a way to contact him sooner.

Joy and I followed Marcus, watching him make it on his motorcycle through a light that forced us to stop. "That Marcus is something," she said, sighing.

With what little information he'd provided that afternoon, I found him even more mysterious. Rougher around the edges. But I didn't want to talk to Joy about it—wanted to keep his vulnerability to myself—so I switched topics. "Who's your date?"

"The guy I met at the gas station." She hesitated. "Edward. No Ethan. I think it was Ethan."

"You're going on a date, and you don't even know his name?"

"So much has gone on lately."

"Where you meeting him?"

"At your house, silly."

I gritted my teeth. "Jesus, Joy. You gave him my address? He could be a—"

"He's not a pervert. Why do you think everyone's a pervert?"

"I do not think everybody's a pervert. Just everybody I don't know. And I was going to say serial killer."

Joy looked at me like she'd made her point. Aggravated beyond belief, I entered the highway and put the radio on, pushing the volume until I knew conversation would be impossible, and I'd be able to think.

So, Hope had ties to Matthew Peterson. Just because she recommended him as an attorney, didn't mean she was dating him. She could have met him in court and picked his brain about my father's tree problem. Damn my dad and his befuddled whiskey brain. Last time I talked to Peterson, he wasn't very helpful, but I had approached him about Harlan Jones, not Hope. I think this little bit of news gave me a reason to try again.

At my house, Joy ran inside to get ready before Ed/Edgar/Ethan arrived. Not wanting any part of it, I stayed outside and pulled a few weeds. I struggled with a deep-rooted one, pulling with both hands and breaking into a sweat. When the top section broke off, I tumbled backward, landing flat on my ass, making my already sore tailbone scream. Of course, this coincided with Marcus pulling up.

I rubbed my raw hands together and prayed he'd missed the show.

He came up the drive with a devilish grin on his face. "That was smooth."

"That sucker must go six feet deep."

Marcus leaned over, gave the weed a yank, and tossed it onto the pile I'd started.

"Show off."

He offered his hand and helped me to my feet. "You got plans tonight?"

Only with a bottle of Chardonnay and whatever I could find on Netflix. "Why?"

"You like Mexican?"

Any other night, I'd dine on dirt if he were my dinner companion, but with Hope missing, it didn't feel right. "I should... you know, until Hope's home..."

He frowned. "The police got this. And you still need to eat. So, you know of a good place?"

I hesitated, but he stood there looking at me with all of his adorable self. I was kind of hungry. "Tia Maria's is authentic. And close."

"Tia Maria's it is."

"Just give me a minute." I turned to go inside. The grin on my face was so wide, it hurt. I hurried to my room, ran a brush through my hair, combed on some mascara, and spritzed myself with a squirt of body splash.

I looked in the mirror and shrugged. Good enough.

When I came out of the bedroom, Joy was greeting the BMW man at the door. He looked normal enough in khakis and a polo shirt. But Joy. Oh. My. God. She wore black fishnet hose, stiletto heels, a black micro mini skirt, and a fuchsia halter top. She would overwhelm the hosts of those makeover shows.

"Casey," she said, giggling. "This is…" She doubled over and pretended to have a coughing fit.

Her date fell for it and offered me his hand. "I'm Howard."

She hadn't even been close. "Hello."

"Where are **you** going?" Joy asked.

"To dinner with Marcus." I couldn't resist rubbing her nose in it.

She narrowed her gaze and pointed to my jeans. "Like that? Guess it's not a date then."

"Depends on how you characterize a date." She was pushing my buttons again, and I was toying with a comeback about her outfit, but Joy cut me off.

"Whatever," she said.

Howard opened the door. "We have reservations. We should be going."

Joy turned and wobbled after him. I followed, locking the door behind me, and joined Marcus in his driveway. We watched Howard open the car door for Joy.

"My cousin has a special fashion sense," I said.

"Didn't notice." Marcus leaned back and looked behind me. "Too busy checking out your ass in those jeans."

I smiled. This was going to be good.

Chapter Twenty

Tia Maria's had been around since the 1950s, and not much had changed. Faded yellow and blue banners hung from dingy orange sherbet-colored walls. It was a bit like walking through a three-day-old fruit salad. The place was packed. Marcus trailed behind me as I squeezed through rows of tables occupied by people laughing and spooning up salsa with fresh-baked tortilla chips. Margaritas poured from pitchers into fish-bowl-sized glasses. Scents of cilantro and cumin drifted from the kitchen where cookware clanked, and Mexican music flitted out the door.

Marcus placed his hand on the small of my back, sending a shiver up my spine.

I found a table in the back, just past a group of women who looked like they shopped at the same store as Joy. I grabbed the seat that would keep my back to the wall and Marcus' attention off the smorgasbord of boobs behind him.

He leaned forward and said, "Great place."

"Foods good." I stared at his hands, which were clasped and resting on the table. He had long fingers with a touch of grease under the nails. Was he a mechanic? I glanced at his face but couldn't hold his intense stare. He had the look of someone who knew something but would make you work hard to find out what it was.

"You never said what brought you to Arizona," I said.

He leaned back in his seat, seeming to contemplate his answer.

The waitress saved him, asking for our drink order. "Corona," I said.

"Make that two." Marcus smiled, and the waitress was putty in his hands.

She beamed at him, leaving me feeling invisible. "I need to see your ID," she said shyly.

We both lay our driver's licenses on the table. She glanced at mine, then picked up Marcus's and studied it. "New Jersey," she said. "What brings you out here?"

"I heard the summers were beautiful," he said.

The waitress laughed. "If you're a lizard." She laid his license on the table and gave him a woeful look before returning to her duties.

I snatched his license before he could put it away. "Marcus Sheldon," I read. "Saddle Brook, New Jersey. Where is that, exactly?"

"About twenty minutes outside New York City." He held out his hand, and I dropped his ID into it after memorizing his date of birth. He was a few months older than me.

The waitress returned with our drinks. I squirted myself in the eye with lime juice as I pushed the sliver of fruit into the bottle. Ouch.

Marcus took a long drink. "Joy tells me you're still pretty torn up after your last breakup. She called you the runaway bride."

I bet she did. Truth was, when I thought of Vincent, I mostly felt relief. "It wasn't like that. I'm fine," I said.

Marcus seemed to consider this. I hadn't forgotten that he dodged my earlier question. "You haven't answered my question."

"What question?"

"What brought you to Arizona?"

He studied me before responding. "It was time to move on."

"Move on?"

He twirled the beer bottle between his hands. "I felt stuck. I needed a change."

I wondered if this change involved a breakup. "Do you know anyone in the area?"

He shrugged. "I'm getting to know people. You, for example."

I took a drink to keep my stupid grin from reappearing. "You have a job?"

"I get by."

"What does that mean?"

"Is this your standard probation interview? Cause I'm starting to feel like I need a lawyer."

"I'm just curious."

Marcus picked up the menu and opened it. "What's good here?"

Guess that was the end of our conversation.

We ate chimichangas and drank beer while I told Marcus most of what happened since Hope's disappearance, including that Betz was helping me out. I hadn't meant to share so much information, but the beer and Marcus' ability to sit and stare at me had me spilling a lot of details. I had sense enough to leave the business card, Ramirez, and the conflict-of-interest thing out of the story.

"I like that about you," he said when I took a break from gabbing to finish my third beer.

"What do you like about me?"

"Many things," he said, with a twinkle in his eye. "But I was referring to you being friends with your ex. I think that says a lot about a person."

After everything I told him, that was what he found interesting? "What about you? Do you have an ex?"

"Doesn't everybody?"

"Are you friends?"

Marcus grinned. "She wishes I were dead."

"Why?"

He shrugged. "It's complicated."

His evasiveness made me want to scream, but then I remembered his comment about him not being one of my probationers.

"You ready to get out of here?" he asked.

I looked at my watch. We'd been eating and talking for two hours. I didn't want to leave, but I didn't have the guts to say so. "Okay."

Marcus pulled a substantial wad of cash out of his jeans pocket and paid the bill. I resisted the urge to question him about the money or make a joke about him being a drug dealer. He was right. Although I wouldn't exactly call this a date, it wasn't an interview either. Still, I wondered why he was so stingy with information. My gut told me something was off about him.

My hormones told my gut to shut the hell up.

Outside, wind whipped palm treetops and dust swirled in the air. While it provided a welcome relief from the scorching sun, the warm air that blew dirt and debris wreaked havoc on my allergies and my hair. Climbing behind Marcus on his motorcycle, I buried my face between his shoulder blades as he drove us home through heavy raindrops that drummed against my helmet, relieved when we pulled into his otherwise empty garage.

Saturated, I slid off the motorcycle and laid the helmet on the seat. Marcus pushed wet hair off his face, leaned forward, and put his lips near my ear. "You coming inside?"

The warmth of his breath made my heart race. Like I could say no.

He took my hand, and butterflies flitted in my belly. He led me through the garage to the kitchen. It looked like my space before Joy had taken over and scattered stuff everywhere. Marcus' counters were clear.

He brought me into the living room, where he left me by a simple beige sofa. The room was empty except for the sofa, a cheap coffee table, and a television. I'd wager fifty bucks that it was rental furniture. "I'll be right back," he said.

I dropped onto the sofa and waited. The back of my wet shirt gave me a chill in the air-conditioned room.

Marcus returned, pulling a dry tee over his head, giving me a good five seconds to admire his abs. He handed me a plain white T-shirt. "You should get out of that wet shirt. House is the spitting image of yours, so you know where the bathroom is."

I took it from him, thinking this was ridiculous. I could easily run next door and get my own clothes. But I didn't want to appear ungrateful, and the fabric sticking to my skin was uncomfortable.

In the bathroom, I took care of business and changed shirts. I couldn't resist a peek inside the medicine cabinet, which was empty. Of course, he'd use the bathroom in the primary bedroom.

When I re-emerged, I found Marcus in the living room. He handed me a glass of white wine. "I saw Chardonnay in your fridge, so I figured you liked it. Hope it's not Joy who likes the stuff."

He prepared for this by buying wine for me? I took the glass. "I really shouldn't," I said. "All that beer and tomorrow..."

He took a step closer and tilted his head like he wanted to kiss me.

"And I have laundry to do..."

His hands cupped my face. "Stop." Then he bent toward me and brushed his lips lightly over mine."

I closed my eyes and stopped talking. I stopped breathing, for goodness sake.

He lingered on my lips, gentle and slow at first. Then his kiss became more urgent, probing. I leaned into him, feeling dizzy. I no longer cared that I knew nothing about him and pushed the bad feeling I had about his vagueness to the furthest corner of my mind. His hand moved off my face and along my throat. I awkwardly clung to my glass of wine as his lips moved down my neck while his hands settled around my waist.

A thunderclap almost stopped my heart, and I dropped my wine glass, Chardonnay splashing both of us as the glass bounced on the carpet. Marcus didn't flinch. He guided me to the sofa and gently pushed me until I was lying down, and he was on top of me. I reached around his waist and rested my hands on the small of his back.

A blood-curdling scream jolted me from the moment.

Marcus pulled back and looked down at me. "Who the hell was that?"

I lay still, trying to catch the breath he'd stolen from me.

Another scream.

I shoved him off me and jumped to my feet. The commotion was coming from the direction of my house.

We ran out the front door and crossed the yard. Howard's car was parked in the driveway. We hurried past it, and I pulled the front door open. Joy ran from the kitchen, arms waiving like propellers. "Help!"

"What's wrong?" I wondered if I should run, too.

She grabbed my arm and patted her heaving chest. She looked frantic. I assumed Howard was in the kitchen, and I tried to imagine what he could have done that would make Joy so upset. Wasn't she up for just about anything?

Howard came out of the bathroom, zipping up his fly. "What's all the screaming about?"

"There…in there…" Joy pointed to the kitchen.

"What?" Marcus asked.

"That lunatic. She's in there."

I walked past her to the kitchen with Marcus in tow. Half the food from my refrigerator was on the counter. The skinny blond from Hope's house crouched between the cabinets in the corner. She had a milk mustache and gripped half a sandwich in one hand and a large kitchen knife in the other.

She looked crazed, her pupils enormous black dots. Stringy blond hair fell onto her face.

I looked back toward Joy and mouthed for her to call 911.

"What?"

I sighed and looked back at the girl, who shifted her weight from foot to foot. She was ready to spring at us. Remembering my trip down Hope's stairs, I took a step back and held up my hands. "Just relax. Nobody's going to hurt you."

She clutched the knife tighter and held it slasher-style. Beads of sweat broke out across her brow.

"Why don't you put the knife down?" I said. "We can talk. You can have another sandwich if you'd like."

"What are you reasoning with her for?" Joy asked. "She broke into your house."

I kept my eyes on the frightened girl. "Look," I said. "You came here for a reason. Let's talk about it."

She straightened and let the knife drop. It clamored against the terra cotta tile. She pushed hair off her face, still shifting her weight like a boxer.

There were only two ways out of the room. Through the fire door to the garage, or through me and Marcus and into the living room. I could see her calculating her chances.

"I can't do this," she said. And just like before, she charged me.

The damn girl must have been part bull. I caught her on the way by, but she wiggled so much, I couldn't keep hold of her. She broke away and started past Marcus. He reached out and grabbed her from behind and wrapped both arms around her, so she was unable to flail about.

"I don't think so," he said.

"Let me go!" she cried. She twisted and tried to kick back at his shins, but Marcus hardly seemed inconvenienced.

"Call the police," Joy said.

"No!" the girl shrieked. "Don't."

"Police?" Howard said. "I'm outta here."

"You can't leave," Joy said.

"Damn straight, I can." He flew out the front door.

Joy sighed and picked up the phone. "You just cost me a date. I'm calling the cops."

"No, please," the girl begged. "Hope sent me, and if you call the police, that's all I'll ever tell you."

Chapter Twenty-One

Marcus sat the girl on the wing-back chair on my patio, and we all stood around her. Her gaze drifted from Marcus to me, like she wasn't sure who was in charge.

That made two of us.

Marcus pulled a pack of cigarettes from his jeans pocket and put one between his lips. He then held out the pack for the girl, and she reached out with a shaking hand to take one.

He lit the girl's cigarette before tending to his own. They both inhaled and seemed to exhale calmness.

"What's your name?" I asked.

Leaning back in the chair, she pulled her knees to her chest. "Beyoncé." Her gaze was hard when she drew the cigarette to her lips.

"That's a new one," Joy said.

Rain spilled into puddles in the yard. I hoped she didn't try to run again because it would be nasty chasing her in the storm.

"You said Hope sent you," I said.

"You're Casey, right?" she asked, motioning to me with a point of her chin.

"I am."

She looked at Joy. "Who's the slutty bitch?"

"That's rude," I said. Only I could call her that.

"Okay, who is the sharp-dressed one?"

"Joy. Hope's sister."

The girl barked a laugh. "You kidding me?"

Joy puffed out her chest and waggled her finger at the girl. "Watch who you're calling bitch, Bitch."

I held up my hand to Joy but kept my attention on the girl. There were marks on her wrists. Was she a cutter? She noticed me looking and pulled down the sleeves of her long-sleeved shirt.

"And the supermodel with the cigs?"

I bit my cheek. "My neighbor."

Like all the females he was around, she weakened and smiled. I felt a tightening in the pit of my stomach. Was I just another fool who had fallen for his powers?

I forced myself to focus. "About Hope, is she all right?"

The girl looked at me squarely. "I saw the news. Her being missing and all. But she's fine. They won't harm her."

"Who's they?" I asked.

"If I had a death wish, I might tell you. But I don't." She puffed on her cigarette.

"Do you know where she is?"

The girl looked at each of us, then held her gaze on Marcus. "I might."

"Care to tell us?" I asked.

"Probably not."

"How old are you?" Marcus asked.

"I'm legal if you're interested." She smiled a seductive smile that looked all wrong on her little girl face.

"You don't look eighteen," Marcus said. "You look like a runaway. And you look like street life isn't agreeing with you."

"What do you know?" she shot back.

Marcus dropped his cigarette, ground it out with the toe of his work boot, and crouched down in front of her. Tucking his hair behind his ear, he reached out and grabbed the girl's forearm, pushed up her sleeve, and exposed raw rope marks on her wrists. "I know you don't get these working at Disneyland," he said. "So why don't you help us help you?"

The girl yanked her arm away, wrapped her arms around her knees, and buried her face against them. She was silent for a moment, then looked up, staring Marcus in the eye. "I need five hundred dollars. Give me that, and

I'll tell you what you need to know."

"And what would you do with five hundred dollars?" Marcus asked.

"Get far away from here," she said. "Maybe I would get a job at Disneyland. What do you care? Nobody cares."

"We should call the cops," Joy said. "Give her the money, and she'll feed us a line of crap anyway."

"Why did Hope send you?" I asked.

"I'm not telling you without the money."

"I will have to call the police," I said. "This is their investigation, and I can't withhold evidence. But we can make it easier on you if you would just talk to us."

"You got nothing on me." The girl dropped the butt of her cigarette at Marcus' feet.

"How about breaking and entering?" Joy asked.

"I think I know what's happening to you," Marcus said. "We can help you get away from that life."

"Like it's that easy," she said.

I wanted to ask her about her ad on the website and her connection to Joel Quinn, but I knew Betz would be mad if I interfered with the police investigation. And I didn't want to bring up Hope's business card in front of Marcus and Joy.

As if reading my mind, Joy said, "This is ridiculous. I'm calling Barry."

The girl sprang to her feet. Marcus stumbled backward but caught himself and stood up, blocking her path. She hid her face against him and then sobbed like the child she was in his arms.

Betz arrived with a female detective from the human trafficking task force named Macey. I'd met her at some cop party when Betz and I were still married. She had the reputation of being good with kids. Within minutes of her arrival, we left Macey and the girl outside talking while Betz spoke to me and Joy inside. Marcus had excused himself just before Betz's arrival, saying he'd be right back. So far, he hadn't returned.

"How'd she get in?" Betz asked.

"Good question," I said. "We've been kind of preoccupied, and I didn't get the chance to look around."

The three of us toured the house and found my bedroom window smashed, the screen bent, and lying on the ground. There were no muddy footprints, which meant she'd entered before the storm had started.

We reconvened in the kitchen. "She sure was hungry," Joy said. "She even ate the piece of cheesecake I was saving for Howard and me."

Howard, who couldn't get out of here fast enough.

I took the garbage can out from under the sink and started to throw out food.

"What are you doing?" Joy asked. "Don't you need pictures or something for evidence?"

"I'm not going to prosecute her for eating my food. The girl has it rough."

"We may need the charge to hold her until she gives up the info on Hope," Betz said.

I lowered the can to the floor.

"If Macey can't get her to talk when we print her at the station, we'll hopefully learn her name," Betz said. "Kid like that is bound to have a record."

"How old do you think she is?" I asked.

Betz shook his head. "Clean her up? Sixteen, maybe. Where's this neighbor of yours? I thought he was coming right back."

I shrugged but couldn't help but wonder why Marcus had made himself as scarce as Howard had at the mention of police. And I hadn't told him about Joel Quinn or the Private Room website where Beyoncé advertised her services, yet he seemed to know she was involved in prostitution. Was he just street-smart, or did he know something about that lifestyle?

At some point, I'd have to get Beyoncé alone so I could ask her about Hope's business card and the mysterious numbers on the back, but now wasn't the time for that.

I spent the next half-hour giving a uniformed officer information for a burglary report. The girl left with the cop, giving me the finger even though her hands were cuffed in front.

"Still says she's Beyoncé," Macey said, joining us in the living room.

"What, this generation never heard of Jane Doe?" Betz said. "She give you anything useful?"

Macey sighed. "Kid is scared out of her wits. Those rope marks on her wrists are from being tied up, kinky shit like that. I'm sure her pimp has used scare tactics that have frightened her into silence. Last case I had like this, pimps threatened to go after the girl's family if she ratted them out. That's how they get these girls to be so loyal. They're trying to protect their loved ones.

"I'm hoping we can learn her name at the station and then contact the family and assure Beyoncé everyone is okay. Maybe then she'll speak to us. Another problem is, these girls don't see themselves as victims, so they think if they talk, and they get in trouble. And they see it as their fault."

"Well, our job is to make her see it's not her fault and that her pimp doesn't give a damn about her, so she stops protecting him," Betz said.

"Unfortunately," Macey said, "It'll take time to reprogram her to trust anybody. She's been taught that she's worthless."

We all stood quiet for a moment. It was hard to imagine living such a life. Maybe Hope was in some way trying to help these girls.

"Anything else?" Betz asked.

Macey flipped open a pocket-sized notepad. "Just the cross-streets for a place called Technerds. You heard of it?"

Betz helped me board up the window, then left with Macey, promising to call me the minute he learned anything new. Joy took a Valium and went to bed. I peered out the window at Marcus' dark house, changed into my nightshirt, and looked out again. Where the hell did he go? I was mad at myself for letting him kiss me. God only knew how things would have progressed had Joy's scream not stopped us. I didn't exactly consider myself impulsive, but I fell hard and fast when it came to guys. It was something I had to work on. Promising myself, I would slow things down with my sketchy neighbor, I climbed into bed. Even with my new resolve, I couldn't help but think about seeing him again. I fell asleep, frustrated as hell.

Chapter Twenty-Two

Sunday morning, I allowed myself the luxury of sleeping until seven. I'd slept like the dead, waking in the same position I dozed off in. The only light in the room came from the bathroom window since my bedroom window was boarded up. I had to get that fixed. Knowing that Beyoncé, or whoever she was, had been in my room felt like a violation. I wondered if she went through my things or if she went straight to the kitchen.

My phone buzzed on my bedside table. I reached for it and brought it in front of my face.

A text message from a blocked number.

They know you have it, watch your back.

My heartbeat quickened. Had it been another time of my life, I might have chalked the message up to a wrong number, might have ignored it. But with Hope missing, I recognized the threat. What was it I had? Ramirez had mentioned me having something as well. Was this message meant to warn me about Diablo? With all that was going on with Hope, I almost forgot about Ramirez being mad at me.

I sat up, staring at the phone. Waiting for it to go off again. When it didn't, I replied. "Who is this?"

When no answer came within a few minutes, I got up. I thought about forwarding the message to Betz, but he had to be sick of hearing from me by now. I'd wait until I had more information. What could he do since it had been sent from a blocked number except worry more about me?

Dressed in my running clothes, I grabbed my pepper spray and my phone, planning to head out for a run before the temperature climbed into the triple digits.

Joy's door was still closed, and I figured the happy pill she'd taken after the police left would keep her in bed at least a few hours longer.

I stepped outside and adjusted my earphones. Marcus' house was lifeless, and I wondered where the heck he went last night.

The Counting Crows motivated me as I maneuvered the quiet streets. I hoped a good run could help me cope with my anxiety. But with each car that passed and every time the bushes swayed in the breeze, I became more uneasy. Sure, my pepper spray offered a bit of protection, but anyone associated with Diablo would laugh it off as Ramirez had. I swayed between not letting them alter my lifestyle, to thinking I should lock myself inside with the blinds closed until this whole thing was over.

My thoughts drifted from Diablo to Hope. With each day that passed without finding my cousin, I was losing faith that we would. The girl last night said my cousin was fine and that they wouldn't hurt her. But what did that mean? I picked up my pace. The girl had those answers and wasn't giving them up. I understood she was a victim in all of this, too, but that didn't get me any closer to finding my cousin.

What connection could my cousin have to a teenage prostitute in the first place? Did Hope send the girl because she didn't have the freedom to contact me herself? There was the website, and Joel also had an unexplained connection with my cousin. Had she stumbled onto the website and tried to help the girls? And how was Harlan Jones involved, and why was he murdered? Hopefully, Macey could get something out of the girl, but she was a tough nut to crack.

As I reached the halfway point in my four-mile route and turned around, my phone buzzed in my pocket. My stomach dropped. I worried that it might be another cryptic message like the one earlier. No, this was a phone call. I answered. "Hello?"

"Is this Casey?" a woman asked.

I tried to breathe normally. "It is."

"This is Mary. You left a message for me to call you."

"Mary McDonnell?" Harlan Jones' girlfriend.

"Yes."

"Thanks for calling me back. I wanted to talk to you about Harlan."

"What about him?" she asked suspiciously.

"Have the police been in contact with you?"

"Police? No, I've been camping and just got back into town," she said. "I really have nothing to do with Harlan anymore. We broke up a few months ago."

Traffic had picked up, and I was having a hard time hearing her. "Would you meet me for coffee anyway? It might be easier…"

Silence.

"My treat," I added.

"Who are you?" she asked.

"I'm a probation officer," I said. "Harlan was mixed up in the disappearance of my cousin, and I'm looking for anything that can help."

"I don't know anything," she said.

"Maybe not, but I'd like to at least give it a shot. You might think something isn't important, but it might help us find my cousin. I'm really worried about her."

She sighed heavily. "There's a Starbucks on Central and Camelback. I can be there in an hour."

I would have to haul ass on the two miles back to my house in order to make it, but with Sunday light traffic, it was doable. "I'll see you there."

The Barista at Starbucks handed me a double mocha Frappuccino that I passed to Mary. I grabbed a bottle of water, and we settled at a metal table outside under a misting system.

Mary was probably in her forties but had the look of having lived a hard life. She had wrinkles worse than a Shar Pei and lines around her mouth from a lifetime of smoking. I thought about getting Marcus to quit but reminded myself that five minutes of making out with the guy didn't give me the right to change him.

Besides, I'd yet to see him again since he ran off the night before.

117

"Why would you think the police want to talk to me?" she asked.

I didn't want to be the one to break the news to her, but felt I had no choice. It wasn't exactly protected information since it had been all over the news while Mary was out of civilization. "I hate to tell you this, but Harlan was shot. He died."

She took a minute. After several deep breaths, her eyes filled with tears. "I'm sorry." She dabbed her eyes with a napkin. "I don't know why this is affecting me so. He wasn't leading a very pure life."

"How do you mean?"

"When we met, he was kind of lost. It was almost endearing. We were in AA together. I'd been sober for ten years, and he'd just started coming to meetings. I knew I should stay away from him. He only had a few months of sobriety under his belt. But he could be sweet, and he got to me."

I nodded and thought of Marcus. It happened to the best of us. Sometimes, the most rational people lost all common sense when it came to matters of the heart.

"Anyways," she said. "We started dating, and things moved pretty fast. Before I knew it, his toothbrush was next to mine, and he was spending a lot of time at my place. He found a job and really seemed to be getting his shit together."

"So why did you break up?"

She twirled the straw in her cup. "We were just sitting around one night watching a movie at Harlan's place, and the front door banged open. A bunch of bikers poured into the room. Harlan turned pale, but I could tell he knew them. They threatened to break his thumbs. I had no idea what was going on. I thought they were going to kill us both.

"They took him outside while one of the bikers sat on the sofa next to me and told me they wouldn't hurt me if I just kept quiet. He helped himself to the bowl of popcorn on the coffee table, and I didn't say a word. I heard a lot of commotion out front, and then they left.

"I found Harlan a bloody mess in the yard. I was terrified but felt sorry for him at the same time. I started to call the police, but he begged me not to. He claimed the men were there to collect an old gambling debt."

CHAPTER TWENTY-TWO

"You didn't believe him?"

"I didn't. He wasn't convincing."

I took a drink of water. "So, you left him after that?"

Mary wiped her nose on the back of her hand. "Should have, but I stuck it out a little longer. There were more red flags. I knew he was on probation and not reporting or doing anything he was supposed to. He seemed to think he had his PO wrapped around his finger. I'm not proud of it, but I didn't leave until a few months later when I found him looking at a website to meet girls."

I sat up straight in my seat. "Go on."

"It wasn't a dating website, which would have been bad enough. The girls were young. They had to be prostitutes, the way they were dressed. He tried to tell me it wasn't what I thought. Said he was totally faithful.

"Harlan wasn't really motivated in the bedroom, so I did find it hard to believe he was trolling for sex elsewhere, but some guys are just into weird shit. I had more questions than he had answers. I broke up with him about then. He took it hard. Kept trying to buy me stuff to win me back. I have no idea where he got the money. He couldn't hold a job to save his life, yet here he was, offering me jewelry, expensive clothes. He even offered to buy me a new washing machine when mine broke. I was suspicious enough to move on."

"The motorcycle guys who beat him up," I asked. "Do you know who they were affiliated with?"

"I don't know much about motorcycle gangs," she said.

"Did you notice any tattoos?"

Mary scrunched up her face while she thought for a moment. "The guy who babysat me while the others roughed up Harlan, he had a pitchfork on his arm. You know, the kind the devil carries."

Diablo. Javier Ramirez's crowd. A shiver tickled my spine even though it was easily 105 degrees.

I sent Betz a text message asking him to call me as soon as he could, then drove home. Traffic was light, and I made good time. I replayed my conversation with Mary on the way. So, Hope had been easy on Harlan. Was there a reason other than that we are all overworked, and sometimes people are just not on our radar as we deal with emergencies? Or was that too much of a coincidence? And if Harlan was involved with Diablo, was my run-in with Javier Ramirez more than just an encounter with a paranoid meth addict? Like Harlan, spending money he didn't have, Hope was living beyond her means. Did she transfer Ramirez to me because she was caught up in the same shit as Harlan? I wanted to throw up.

After I parked in the garage, I stepped outside and looked over at Marcus' house, still silent. I walked over and rang the doorbell. Nothing.

With a heavy sigh, I returned home.

Pushing the door open, I started to kick off my shoes when the flash of a muzzle across the room startled me even before the sound of a gunshot exploded in my head.

Chapter Twenty-Three

A stinging sensation prickled my upper arm. I ducked down, throwing my hands over my face.

I spun around and pulled the door open, about to scamper back outside and brace for another gunshot to my back, when I heard Joy shriek. "Oh my God! Casey?"

Turning around, I peeked through my fingers. Joy stood across the room, a handgun gripped in trembling hands.

"Jesus, Joy," I said. "Put that thing down."

She dropped the gun on the table beside her, then fanned herself with her hands. "Oh, God, I shot you."

I looked down at my arm. Blood trickled from my bicep to my elbow, where it gathered before dropping onto my tile floor.

"I don't want to go to prison!" Joy wailed. "Please, Casey, don't turn me in."

I leaned against the wall, then slid down until I was sitting on the floor.

"Women like me don't do well in prison." Crocodile tears splashed down her face.

"Shut up," I said. "And get me a towel."

Marcus rushed through the open door. "Was that a gunshot?" He crouched down before me. "Casey, are you okay?"

I rested my head against the wall and looked at him squarely. "She shot me." I started to hyperventilate. I told myself to calm down. People didn't die from being shot in the arm. Unless she hit a main artery. My vision became fuzzy, and Marcus' face started to go out of focus.

Marcus reached out and pushed the sleeve of my shirt up, revealing my wound. He looked at me, trying to suppress a grin. "You weren't shot. But she definitely killed the vase."

I turned my head to look at the pile of shattered glass from the vase that had been sitting on the table next to the door.

"I think you got hit by a little flying glass." He stood up and offered me his hand, helping me to my feet. "Let me help you clean up."

He led me by the hand to my bathroom, where I sat on the edge of the tub. He took the towel Joy handed him, wet it with warm water, then dabbed the blood away. "Just a small cut. You have any Band-Aids?"

Band-Aids? A few seconds ago, I thought I might bleed to death, and now he was patching me up with a half-inch of gauze?

I pointed to the medicine cabinet and waited while he took out a Band-Aid and placed it on my arm. "There," he said. "Want me to kiss it and make it better?"

I rolled my eyes, then looked past him to Joy, who stood in the doorway biting her lip.

"You see," she said. "Just an itsy-bitsy little cut. No need to call the police."

"What the hell were you doing?" Anger welled in my chest and pounded in my head. Here I was afraid of Diablo and my own cousin almost blew me away. "You could have killed me."

"I thought you were that girl. You know, that bitch who keeps turning up."

"The girl who hasn't hurt anybody?" I asked. "You were going to shoot her?"

Joy put on a pout worthy of an Oscar nomination. "She frightens me."

"Oh, brother." I pointed to the door. "Out. I'm going to take a shower. Please don't shoot me when I return."

Marcus turned and guided Joy out of the room. "Come on, Annie Oakley, let's clean up the mess."

I emerged from my bedroom to find Joy sitting on my living room sofa, her foot on the coffee table as she painted her toenails purple. "Where were you coming from before I...you know... before the accident?"

I plopped onto the chair next to the couch. "Out." I was still processing what I'd learned and was not ready for a psychic's opinion.

"You could have left a note," she said. "I was worried."

I missed living alone. "Where did you get the gun, Joy?"

She twisted up her face, as if trying to decide if she should be truthful. "The Internet. Someone a few blocks over had it for sale. It's legit."

"So, you bought it today?"

"This morning."

"Have you ever shot a gun before?"

Joy concentrated on painting her toes. "You just point and shoot. Any idiot can do it."

"Believe it or not, there is some skill involved. You'd think my shattered vase would be enough to prove that to you. Please get rid of it. I don't want a gun in the house."

"You'd think with all that's been happening, you would want the protection," she said.

If either of us were trained on firing the damn thing, I might agree. "Do you remember how my mother died?" I said. "I hate guns."

"All right," she said. "I understand. Can we stop talking about it? I had such crazy dreams last night. I can't figure out what that girl has to do with Hope. Have you heard from Barry?"

I hadn't, which was odd. We'd pretty much been in constant contact the last few days. I took my cell phone out of my pocket and checked for messages. None from Betz, but Hope's friend Elise had left one.

I played the message. "Casey, it's Elise. I got your message. I'm so sorry about Hope. I pray she's okay. I'm back from vacation, so feel free to call me."

I walked into my bedroom, closed the door, and pushed redial. "Casey," she said.

"So, you heard about Hope?"

"I was out of town, and it didn't make the news there, but Jerski posted it on Facebook. Then, I did a little research and read the news stories. Is there anything I can do?"

"I'd like to ask you a few questions."

"Anything."

"When was the last time you spoke to her?"

"Gosh, not since I went on vacation two weeks ago."

I paced my room. "Is that unusual?"

"A year ago, it would've been. We used to talk several times a day, go shopping, do happy hour, that sort of stuff."

"What changed?"

Elise hesitated. When she spoke, she sounded incredibly sad. "Hope did. She became so secretive. And she started showing up with all these expensive things. Jewelry, a Coach bag, a fancy new car."

"Did she explain how she afforded them?"

"That's where the secretive part comes in. At first, she was vague. Then she flat-out told me to mind my own business. Her work started to suffer. I tried to cover for her. I even did a few warrants on her caseload since they were overdue. Hope freaked when she saw I did one on a particular client. She tore it up and said if she wanted my help, she would ask for it."

"Who was the warrant for?" I asked.

"Harlan Jones," she said. "The guy whose house she went missing from."

I emerged from my bedroom, deep in thought. Joy was still on the sofa, this time on the phone to one of her many men. In the kitchen, I called Betz. "You working?" I asked.

"I am, but I could use a break. The investigation into your cousin has kind of come to a standstill."

"Wanna meet for a drink? I got some stuff to tell you."

"Sure," Betz said, sounding skeptical. "Just let me finish a few things. Why don't you come to the office? I should be done by the time you get here."

"Be there in fifteen."

Chapter Twenty-Four

I parked at a meter, shook my head no when a homeless man held out his hand for change and darted inside the precinct. After flashing my badge at the cop behind the information desk, I took the elevator to Betz's office. Since it was Sunday and no one manned the reception desk, I text messaged Betz that I had arrived. Within minutes, he opened the door and ushered me inside.

He led me to a break room with a couch. A bed pillow was crunched up on the sofa, and a duffel bag sat on the floor. I raised my eyes at Betz.

"I try to grab a little sleep when I can," he said. "And I have to admit, home is not that appealing right now. My sister is staying with me, having problems with her girlfriend. They're trying to work things out, and I'm in the way."

Guilt gnawed at me. Here I'd been out to dinner with my gorgeous neighbor and sleeping in my own bed while Betz was working his ass off. Granted, he had help, but he didn't relinquish responsibilities too well, so he was likely overseeing the investigation and probably covering for Jasmine while she dealt with her personal problems. And I knew he hated that these things took time and there wasn't instant gratification like there was on TV. Investigations involved lots of legwork and interviews and not a lot of action. Then, add that the pressure was up since Hope was family, and I was constantly asking for updates…

"I have some pretty good information," I told him. "Want me to tell you here, or are you at the point you need a break?"

"Funny you should say that," he said. "Not ten minutes ago, my sister ordered me to eat something."

"That rat hole down the street been condemned yet?"

"No, and the roaches still outnumber paying customers, but it's close enough that we can walk."

I waited while Betz placed his gun in his shoulder holster and slipped on a button-down shirt that he left open. Once that was done, you couldn't tell he was packing. I followed him down three flights of stairs and out onto the street.

Outside, we passed the same poor guy begging for booze money, and Betz dropped a few dollars into his hand. Smokey's came by its name honorably. Cigarette smoke was so thick it took effort to wade through. Betz went straight to a booth at the back of the bar. A waitress appeared before I had the chance to sit down. Betz ordered us both a Sam Adams, and I added an order of fries. I did skip lunch, after all.

Our beers arrived instantly.

"I half-expected you to be on leave," I said.

"If one of us pulled the trigger, I would be." Betz took a swig of beer. "And we're so short-staffed, I doubt they could spare me."

We sat silent for a moment. The image of Joel Quinn dead on the floor was a hard one to clear from my head.

"So," I said with a sigh. "I found out a few things since we last spoke."

"Yeah?" Betz looked uneasy.

"I did everything safely," I assured him. "I talked to Hope's best friend Elise. Seems Hope didn't want a warrant done on Harlan Jones even though he needed one."

"That's interesting," Betz said.

"There's more. Harlan Jones was mixed up with Diablo."

Betz tipped his beer bottle and took another drink. "And how do you know that?"

"I had coffee with his ex-girlfriend. She also told me she caught Jones looking at a website that sounds a lot like the one Beyoncé was on."

The waitress appeared with a plate of French fries. I stuffed one in my mouth. It was so greasy, I hardly had to chew it to get it down. "Speaking of our little liar?" I said.

Betz helped himself to a handful of fries. "Real name is Melissa King. She's a throwaway kid. Been missing for over a year, but her family didn't report it. Been hooking for the past six months but hasn't given up her pimp yet or her connection to Hope. Seems she has a younger sister she's worried about. Macey is still working on her. But it's delicate."

"Hope's knee-deep in this, isn't she?" I asked.

Betz sighed. "Certainly looks like it. Joel Quinn was the administrator for the Private Room website Beyoncé was working from. We interviewed his wife and she said everything changed after he got into a fender bender with a biker and didn't have the money to fix the guy's Harley. Said he was doing a job to work off the debt. I'm thinking that the biker was a Diablo member, and he cashed in on Quinn's computer knowledge. There's no record of the accident, so it doesn't look like police were involved.

"I've been interviewing every Diablo member I can find, but, big surprise, no one's talking. We've been to their club, but it seems they have someplace they are working from that's not on our radar. We got officers following them, but so far, no luck."

I leaned back in my seat and tried to digest what Betz told me. With all that had happened today, I had forgotten about the sinister text I'd received that morning. I shared the story with Betz.

"You get any more messages?" he asked.

I shook my head.

"I don't like this whole thing and how it seems to keep touching you. Now that we know there is a link to Diablo, I'm thinking your run-in with Ramirez is related to Hope's disappearance. I'd offer you protection, but we just don't have the manpower. Which means—"

"That I need to be careful. I know. And I am, as much as I can be. I don't have the funds to hire a bodyguard."

Betz slid another fry off the plate. "I wish you'd get a gun."

"You know my stance on that." And that became more sold after almost getting shot that morning. I thought it best not to tell Betz about that. It would put him in a compromising position, and as much as Joy drove me nuts, I didn't want her hauled off to jail.

"How about a dog?" he said. "A dog can be a good alarm system."

"I could live with a dog. Except I'd have to remember to feed it. And I'm no good with those kinds of things. Remember the frogs we had? I forgot to feed them, and one ate the other."

"That was pretty traumatic."

"Especially for the frog."

Betz took a last tug of beer and ordered another round.

It was after nine when we emerged onto the dark city street. I gulped fresh air. Fresh compared to inside Smokey's, not so fresh if you looked at the EPA air quality reports.

"Look," he said. "With all that's going on, I don't want you to be alone. Why don't you come to my place? I have a pretty nice guestroom."

"I'm not comfortable getting in the middle of Jasmine's personal life," I said. "Besides, then Joy will be alone. I'll be fine."

"Nope," he said. "I'm not backing off on this. Either you stay somewhere safe, or I'm inviting myself over."

"I do have a pretty comfortable couch." I suppressed a smile.

"My back is killing me. That office sofa is lumpy as hell."

"So, what are you waiting for? Get your stuff."

Betz followed me to my house in his SUV. My street was quiet. Most of the houses, including Marcus's, were dark. I pulled into the garage while Betz parked in the driveway behind me.

I held the door to the kitchen open for him as he passed through, holding his duffel bag in front of him as I led the way into my living room, flicking on the kitchen light as I passed.

"Holy shit," I said.

My cabinets and drawers were open, the contents dumped on the floor. Pillows and sofa cushions were strewn about. We looked at each other wide-eyed. A thump sounded in my bedroom.

Betz soundlessly put his bag on the floor and reached for his gun. He moved down the hallway, holding his weapon at the ready.

I tiptoed behind him.

He flipped on my bedroom light as we stepped into the room. At the same instant, I saw a boot disappearing through my open bathroom window as the intruder slipped outside. Betz darted across the room and out the window after him. I took my cell out of my pocket and punched in 911.

"Someone broke into my house," I said. "An off-duty cop is pursuing him."

I stayed on the phone with the 911 operator while checking the rest of the house and looking for Joy. She wasn't home. I paced, chewing my nails until there was a knock at the front door. "Our officers have arrived at your address," the dispatcher said.

I thanked her and disconnected, letting two female cops inside.

"What we got?" the stocky one asked.

"Someone broke in," I said. "My, uh, my friend and I surprised him when we came home. He escaped through my bedroom window. My, uh, friend followed him."

"The off-duty cop?"

"Detective Betz."

"How do you know our suspect is male?" the officer asked.

"I saw his boot. It was a large man's boot."

About five seconds later, Betz appeared breathless in the doorway. "I lost him," he said. "I hopped a few walls to keep up, but he took off in a dark-colored van waiting on the next street over. I got the plate." He asked the officer to run it and then handed me a file. "He dropped this."

I recognized it right away. It was the file on Harlan Jones I'd taken from Hope's office. Only Hope's kidnappers would be interested in Jones' file.

The second officer relayed Betz's information onto the radio so anyone in the area could look for the van. The older one took out a pen and notepad. "Anything else missing?"

I looked around and did a quick inventory. The TV and my tablet were still in place. I crouched on the floor where my mail had been dumped off the table. I hadn't opened any of the envelopes. I had the bad habit of not opening mail until the beginning of the month when I paid my bills. I rarely even got it from the mailbox. I restacked the pile and put it on the table.

"Not that I can tell."

"We'll dust for prints," the cop said. "Maybe something will come up. Probably a drug addict looking for money or a check that came in the mail he could forge."

Except why would they take Harlan's file?

"Point of entry was here," the cop said, fiddling with the lock on my patio door. "These locks are so easy to pick. It's a cinch to break into these houses."

That made me feel a whole lot better.

"Plate came back stolen," the other cop informed us.

While the cops did their thing, I motioned Betz out back. "This has to be connected to Hope. Why take Harlan's file if you're looking to score something you can use to buy drugs."

Betz took the file from me and paged through it. "What's in these files?"

"Since everything is electronic these days, it's mostly the reporting forms clients fill out when they report. Stuff we had to have them sign, like the conditions of their probation."

Betz followed the numbered conditions with his finger. "Number one," he read. "Obey all laws. Any of them do that?"

I arched my brow. "A few. Usually takes something big to hold them accountable, though."

"So, the file wouldn't be useful to whoever killed Jones, but maybe whoever took it wouldn't know that until they looked through it."

I text messaged Joy. "Where are you?"

"On a date," she messaged back. "Why?"

"Just be careful," I returned.

"What time will Joy be home?" Betz asked.

"I have no idea." I wouldn't put it past her to spend the night wherever she was. I was thankful *my friend* was sleeping on my couch tonight.

Once the cops left, Betz and I secured the back door by sliding a piece of wood into the track. I text messaged Joy to make sure she was still okay, and she assured me she was on a very hot date and to please stop bugging her.

We spent the next half-hour picking up the mess left by the intruder. The glass and frame of my sliding glass door, my tabletops, and my bathroom window were all covered with a fine mist of black fingerprint powder where the cops had dusted. They found a lot of prints, but if I had to hazard a guess, I'd bet they belonged to me and Joy. It had been a while since I went wild with Windex. Around midnight, I made up the sofa with sheets and a pillow.

As I got ready for bed, I tried not to think about the stranger who had been in my house, in my bedroom, a few hours earlier. But think about it or not, every muscle in my body was wound tight from the violation. Anger was part of it—but mostly, I was terrified that he'd come back. And that Hope could be lost to me forever.

After getting ready for bed, I checked to see if Betz needed anything before I turned in for the night.

He stood in the middle of the room, his shirt off and jeans undone. I sucked in a big breath. A smile spread his lips. I felt a little homesick looking at him like that, remembering when it was the most natural thing in the world to wrap my arms around him. So much had changed between us. Divorce did that, I suppose.

"You okay?" he asked.

I took a step toward him; he took one toward me. I could almost feel the smooth skin of his chest against my face, his strong hands on my back. My cell phone rang before I could make my fantasy a reality. Betz cocked his head. "Better get that."

I took the call. "Hello?"

"I saw the lights on in your house and thought you might still be up."

Marcus. My already pounding heart thumped harder in my chest. I blushed and looked at Betz. "Excuse me," I mouthed and hurried back to my bedroom. Closing the door, I sat on the edge of my bed.

"Just wanted to make sure you were okay?"

"I don't remember giving you my number."

"Joy did. Hope you don't mind. You okay?"

I didn't want to talk about Joy or Hope or break-ins. I didn't want to tell him my ex-husband was half-naked in the other room. But all I could think of was Betz standing shirtless in my living room. "Everything's okay," I said.

Just too much forbidden fruit around for a girl to get any rest. I thought about questioning him about his disappearance last night and how he showed up after Joy tried to shoot me, but I was too tired for that. We said goodnight, and I tried not to think about him as I drifted off to sleep.

Chapter Twenty-Five

I wanted to stay snuggled in bed where I felt safe. Sleep was an appealing alternative to the madness that had become my life. And I still felt exhausted after a night of strange dreams about Marcus and Betz. But my bladder was unforgiving. Peeking out from under the covers, I focused on the bedside clock.

Nine thirty! I couldn't remember the last time I slept that late. I shot out of bed and raced for the bathroom.

After, I checked in with my office. My job afforded me a flexible schedule, but I liked to let them know what I was up to during business hours. And good thing. Tracy reminded me I had a court appearance.

Once I'd showered and dressed, I found Betz had left for the day, but he'd taken the sheets off the sofa and left them neatly folded on the coffee table. In the kitchen, a bag of bagels and a six-pack of Diet Coke sat on the counter. Leaning against it was a note. *Thanks for letting me crash here last night. Be super careful today. I'll call you later.*

I put the soda in the refrigerator, grabbed a sesame bagel, and munched on it as I returned to the living room. Betz had taken his bag with him. Drat. I wouldn't have minded a semi-permanent arrangement—at least until Hope was found.

Finding Matthew Peterson's number, I punched it into my phone. A receptionist told me he was in court all morning but offered his voicemail. I left a message, claiming it was urgent that we speak, but I didn't offer the reason in case it gave him cause not to return my call.

With a bit before court, I called a locksmith to repair the broken lock on my patio door and a handyman for the bedroom window, and spent the next twenty minutes wiping off fingerprint powder.

Figuring Joy had a late night, and I didn't hear her come in, I waited until close to ten-thirty before tapping on her door. When she didn't answer, I eased it open and peered inside to find the bed neatly made.

I grabbed my phone and sent her a message. "You okay?"

A few minutes later, I got a reply. "Fine."

I breathed a sigh of relief and sorted through my mail, separating the junk from the bills. Remembering I hadn't checked my mailbox for the better part of a week, I retrieved my keys and walked down the street to the bank of mailboxes.

As predicted, my box was full. I pulled out the contents and started shuffling through the pile of mostly junk when my cell phone chirped with a text. I tucked the stack of mail under my arm and looked to see if it was Betz. I half-hoped he was checking on me again.

Don't be the next victim. Again, from an unknown number.

My face flushed with anger. Really? What the hell were these cryptic messages about? *What the hell does that mean?* I typed back.

The alarm on my phone startled me. Court was in thirty minutes. When I set it, I assumed I'd be on my normal schedule and sitting in my cubicle. Making it downtown from home would take some favors from the traffic gods. I jogged back to my house, stuffed the mail in my bag to sort through later, and headed to my Jeep.

As I drove toward the courthouse, I mentally prepared for the hearing ahead of me. Lindsey Sejour had violated her probation by leaving a residential treatment program while she was seven months pregnant and then failed to inform me of her whereabouts. Police picked her up the week before while she was in the company of a guy in possession of methamphetamine, Lindsey's drug of choice. I'd recommended probation be reinstated after she served six months in jail. That way, the baby could be born without its mom ingesting any more drugs. Child Protective Services would take the baby, and Lindsey would have some time to get clean before she returned to the community and regained custody of her child.

I hated cases where children were involved. In this situation, one yet to be born. Her attorney thought my recommendation was harsh since it was Lindsay's first alleged probation violation. That was why we were having a hearing.

I made it to the 4th Avenue Jail in just under thirty minutes. I parked at a meter a few blocks away and jogged to the building.

Once I'd cleared security, I hurried to the courtroom which was already in session. Another inmate pled his case to the judge, so I still had time. The court usually heard probation admissions to violations before they held contested hearings.

I took in the familiar setting. Inmates to the side, counsel for the state and the defense at their respective tables. The judge sat at her seat on the bench. Court was usually a high-stress situation for me, but flashbacks from my recent appearance before Judge Dorfman made it much worse.

While a defendant went on and on about what a great support system he had at home, Alan Wonder, the Ken doll county attorney, stood and came over to me. "Casey?"

I nodded, and he motioned for me to follow him to a small room at the back of the courtroom attorneys used to confer with witnesses before hearings. "She's willing to admit if you change your recommendation from six months to three."

Except six months would allow her to complete a treatment program offered in jail. "If she doesn't get a substantial amount of sobriety time under her belt before she hits the streets, I don't think she's going to make it."

The Ken doll nodded. "Understand your reasoning. Problem is that the defense has a witness to testify she left treatment after an abusive ex-boyfriend tracked her down and threatened her."

It was the first I'd heard of that development. "No matter why she left, she should have contacted me and informed me of her whereabouts once she went AWOL. She was on abscond status for two weeks."

He shrugged. "This judge hardly ever gives jail. Three months is a success in this court."

"She's pregnant."

"And due in two months. She'd still have the baby while in custody. If the baby has meth in her system, CPS will step in and take the baby."

"In two months, there won't be meth in the baby's system."

"The system isn't perfect, Casey."

But the system didn't have to supervise her and deal with the fallout. I did. "I'm standing by my recommendation, Alan."

I testified first. My part was easy. Lindsey was pregnant, a meth addict, had left treatment without permission, and had been on the run for two weeks. I had a discharge summary from the treatment program that backed my testimony.

Then Lindsey took the stand. She was tearful and respectful to the judge. She swore she hadn't used while on the run. "I've been clean for five months," she said. "I wouldn't put my baby's well-being in jeopardy."

I hoped that was true, but experience told me it was iffy at best.

"Tell us what happened to cause you to leave treatment," her lawyer asked.

"I wasn't safe there." She hung her head. "I was scared."

"You were already in the program for close to five months," her attorney said. "Why did you decide after all that time it wasn't safe?"

"They were building a website for the program," she said. "They hired a company to design it. The man that came, he was from my past."

At the word website, I straightened in my seat.

"And you were fearful of this man?" the Attorney asked.

Lindsey nodded. Then she went very pale as she stared at the back of the room.

I twisted in my seat and looked behind me. Two men dressed in black with Diablo tattoos on their bulging biceps stood at the door, their arms crossed against broad chests. The scrawny man standing next to them was so unremarkable, I almost missed him. Michael Crowne: the client who saw me berated in Judge Dorfman's courtroom and was so inappropriate when he reported. What was he doing here? And why was he with Diablo? He didn't strike me as the type of guy the gang would give the time of day.

I turned my back before the gang members noticed me and leaned over and whispered to Ken. "Gang members in the back of the room."

He checked over his shoulder, then looked at me and nodded.

"Why were you fearful?" Lindsey's lawyer asked, unaware of Diablo's presence.

Lindsey looked down at her lap and wrung her hands. She didn't respond.

"Ms. Sejour?" the judge said.

Lindsey looked up, tears glistening in her eyes. "I don't remember."

Her lawyer looked taken aback. "Ms. Sejour, you are under oath."

"I left, okay? Just put me in jail. I don't want to testify anymore."

I chanced a glance back at the Diablos, but they were leaving. Michael Crowne caught my eye and blew me a kiss before following the goons out the door.

A shiver ran up my spine. Was the show for my benefit or Lindsey's? I prayed Ramirez hadn't been able to alert his buddies about my existence and figured Michael Crowne would have no idea about our connection. Still, I felt unnerved.

The judge shook her head. "Miss Sejour, do you know what's at stake here?"

Lindsey nodded. Tears dribbled down her face.

"Okay," the judge said, shrugging her shoulders. "I find the defendant in violation of her probation, and I sentence her to four months in jail with early release to residential treatment. Furthermore, I'm continuing probation for one year. Ms. Sejour, I hope you complete treatment this time. Your child will need you."

We all stood as the judge strode out of the room. I asked the deputy if I could have a moment with Lindsey before he took her away.

"What was that about?" I asked out of earshot of everyone around us.

Lindsey shrugged. "If you really want to help me, you'll leave this alone."

"Are you mixed up with Diablo?"

Lindsey laughed. "Aren't you the master investigator. If you know anything about Diablo, you know that answering that question could leave me dead."

"I can help you."

She shook her head. "Nobody can help me." She turned to the deputy, who had been standing several feet back to give us some privacy. "I'm ready to go."

He came forward and led her toward the door.

"The man who built the website," I called after her. "What was his name?"

She looked over her shoulder. "What does it matter?"

"Was it Joel Quinn?"

A shadow passed over her face, giving me my answer, but she turned her back on me and didn't say more.

Lindsey's connection to Diablo left me wondering if she also had a connection to Hope.

Chapter Twenty-Six

I hadn't finished my bagel earlier, and my stomach growled. I needed to walk a petition through at the main courthouse, which was a few blocks down the street. The search for Hope had stalled, and I couldn't think of anything else to do to help. At least work continued to be somewhat of a distraction.

At the courthouse, I headed for the cafeteria first. It was just past noon, and the place was packed with court employees, jurors, witnesses, and defendants. I picked up a pre-made turkey sandwich and a bottle of water and got in the shortest of three lines.

Bending down to tie my shoe, I balanced my sandwich on my knee.

"You do spend a lot of time around here, Ms. Carson," a voice said from behind.

I turned toward the voice. I almost didn't recognize Judge Dorfman without his robe. He wasn't quite as imposing in gray dress slacks, white shirt, and blue tie. He smiled at me. Most people would have seen kindness. I saw a killer whale playing with his food before he devoured his dinner.

"Hello," I said as I stood.

The person in front of me moved ahead a foot, and I did the same, turning my back to the judge. As far as I was concerned, the conversation was over.

I felt as if his eyes were burning a hole through my back. It seemed to take forever for it to be my turn at the register.

When I reached the cashier, she scanned my items and said, "Five forty-nine, please."

I pulled the last five-dollar bill from my purse and dug for change. Coming up empty, I took out my debit card and held it out for her.

"Sorry." She pointed to a sign. "Our system is down. It's cash only."

I sighed and took another try at finding change in the bottom of my bag. But all I came up with was an old Tic Tac. I gave her the five-dollar bill. "I'll just take the sandwich."

She gave me my change, and I found an unoccupied waist-high table. Settling on a stool, I unwrapped my sandwich. As I took a bite, a bottle of water was placed on the table in front of me.

I looked up, startled to see Judge Dorfman. "Let's call it a peace offering," he said. He lowered a salad with grilled chicken and another bottle of water on the table and sat across from me.

I swallowed dry turkey. "Not necessary."

"It's a bottle of water," he said. "Don't make a big deal out of it."

I would have argued, but a lump of lunch meat was stuck in my throat. Reluctantly, I opened the bottle and took a sip. "I'll pay you back."

"If you insist." He looked quite proud of himself.

I lost my appetite and thought about tossing my sandwich and leaving, but I didn't want to give him the satisfaction of knowing that he got to me.

"So, what brings you to my neck of the woods today?" he asked, spearing a piece of chicken with his fork.

"I have to walk through a petition," I said.

"Petition for what?"

"To delete a jail term."

"Which judge are you looking for?"

I fought to keep the irritation from my voice. "Judge Pudis."

"She's on vacation." He held out his hand. "Let me save you the trouble of finding someone."

Oh God. I just knew he'd find something to question and berate me about. But I saw no graceful way of declining his offer. I took the petition out of my bag and slid it across the table.

Dorfman perched bifocals on his narrow nose, glanced at the paper before him, took a pen from his pocket, and scribbled his signature. "Any time I can help," he said. "I know you officers are overworked."

Talk about a personality disorder. I'd never had a judge shoot the breeze with me. What could his angle be?

"I saw a story on the news about the missing probation officer. Same last name. You related?"

"She's my cousin."

"Oh, my," he said. "That must be hard for you. I hope she turns up soon and in one piece."

"Thank you." I took the petition back, rewrapped the remainder of my sandwich, and stuffed both in my purse. I stood. "I'll interoffice you the money for the water."

"You didn't finish your lunch."

"Like you said, officers are busy."

He reached out and placed a hand on my arm. "Please," he said. "Sit."

I stiffened.

He laughed. "Judges don't bite, you know."

I was pretty sure this one did.

He reached into his pocket and pulled out a business card. After scribbling a number on the back, he handed it to me. "If you need anything, please call. That's my private cell." And he winked at me. Was he hitting on me? I doubted I was his type, and he certainly wasn't mine, but I couldn't think of another reason for him to give me his number.

He refastened the lid on his salad. "I need to get back for a hearing anyway."

Oh, thank God. I took the card and got out of there before Dorfman could follow me.

Squeezing through the crowd at the entryway, I walked the wide first-floor courtroom hallway, weaving through attorneys, court staff, and the public as they hurried to their destinations. What was wrong with that man? He was all over the place, berating me one minute and acting like he wanted to be besties the next. What did he care what I thought of him? He obviously had a God complex, and I was insignificant to him. Did he feel bad after seeing Hope's story on the news? Or did he just enjoy messing with me? Although I tried, I was pretty sure I hadn't hidden how uncomfortable he made me, and that just pissed me off.

A line of people stood at the metal detectors, waiting for their turn through security. I looked up just in time to see Matthew Peterson bypass the crowd and scrutiny by showing his court ID.

I hung back for a minute, then followed. Peterson strode past the elevator and took the stairs. I waited a moment, then entered the stairwell a few paces behind him, making my footsteps as soundless as I could.

He took the stairs two at a time. A door opened two floors above me and then swung shut. I exited on the same floor and came to a corridor that led to four courtrooms. Peterson wasn't there. I approached each room in turn, studying the docket that hung on the wall. Scanning the lists for Peterson's name, my heart stopped when I found it at room 403. It was Dorfman's courtroom.

My heart started beating again, but into overdrive. He was here representing Javier Ramirez. That meant Ramirez was in the building.

I whirled around at the sound of footsteps. Peterson stood behind me. "Ms. Carson," he said, like he wasn't all that surprised to see me. "This is just a show cause hearing. You don't need to be here."

"Actually," I said. "I wanted to talk to you about my cousin Hope."

He looked confused or uncomfortable. I wasn't sure which.

"Apparently, you gave her your business card, and it made its way to my father for some legal advice. You must know her."

A flicker of concern clouded his face, but he quickly regained his lawyer's composure. "I give my card to a lot of people. I'm sorry about your cousin, but I really can't help you. In fact, I'm afraid even speaking with you is a conflict of interest. Not only am I representing Mr. Ramirez in a case in which you are the supposed victim, I'm representing him in a case where you are the defendant."

"Defendant?" I squeaked.

"Mr. Ramirez intends to sue you. You can't stick a handcuff key in an unarmed man's eye socket and not expect repercussions." He squared his shoulders. "Now, if you'll excuse me. I have a hearing to attend."

Peterson disappeared through the swinging double doors and into the courtroom, leaving me speechless. I didn't see that one coming.

I struggled to right my breathing. Ramirez could sue me, but could he win? I was defending myself when I knocked his glass eye out and stabbed my keys into the empty socket. Okay, when I thought about it like that, it did sound bad. Mentally reviewing our use of force policy, I was in the right. Ramirez's size and strength gave him the means and ability to knock me into next week, if not worse. I should contact my union rep and head to the County Attorney's Office and talk to the probation department's lawyer, but I didn't feel up to facing the newest development. Since I hadn't been served with a complaint, it could wait. Eventually, they would come to me anyway.

I had to get out of there. If Ramirez had a hearing, his buddies might attend, and I couldn't risk him pointing me out to them.

But I was too late. Three massive thugs strutted in my direction. Dressed in black jeans and black T-shirts, their tats made their affiliation painfully obvious. Unfortunately, Dorfman's courtroom was at the end of the hall, and I had nowhere to go but through the thugs or into the courtroom.

I opted for the second choice, eased the heavy wooden door open, and squeezed inside. I yanked my hair out of its ponytail, fluffed it, and let it fall around my face, hoping it would help conceal my identity.

The courtroom was standing room only. I squeezed through the crowd and wedged myself in the corner where I could keep watch and hopefully blend into the cluster of people. The three thugs came inside and stood at the back of the room, their attention on Ramirez.

Peterson took his place at the defense table where Ramirez was already seated and wearing jail stripes and an eye patch. Court was called into session as Dorfman sauntered in from his chambers and took a seat at the bench.

"Call the first case," Dorfman said.

With the distraction, I started to squeeze through the crowd toward the door. Diablo's disciples were intent on watching the hearing, and I figured I could sneak out behind them. They hadn't recognized me, but if Peterson, Dorfman, or even Ramirez alerted them, things could get ugly fast.

I was almost to the door when one of Diablo yelled, "Now!" The crowd pushed forward like an incoming wave, taking me with them.

"Order," Dorfman barked.

But it was utter chaos. People pushed and shoved, and the three heavily muscled thugs jumped over the three-foot partition that separated the public seating from the lawyer's tables. One of the gangsters pulled a handgun from a sack and dropped the bag on the floor.

I squatted, using the bench as cover, and dared a peek over the seat. The biggest thug wrapped his arm around the female deputy, immobilizing her so she couldn't reach for her gun. He pointed his weapon at her head and dared the second deputy, who had time to draw his weapon, to use it and threatened to shoot the woman in the head.

I dropped flat to the floor and belly-crawled toward the door, getting kicked twice in the head on my way there. I was close, but I didn't make it.

People screamed and scattered. From my vantage point, I could only see feet as people moved toward the door. Some made it and escaped. Others crouched behind benches.

The room went quiet.

"Let's get the hell out of here," a deep voice said. "Grab a hostage."

They'd only have to get by the two deputies in the courtroom, and they'd be free to escape since the exits weren't manned.

"Please," a meek voice begged. "I have a baby at home."

I wanted desperately to help her, but knew I had less chance of surviving an encounter with Diablo than she probably did. Hoping the bench concealed me, I reached in my pocket and brought my cell phone in front of my face.

I thought about calling 911 but couldn't risk Diablo hearing me make the call. *Under attack in Judge Dorfman's courtroom*, I banged out in a text message. *Ramirez is escaping.* I hit send and hoped Betz had his phone with him.

Heavy boots sounded toward the door. I risked a glimpse in time to see one of the Diablos squeeze off a round at the deputy, holding his gun at the ready as the other deputy was let go. As he fell to the ground, I saw the backs of Ramirez and his gang as they pushed through the double doors, pulling a pleading court staff with them.

I wiggled out from under the bench and got to my feet. The courtroom looked like a battlefield. Chairs were overturned, files strewn across the floor, and a deputy lay on his back gasping as he held a hand to his blood-soaked belly. Two prisoners, still chained together, huddled on the floor where the inmates sat. The county attorney sat cross-legged and crying under the prosecutor's table. Spectators stood trying to console each other.

I hurried over to the female deputy who tended to the wounded deputy on the floor. I looked to the lawyer, who seemed frozen to the spot. "Call 911," I said.

Leaning over the deputy on the floor, I held his terrified gaze. "Hold on." I put pressure on the wound with my hands and glanced up at the second deputy. "It's going to be okay, Joe," she said.

The attorney was still frozen under the desk, watching me with wild eyes. Peterson and Dorfman were nowhere to be found. "Get help!" I yelled.

She seemed to come to her senses and crawled out from under the table and then ran for the judge's chambers.

I pressed harder on the deputy's wound. His eyes were frantic. "Hey, Joe," I said. "We need you to stay with us. Help is on the way."

His eyes showed gratitude.

"You got this, Joe," the other deputy said. She took his hand and squeezed it.

A young judicial assistant crouched beside me and handed me a towel. I placed it over the hole in Joe's stomach and applied more pressure. His eyes fluttered shut. "I need you to stay awake. Can you do that for me, Joe?"

He blinked and forced his eyes open. Deputies poured into the room. Paramedics knelt beside me, and hands on my shoulders gently pulled me away. "We'll take over," a young man said.

I stumbled back, staring down at my blood-soaked shirt, my hands stained dark red. Tremors ran through my body like an electric current. Ramirez was on the loose. It wouldn't be long before Diablo came for me.

Chapter Twenty-Seven

The corridor outside the courtroom was set up as a triage center. I wandered about aimlessly, taking in my surroundings. Deputy Joe had been brought out on a stretcher moments earlier. Those who had been in the courtroom were checked out by medics, and the Phoenix Police crisis response team was there in full force, offering mental health assistance.

Deputies stopped people from leaving so they could be interviewed as part of the investigation.

The same woman who had knelt beside me while I tried to comfort Joe came out of a side door and touched my arm. "Casey?" she asked.

I turned and nodded.

"My name is Kathy. Judge Dorfman sent me out to get you. Please wait in chambers with us. It's much more comfortable."

I didn't think anything related to Dorfman could be comfortable. "I'm fine out here," I said. But my legs nearly buckled beneath me, and I had to put my hand on the wall to steady myself.

"Come on," she said. "There's a restroom in there. You can clean up a bit."

I looked down at my stained, shaking hands. I didn't recognize them.

Without speaking, I followed Kathy through the door.

In chambers, Dorfman sat at his desk, his robe open, a glass of water in his hand. Matthew Peterson leaned against the wall, constantly running his hand through his hair. The county attorney, who had taken refuge under the table during the attack, sat in a chair with her head in her hands.

Dorfman looked up at me. "The washroom is over there." He motioned across the room.

I went into the room and closed the door. Swallowing hard, I took deep breaths. The scene from the courtroom replayed in my head. Vomit rose in my throat, and I made it to the toilet just in time. The vile taste in my mouth momentarily distracted me, and I was almost grateful. Rising on shaky legs, I flushed the toilet and stood before the sink. Turning on the water, I put my hands under the stream and watched the water turn red as it cascaded over my skin. When the water finally ran clear, I slathered on liquid soap and scrubbed until my hands were raw. When I felt my hands were clean, I cupped them under the faucet and gulped water until the rancid taste in my mouth was gone.

Looking up, I caught my reflection in the mirror. Blood smudged my face. I grabbed a towel and rubbed the skin on my cheek until there was no more evidence of the ambush I had witnessed. There wasn't much I could do about my shirt.

I opened the door and emerged feeling slightly better. The scene was pretty much as I'd left it, except all eyes turned on me.

"I want to thank you, Ms. Carson," Dorfman said, "for helping Deputy Whitlow. He's been a member of my team as long as I can remember. Unfortunately, protocol kept me from helping too."

I nodded and looked at Peterson, trying to read him. Had he known what Diablo's plans were? Security was tight at the courthouse, but his ID allowed him to bypass it. Getting a gun through, while not impossible, would be very difficult for anybody who didn't have employee access.

"How did Diablo get the gun past security, Mr. Peterson?" I asked.

He looked at me, his gaze hard. "How the hell would I know? I was taken off guard just like everyone else."

"It's happened before," Dorfman said. "Not here that I can remember, but no system is perfect. Some security guard is probably on the take. I can assure all of you I will not rest until that person is identified and brought to justice."

Kathy walked in from the adjoining office with a T-shirt in her hand. "Why don't you change into this. It was in my gym bag, so it's kind of wrinkled, but it's better than what you have on."

"Thank you." I took the shirt and returned to the bathroom. Pulling my blood-soaked tee over my head, I threw it in the trash, then took the towel I had used earlier and ran it over my torso. Before I could put Kathy's shirt on, my phone buzzed in my pocket.

I took it out and looked at the screen. There were twelve messages, all from Betz. I looked at the last one. "Where are you? I'm outside the courtroom."

I pulled the shirt over my head and hurried to the door. "Thank you," I said, mostly to Dorfman and Kathy. The others hadn't done anything. "But I have to go."

Before they could respond, I opened the door and stepped out into the hall.

Betz paced a few yards down, his cell phone to his ear. When he saw me, he dropped the phone to his side and crossed over to me. Pulling me into a tight hug, he said, "Jesus, are you all right?"

I took a deep breath, inhaling his fresh shampoo scent. So much better than the iron blood smell that clung to my skin despite my attempt to clean up.

"It was awful," I said into his shirt. "A deputy was shot."

"I know," he said. "What the hell happened?"

He led me to a bench just around the corner from the command center in front of the courtroom. We sat, our legs touching, him rubbing my back as I told him everything that had transpired, my words jumbled, the order of events all off, but he just nodded and kept rubbing my back.

"You're lucky Diablo didn't recognize you," he said. "I was sure they had you when I got your text, and you didn't respond."

"But they did take a hostage."

"The court staff," he said. "They released her on the street. She's shaken up, but okay."

"Thank God."

"This is the Sheriff's Office investigation," he said. "Has anyone interviewed you yet?"

I shook my head. "God, I know I'm going to have to answer a bunch of questions, but there's something about Matthew Peterson that has me on edge," I said. "I'm not sure how he gets assigned cases, but this isn't the first client he's representing who has ties to Diablo."

"Harlan Jones was not a Diablo gang member," he said. "But he was an associate."

"So, there was a connection." And then there was Michael Crowne.

"I'm sure the Sheriff's Office will look at the lawyer. I'll do what I can, but technically, this is their investigation. There's a manhunt on for Ramirez and Diablo. Every agency in the valley is on it. News vans are three-deep out front."

A man in dress pants and a button-down shirt came to stand in front of us, a MCSO shield clamped to his belt. Betz stood up and pumped his hand. "How you doing, Carl?"

"Been better, Betz." He turned his attention to me. "We need to chat."

I stood and followed him down the hall.

Two hours later, I emerged from the detective's office, thankful to find Betz waiting for me. The questioning was brutal, the same basic things asked a hundred different ways. There was a lot of waiting between interviews, and I managed to call Alma to let her know what was going on. Technically, I was on the clock when it happened. Since Ramirez was on probation, upper management needed to be aware before the press got to them.

Joy texted me to make sure I was okay because she'd seen Ramirez's escape on the news and me looking shell-shocked in the background of the footage they ran over and over. I sent her a message in return suggesting she not be home alone. She assured me she was at her date's house and perfectly safe. I also returned a quick call to Kate, promising her I would get back to her after I got some sleep and could think clearly.

Betz had the wherewithal to sneak me out a side door so I could avoid further news coverage since all the major channels were parked out front. The shooting of a deputy and the escape of an inmate upped us to national coverage. I was okay with that if it meant more people were looking for Ramirez and possibly for Hope. I didn't know how she fit in on all this, but it looked like the two were connected.

Betz took me home, stopping for pizza and beer along the way. I showered and then joined him in the living room, where we ate cold pizza and drank lukewarm beer. Neither tasted very good, but I was famished and managed to choke some of both down.

"I requested police protection for you," Betz said.

My stomach knotted. On one hand, I was grateful. On the other, having someone watching me felt creepy.

"They said no," he said. "Since Ramirez hasn't directly threatened you."

"So, I have to wait for something to happen to get protection?"

Betz rubbed the back of his neck. "I'm staying here tonight." He rose and set our empty beer bottles in the recyclable bin.

I felt bad for monopolizing Betz. I wasn't his responsibility. "I won't be alone. Joy will be here."

"Not my idea of a bodyguard. Just somebody else for you to look after."

I refrained from telling him she was packing these days. "Maybe I can stay in a motel or something," I said, yawning. "I can't even think straight tonight."

"Sounds like you don't want me here."

"No," I said. "It's not that." But I had to admit having him around so much was weird. It was getting difficult for me to keep my feelings in check. I was tired of reminding myself that we divorced for a reason. And being as tired as I was, it was hard to remember what that reason was.

"Go to bed," he said. "I'll be right here if you need anything. And I think you should go to work tomorrow. That's probably the safest place for you to be right now. But stay in the office. Don't go out alone."

I squeezed his shoulder on the way to my room—too tired to argue. I'd need sleep if I intended to be on my game if Ramirez or his goons found me.

Chapter Twenty-Eight

The next morning, before we went our separate ways to work, Betz made me promise not to go anywhere alone. As much as I liked having him around, I remembered why things didn't work out for us. He hovered, and it made me crazy. I got to age thirty, working in what many would consider a dangerous profession without getting myself killed. I had no interest in messing with that statistic. And I didn't need him to remind me of how to conduct myself.

After my promise to behave, the minutes ticked by like molasses. At my office, the first thing I did was go on the Internet and read all the news stories I could find about Ramirez's escape. It had made all the major networks. I couldn't bring myself to watch the video of the aftermath. The latest story listed Deputy Joe Whitman in stable condition. I said a silent prayer of thanks.

I walked to Alma's office half a dozen times, but she hadn't yet arrived.

Back at my desk, I drummed my fingers on the desktop. It was still early, so most of the cubicles around me were empty, but slowly, the office came to life. When Claire came in, she dropped her stuff at her desk and came straight for me, arms out for a hug.

I stiffened as she wrapped those mama bear arms around me, and I patted her on the back before pulling away.

"I heard what happened yesterday. I'm so sorry, Case. That must have been horrible." She stepped back and looked me over. "What are you doing here? You should be home, taking it easy."

"I have to stay busy," I said. "And I'm fine, really. It didn't happen to me, it happened to that poor deputy."

"Still, you were there. It must have been terrifying."

My phone buzzed, saving me from a deep dive into my emotions, which I'd walled off. But I had to admit the wall was cracking, and it wouldn't take much to send me over the edge. "I have to take this."

It was Betz. "You sitting down?"

"Yes."

"Prints are back from your break-in."

"That was fast."

"I pulled a few strings. Anyway, nothing matching anyone with Diablo. But some came back for a Marcus Sheldon. Isn't he your neighbor?"

"He is, and it makes sense his prints would be in my house. He was there." Then it dawned on me. "Why are his prints in the system in the first place?"

"Now you're asking the right question. He has a record."

It felt like a punch to my stomach. "For what?"

"Assault. From New Jersey."

"You have any details?"

"Not yet. Listen, Case, I got another call. But I don't like this Marcus already. Be careful around him."

I hung up, biting my lip. And Betz didn't even know we'd had a makeout session.

Bringing up the Internet, I looked up Saddle Brook, which was the address listed on Marcus' driver's license.

Using our database and my credentials to gather information for personal use was a major no-no. It could result in termination of employment. The fact that the guy's tongue had been in my mouth did not make a stronger case for violating the rules. But going to a website, like any civilian could, was perfectly legit. I found a list of counties and learned Saddle Brooke was in Bergen County. Finding the superior court website, I then did a public records search.

While the computer did its thing, I thought about Marcus. My gut had tried to warn me about him. How convenient he'd shown up just after Hope disappeared, and then he wormed his way into my life. He offered no information about himself yet seemed adept when dealing with Melissa King/Beyoncé. I wasn't half-bad looking and had been called pretty by most who commented on my appearance. But Marcus was in another category and could have any woman he wanted. Sure, I felt chemistry, but something had nagged at me. I should have trusted my intuition.

After being led to several sites that promised to find records for a fee, I found the Bergen County public information page. I typed in Marcus' name and date of birth and waited.

And there it was. Marcus Sheldon. A case number and a conviction date of just six months ago. The charge: Assault. A felony.

I gulped air and sat back in my chair. If Marcus was convicted just six months ago, he had to be on probation. And if he was on probation in New Jersey, what the hell was he doing here? Probationers weren't allowed to leave the state without a good reason and a travel permit. And that was for a visit. Marcus had moved here.

I minimized the website and checked our system to see if we were supervising him through Interstate Compact, a program that allowed departments to supervise people from other states if they moved while on probation. I found no record of him in our system.

I closed out of our system and maximized the Internet page. A search for the probation department in Bergen County gave me the number. I dialed. The ethics train was still in the station, and I'd found the information on Marcus as any civilian would. Nothing unethical about calling someone's PO. Making out with a convicted felon? That was another story.

It took three phone calls to track down his probation officer, a woman named Charlotte Manley. I got her voicemail but didn't leave a message. What would I even say? I was on the verge of having sex with this guy the other night, and now I found out he was on probation? No, I didn't think that would fly.

I'd try her again later, as I felt I had a duty to report that Marcus had probably absconded his New Jersey supervision.

Alma appeared at my desk.

I closed my laptop. "What's up?" I had Marcus on my mind and no longer felt like a check-in with my supervisor.

"Come to my office."

I got up and followed her. She ushered me through her door and shut it behind us.

Not a good sign.

Alma settled on the chair behind her desk. I sunk into the chair across from her.

"How are you?" Alma asked. "After yesterday? After everything?"

I sighed, exhaling the weight of the last few days. "I'm trying to forget." If she made me talk about it, it wouldn't be pretty.

"You need to take some time off."

"Work is the only thing keeping me sane."

Alma gathered her hair into a bun and leaned forward. "I'm sorry, Casey. You don't really have a choice right now."

"What does that mean?"

Alma let her hair fall and leaned back in her seat. "The department is investigating Ramirez's grievance against you. I know it's bullshit, that you had every right to defend yourself, but while it's being investigated, you've been placed on administrative leave."

"Oh, that," I said, slouching in my seat.

"You knew?"

"Ramirez's attorney told me he was suing me." After what happened at the courthouse, I'd forgotten about it. Now, my stomach clenched at the thought of being investigated. "Admin leave? Is that really necessary?"

"It's standard procedure in a situation like this. I'm not supposed to suggest you call your union rep, but call your union rep," Alma said. "The union has their own attorney. Your dues pay for it. Might as well use them."

I put my head back and closed my eyes. For just a moment, I let my mind wander to what if? What if I lost my job over this? What if charges really led to a conviction? The rational me said that couldn't happen—my actions had been justified. But if recent events taught me anything, it was that life was not fair and justice wasn't always served.

I opened my eyes and looked at the ceiling so I wouldn't cry.

"I'm sure this will be cleared up quickly," Alma said. "Ramirez's escape greatly affects his credibility."

I nodded and stood, smoothed my hands over my jeans. "So, I just don't come to work?"

"Not until I call you and tell you to. Hopefully, it won't be long. Leave your equipment, including your work cell on your desk. And please write down your security codes to your phone and laptop so we can access your calendar and files."

"I have appointments. Stuff due..."

"We'll take care of it," Alma said. She stood, circling the desk, and drew me into a tight hug. "I'm behind you all the way."

I pulled back, wiped my eyes with the back of my hand, and headed out the door.

The laminate card the union rep had given me when I was hired had been tucked in my wallet for years. Now, I held it to my chest as I sat in my Jeep. Dan Millard was still the president. Since Alma made me leave my work phone behind, I dug through the glove compartment for my personal cell— an old flip phone that I hadn't used for years. I'd intended to get rid of it because it didn't hold a charge, but then the county assigned us smartphones, and I only kept the old one for emergencies. The only reason I still had a plan was that I never got around to canceling it. Sometimes, procrastination was a good thing.

Fishing out my old charger, I plugged it in and waited for it to get enough power to work. Sitting in a daze, my thoughts drifted to my mother and how much I wished I could reach out to her for advice. As I dwelled on all the awful stuff that happened, I didn't even notice time slipping away until the screen on my phone lit up, letting me know I had enough of a charge to make a call.

I studied Dan's number on the business card and then punched it into my phone. News had traveled fast, and he was, to my surprise, waiting for my call. We arranged to meet at the county attorney's office as he was there for a meeting. We'd walk over to the union lawyer's office together and chat on the way.

I found a spot two blocks from the office and stared at the building in the distance. Memories of meeting my mother for lunch or even a Diet Coke break flooded my mind. What I wouldn't give for one more day. She would have known what to do. Would have gone with me to my meeting with Dan and the union lawyer, then taken me out for a drink and a debrief afterward. But I had to do this on my own.

Outside my Jeep, I glanced in the back window on the way by and noticed my gear bag. Alma had asked me to leave my equipment. I would drop it off later as I couldn't bring myself to return to the office right now.

I walked the two blocks, barely noticing the blazing sun that scorched my skull and left me damp with sweat. Inside the building, air conditioning blasted, causing goosebumps to prickle my skin. I reached for my ID to flash at the security guard, but then remembered I'd left it on Alma's desk as instructed. I passed through the metal detectors like an ordinary citizen and was granted access to the building.

I rode the elevator to the third floor. My mother's office had been at the opposite end of the hall, and I started to wander that way out of habit. When the door to the employee entrance to her office bounced open, I stopped short, half expecting my mother to greet me. But it was her assistant, Mabel Sutter, who stepped into the hall. Mabel had the highest seniority in the county, and my mother used to fear she would find her dead at her desk one day. But it was Mabel who found my mother. Afterward, she experienced some sort of mental breakdown and had taken an extended leave of absence in Europe to recover. I'd assumed she'd retired, but here she was.

Mable was stooped over from osteoarthritis and had to tilt her head to meet my eyes. She wore orthopedic shoes and a plain blue dress. Her gray hair was cropped short; enormous curls cupped her head like a curled-up cat. She always reminded me of a 1950s sitcom grandma.

"Casey." Her hand flew to her mouth like she'd just witnessed something horrible all over again. "For a minute, I thought you were your mother."

I met her halfway and gave her a big hug. "Mabel, it's good to see you."

"You too, Sweetheart. I've been meaning to call you. How've you been?"

156

CHAPTER TWENTY-EIGHT

I shrugged. "Good days and bad. How about you?"

"I'm okay." She took me by the elbow and steered me away from the door and into the ladies' room across the hall. After checking the stalls to make sure we were alone, she faced me.

"Something's been bothering me. I tried to convince myself it was nothing, but the more I think about it…I don't know how to say this without upsetting you, dear." She wrung her gnarled hands. "I've been struggling with the finding that your mother committed suicide. That would be so unlike Carissa. We worked together for fifteen years. She would never want me to find her like I did. People try to tell me that when people are suicidal, they aren't thinking clearly. But it just doesn't sit well with me."

"Me either," I said.

"She was working on something before she died, something she was very nervous about. It was strange for her not to include me in an investigation. I kept all of her notes. But not this time. She kept a file that was with her always. Kept it in that battered briefcase she carried around. I was so shocked when I found her…when she died…that I couldn't think straight for a while. But looking back on it, I can't help but wonder if she met with foul play."

I sucked in a deep breath. Is that why Hope wanted the briefcase? Could my mother's death somehow be connected to this whole Diablo mess? And if so, did it have anything to do with Hope's disappearance?

I didn't have a quick answer for that, but it was a relief to find someone who also believed my mother wouldn't kill herself. But the thought of someone else ending her life was, in some ways, even harder to swallow. "You said you didn't know much about what she was working on. So, you knew something?"

Mable shrugged. "It was more of a feeling, really. She was jumpy, would minimize a file on her computer when I walked in the room. I'm ashamed to admit that at first, I thought she was having an affair; she had become so secretive. She used to confide in me about most everything. And then one day I heard her on the phone. It was late, and I think she thought I'd gone home for the day. She was setting up a meeting. Said she had information that was inflammatory. When I walked in the room, she jumped and quickly ended the call. A business card fell to the floor. I bent down to retrieve it for her and saw it was for an FBI agent. She snatched it out of my hand before I could read the name."

"Was it rare for her to connect with the FBI?"

"Kind of. I probably wouldn't have thought much of it had she not reacted so strangely. I told our boss, Ryan, after she died, and he said he'd look into it."

"But then Ryan had that fishing accident," I said. "I remember seeing it on the news and thinking how bad it was for your office to lose two employees so close together."

Mable reached out and took my hand, holding it between hers and staring me directly in the eye. "Makes me wonder if Ryan's accident was an accident after all."

The beginnings of a headache threatened me. But my skin prickled at the verification of my suspicion surrounding my mother's death. Why had I let people convince me it was a suicide when it went against everything I knew about my mother? Hugging Mabel goodbye, I promised to stay in touch and hurried down the hall. I caught Dan, the union president, as he was walking out of another office.

"Thought you stood me up," he said.

We walked to Annie Nguyen's law office a block away. During the walk, we reviewed what happened thus far. I tried to push the conversation with Mable to the back of my mind and concentrate on the matter at hand, but it wasn't easy. I'd been put on admin leave, and the department's investigator would investigate Ramirez's claim that I assaulted him to see if I violated any policies or code of ethics, and the police might conduct their own investigation. I wasn't to answer any questions without Dan or Annie present.

Annie was a petite powerhouse who paced the entire time she spoke. "What we have here," she said, "sounds like self-defense to me. I need a copy of the incident report and the report from your doctor. Hopefully, he recorded bruising that is consistent with your reporting of events. Nobody would probably even touch this if they weren't under such scrutiny with all the recent allegations of police brutality across the country. When can you get me a copy of the incident report?"

"Soon." I tried to follow her, but my thoughts were with my mother. Nothing else really mattered to me at the moment.

"Ramirez's escape helps your case. Shows what he's capable of."

I nodded some more.

"Look at the use of force continuum and be able to articulate how you followed it. We'll need to get together in the next few days and go over everything. Sooner we get this settled, the sooner you can go back to work." She handed me her business card. "Email me the incident report, and we'll go from there." She took a call as she waved us out the door.

"Wham, bam, thank you, ma'am," I muttered under my breath.

Chapter Twenty-Nine

I rested my head on the steering wheel of my Jeep, but quickly jerked upright when the leather burned my skin. I checked my forehead in my rearview mirror. A small welt had already appeared. Life just kept getting better and better.

I surveyed the area, looking for anyone who might be watching me. I lingered on a van a few spaces back, but then an elderly man got out and unloaded a scooter. Harmless.

Satisfied I was safe for the moment, I started a mental to-do list as the air cooled off the Jeep enough so I could touch the steering wheel. I could access my work email from my personal computer and forward Annie Nguyen the incident report I'd written following my episode with Ramirez, but that could wait.

Mabel's thoughts on my mother's death were all I could concentrate on. Had my mother been involved in something that got her killed? Who was this FBI agent? I didn't have Internet on my cheap ass phone, or I would have given the FBI a call to see if an agent had been working with my mother. Like they would even tell me.

I wondered about the files my mother so closely guarded. I assumed her employer kept those as they would have confidential information. I would ask Mable to see if she could find out what happened to them.

But there was something I wanted to do first. I put the Jeep in gear and started driving. Thirty minutes later, I pulled up outside Hope's house.

With the key I'd lifted a few days ago, I let myself in. The house was eerily quiet. No one appeared to have been inside since Beyoncé had knocked me down the stairs. The air had been left at a comfortable temperature. I turned it up as I made my way toward the stairs. It didn't seem like Hope had to worry about such things as electric bills, but I felt it was wasteful just the same to run it when no one was home.

I eased up the stairs, listening for odd sounds and waiting for someone to jump out at me. But no one appeared.

In the office, I went straight for my mother's briefcase, still sitting on the chair. I laid it on the desk, turning on the lamp so I could see better. When I'd glanced inside the last time, it looked empty, but I hoped I might have missed something.

Today, I stuck my hand through the compartments and felt every inch.

My mom had kept a day planner, and there were always files. Because of the classified nature of her job, I didn't expect to find those.

I was about to give up when my thumb scratched the corner of something. I yanked my hand out, put my thumb in my mouth, and sucked on the paper cut. Widening the opening of the bag, I held it under the light and saw a tiny corner of a card or piece of paper sticking out from a torn seam in the leather. It was so small, it would be easily missed. I reached in with my other hand but couldn't get hold of it. I ran into her bathroom, found a pair of tweezers, and returned to the office. It took a good five minutes to cox the card out, but with a lot of wiggling, it came free.

A business card. I held it under the lamp. Joshua Madison, Lead Investigator, Federal Bureau of Investigations.

I pulled out my cell and punched in the telephone number listed. It rang four times before a voice came on the line.

"Madison," he said.

"Agent Madison," I stammered. "My name is Casey Carson. I was wondering if you knew my mother, Carissa Carson."

"What's this about?" he asked.

"My mother died recently, and it seems she was in contact with you shortly before her death. It would have been about nine months ago."

Madison cleared his throat. "Let me look through my calendar." I could hear him typing, then a pause. "Oh, here it is, yeah. We had an appointment.

But she never showed. I didn't realize she'd passed. I'm sorry."

"What was the meeting about?" I asked.

"Unfortunately," he said. "we never got that far."

"What division do you work for?"

"The Public Corruption Task Force," he said. "Sorry, I wish I had more to tell you."

Briefcase in hand, I checked the area from Hope's front window before leaving her house. Hopefully, Ramirez was held up in a cave somewhere or had left the country to avoid going back to jail, but I had a hard time believing he wouldn't want to exact revenge on me for the whole eye thing. Gangs were about retribution.

For the moment, it seemed safe to go outside. Driving home, I turned the new information I'd learned over in my mind. Public Corruption? My mom was an investigator. She worked with attorneys every day. Had she witnessed something that didn't sit right and planned to turn the information over to the feds? Maybe Mable could remember more about the cases she'd been working on, and we could look at the attorneys involved and start asking questions. Somebody had to know something. I couldn't help but think of Matthew Peterson.

I called Mable, but when I got her voicemail, I opted not to leave a message. I didn't trust that someone wasn't listening.

I sat in my driveway, the engine running as I pushed the garage door opener. I wished I had another place to go than inside, but I couldn't pull Kate and her family into this mess. I'd been concentrating on my mom this afternoon, but I knew Diablo was still a threat, and we had no leads on Hope's disappearance of late. Although the kidnappings and Ramirez's disappearance were all over the news, the department had thus far been able to keep my name out of it. Still, I didn't feel safe.

I was relieved when I saw a patrol car pull up out front. The officer got out and walked over to me. I unzipped the window so I could talk to him.

"Just checking on you, Ms. Carson. Everything okay."

I nodded. "I thought having protection wasn't in the budget."

The cop rested his hands on his gun belt. "It's not official. Detective Betz mentioned it might be a good idea if I had the time."

"Thank you. I was just about to go inside."

"How about I go with you. Just to make sure everything's okay."

I pulled into the garage and then led the officer through the house. There were no gangsters or runaways hiding in closets. "I appreciate this," I said.

"I'm on duty until midnight," he said. "I'll drive by as much as I can."

"Thank you."

I locked the door behind him, grabbed a Diet Coke from the refrigerator, scooped up my iPad, and settled on the couch. Bringing up my work email, I found the incident report about Ramirez and forwarded it to my attorney and the union rep. I had several unopened emails and had to remind myself I was on mandatory suspension. There was no reason to check them. Alma had made it clear my caseload would be handled. But as my finger hovered over the button to close the screen, one of the subject lines caught my eye. "Without Hope, there is no Joy."

My finger shook as I lowered it to open the email, my heart thudding hard in my chest.

Chapter Thirty

Up popped a photo of Joy. She wore a negligee and was tied to a four-poster bed. A gag stretched across her mouth, a look of terror in her eyes. The contents of my stomach threatened to make an appearance. I swallowed hard and read the note above the photo. "Give us the video, or you're next." It said to wait for further instructions. No cops.

What video? They clearly thought I had something I didn't.

The photo was cropped, so Joy took up much of the frame. The bed was wrought iron. The comforter, red satin. There were no other details except the look of panic on Joy's face.

I reached for my cell phone and called Betz.

"Detective Betz." He sounded distracted.

"They've got Joy."

"What? Oh, shit. Who?"

"I don't know. I got an email with a picture and a note." I read him the short message.

"No cops, my ass. Forward it to me."

My fingers were flying on the keyboard before he could finish his sentence. "Done."

"When did you last see her?"

Good question. I hadn't seen her for a while and had no idea who she had been out with. "We texted, but anybody could have sent those messages."

He was quiet for a moment, and I could picture him rubbing the back of his neck. "Call your sister and have her pick you up. Stay with her until this thing is resolved."

"I don't want to bring Kate into this." I knew my sister, Kevin, and the kids were going to San Diego, and I was glad they'd be out of town for a few days. I could stay at their house, but if they had Joy, they knew about my family. They could find me there.

Betz sighed. "Then who, Casey? Cause I don't want you to be alone."

I thought of Marcus. Strange, he should be the first person to pop into my mind. Strange and crazy. I hadn't gotten the chance to confront him about being a felon on the run. I scratched him from the list. My dad couldn't defend me from anything. Being on leave, I couldn't go back to the office. I was ashamed to admit it, but I really didn't have anywhere to go.

"I'm coming over then," he said. "I have to wrap something up, but I'll be there within the hour. If there's an available unit, I'll have them come by. In the meantime, lock your doors and stay put."

I hated to rely on him. I felt needy, and it wasn't a comfortable place for me. But I didn't want to be alone either.

While I waited for Betz, I put my iPad aside and tried not to think about how terrified Joy looked or what her kidnappers could be doing to her, but it was all I could think about. Diablo proved yesterday that they would go to any length to ensure their agenda, whatever that was. They wanted a video. I didn't have a damn video.

I should have paid more attention to Joy. Should have gotten more information about Howard.

My only comforting thought was that Joy might be with Hope. If Hope was still alive. If Joy was.

I called Kate to make sure she was okay. "Packing," she said before I could speak. "We leave first thing in the morning. What are you up to?"

"Joy was kidnapped," I told her.

"What?"

I filled her in on the email. I didn't tell her about being on administrative leave or what Mabel had shared with me about our mother. Why upset her more than necessary until I had more information?

"We should cancel our trip," Kate said. "I can't go to San Diego while our cousins are missing."

"That's precisely why you should go. It's not safe here."

"Then come with us."

"I can't right now, but maybe soon... I don't know. What about Dad?" I asked.

"We'll take him with us," she said. "He'll kick and scream, but I don't want him alone right now."

"Good."

By the time we had talked through Joy's kidnapping, Betz was at my door. I made Kate promise to be extra vigilant, and she made me promise to do the same. I disconnected as I pulled the door open.

He stepped inside and drew me into a tight hug. I lingered in his hold as long as I could, but then the tears threatened to come, so I pulled away.

"Show me her room," he said.

Joy's bedroom was a disaster. Suitcases lay open on the floor. Colorful clothes were strewn about the room like candy beaten out of a piñata. Her bed was unmade, the sheets a crumpled mess.

I stepped over piles of spandex and made my way to the nightstand. Two speeding tickets topped a stack of receipts. Both happened while she was driving my Jeep. Heat crept up my neck at her nerve, but then I remembered how terrified she looked in the photo, and my irritation dissipated as quickly as it had come. I sat on the bed and shuffled through the pile.

"Joy's been on a shopping spree," I said. "Most of these receipts are from the mall."

I opened the nightstand drawer and rifled through sixteen shades of eye shadow and about a dozen tubes of lipstick.

"These hers?" Betz pointed to a stack of magazines. "Can't remember you reading this kind of stuff."

I picked up the pile of beauty magazines. A phone number had been written on the cover of *InStyle*.

Betz read the numbers aloud as I punched them in and put my phone on speaker mode. "Anthony's Restaurant," a female voice said.

"I'm trying to find my cousin, and I think she might have been at your restaurant last night. Is there someone there who would have worked that shift I could talk to?"

"I was here until ten," she said.

"Do you remember a woman and man on a date?"

"That describes ninety percent of our customers."

"The woman would have stood out. She would have been dressed in a lot of Spandex, really short skirt, nose-bleed heels."

"Oh yes, her. She was all over her date. I almost asked them to leave. We have kids in here sometimes."

"Did they pay with a credit card?" Betz asked.

"I don't know. I mean, I could look, but I can't just give out that kind of information."

"Did you see them leave? Did you notice the car?" I asked.

"This is making me uncomfortable. I don't think I can help you." She hung up.

"I'll drive out there," Betz said. "See if my badge makes her more comfortable."

"Okay, I'll keep looking through her stuff."

"Not alone, you won't."

I sighed. "It's daytime. I'll be fine."

"Is there some rule that kidnappers can't strike in daylight I don't know about? You're too much. I really wish you'd get a gun."

"I hate guns."

Betz snatched my phone and scrolled through my contacts.

"What are you doing?"

"Calling your sister. I'm not leaving you alone."

I rolled my eyes and grabbed my phone back. Reluctantly, I dialed my sister's home phone. Kevin answered and told me Kate was running errands in preparation for their trip to San Diego. Kate had told him about Joy's disappearance, and he suggested coming to get me before I could even ask. He said he'd be over soon.

I disconnected and slipped my phone in my pocket. "Kevin's on his way. You happy?"

"Ecstatic." His cell phone rang. He answered it and listened to the caller, frustration knitting his brow. "I'll be right there." He shut the phone and stuffed it in his pocket. "I have to go. How long until Kevin gets here?"

"Is it something about Hope and Joy?"

"No. It's another case." He checked his watch. "How long?"

"Any minute."

"Lock up," Betz said.

"I will." I tried to act brave, but the moment the door closed behind him, I checked all the locks, then grabbed the baseball bat I kept next to the bed.

Back in Joy's room, I went through all her bags. Not many surprises, just more Spandex, makeup, and a supply of condoms that would last me six lifetimes. My guess was that anything of interest was probably in Joy's purse, which was most likely with her when she was taken.

Not knowing what else to do in the search for Joy, I packed an overnight bag and placed it by the door. I heard a car drive by and peeked out the window, but it wasn't Kevin. Grabbing my iPad, I checked to see if the kidnappers had sent any more emails. They hadn't. Trying to distract myself and keep busy, I went to my Internet homepage and typed Marcus' name in the search engine.

I had no idea how big Saddle Brook, New Jersey, was or if it had its own newspaper. I typed in the town's name and found a link to the *Bergen Record.* Once on their site, I went to the archives and typed in Marcus' name. I was quickly informed there were fifty hits with the name Sheldon in the title. I scrolled past stories about a politician named Sheldon Graham. Two pages later, I stopped on an article titled "Still Missing: 15-year-old Courtney Sheldon has been gone for twelve days now..."

I clicked on the story, and a photo of a pretty young girl smiling brightly in a snapshot filled my screen. The word "missing" was stamped across the photo. My heart quickened as I flashed back to the night in the parking lot at Technerds. The girl's expression of pure hopelessness had made my blood run cold. Was that girl related to Marcus? I read the story:

Fifteen-year-old Courtney Sheldon didn't come home from her job at the local Safeway on April 23rd. A family friend admitted the girl had been talking to a man over the Internet and may have met with him. So far, police have not learned the man's identity. Detectives would like to warn teenagers about the dangers of arranging to meet people alone who they have previously contacted through the Internet.

I reached into my purse for a pen so I could take notes. The mail I had stuffed in my bag earlier fell onto the floor. I was going to ignore it and keep fishing for my pen, but then I saw the manila envelope with my name and address handwritten on it. All I seemed to get was junk mail, but this was addressed by a real live person. I picked it up, my hands shaking.

The handwriting belonged to Hope. The postmark was dated the day before she disappeared. Why wouldn't she just give it to me at our dinner date that never happened? Had she known she was in danger and that it was a possibility she wouldn't make it?

I tore the envelope open and found a piece of cardboard with a thumb drive taped to it. I raced to my laptop and plugged the thumb drive in, and a screen popped up that read "Enter Passcode." Was this the video the kidnapper so desperately wanted?

And if it was—why hadn't Hope given me the damn passcode?

I rubbed my eyes, trying to come up with some options. First, I took a stab at entering random numbers and letters. Then I tried Hope's birthdate, the name of her childhood dog, anything I could think of. Nothing worked. I sent the Probation Department's forensic person an email asking if a program existed to get past the protection without a code, but I got an out-of-office reply that said she wouldn't be back for a week.

When Kevin got here, our first stop would be the police station. Surely, they had the technology to crack or bypass the code.

I checked my watch. What was taking Kevin so long? My mind swirled with thoughts of Hope, runaway Melissa King, my client Lindsey Sijour, and Diablo. Then there was Ramirez on the loose and suing me. And now Joy had been kidnapped, and I had a tangible clue that Hope sent me. My suspicions about my mother's death suddenly seemed justified. And then there was Marcus. For a moment, I felt paralyzed. I couldn't handle one more thing.

My cell phone chirped, and I just about flew out of my seat. I was so engrossed in my thoughts. I pulled my phone from my pocket. It was from a blocked number. "Hello?"

"Did you get my note?" a muffled male voice asked.

A chill tickled my spine. "I did."

"I'm quite proud of the photo," he said. "Do you wear leopard-print panties like your cousin? What do you have on under those sexy jeans you're wearing right now?"

I spun about, looking from the front door to the patio door at the back of my house. Was he watching me? It was getting dark, and my back patio looked grainy through the sunscreens. I squinted as I moved toward it and quickly pulled the blinds shut. Next, I moved toward the only uncovered window in the living room and closed those blinds as well. "Where are you?"

The man laughed. "Are you scared, Casey? Because you should be. You should be scared shitless."

Chapter Thirty-One

I pressed the end button and then called the police emergency line.

"Nine-one-one, what's your emergency?"

"Someone claims to be watching me. It's a long story, but I think I'm in imminent danger. Please send someone."

"What's your location?"

I gave her my address and picked up the baseball bat I'd left by the door. With the dispatcher on the line, I crept from room to room, pulling open closet doors and peeking under beds. No boogie man. Just the biggest dust bunny I'd ever seen. I hoped I lived long enough to vacuum it up.

The crunching of gravel outside my bedroom window made my blood run cold. "He's out back," I said.

"Hold on, Honey," the dispatcher said. "An officer is en route."

A creaking noise came from my bedroom window as the board Betz had placed over the broken glass moved.

I froze while the board splintered as it was being tugged on. I thought about joining the dust bunny under the bed until the police came looking for me. Then I remembered Kevin was on his way. What if he walked into a trap before the officer could get here?

If my intruder was out back, I could slip out front. Run to my neighbors and wait for help while watching for Kevin at the same time.

I tiptoed over to the front door and slowly pulled it open. Night had fallen, and my front walkway was dark. I slipped out the door and closed it gently behind me, whispering my plan to the dispatcher all the while. A breeze rustled the palm tree between my house and Marcus's. I took two steps from the door, thinking I'd run to the house directly across from mine and pound on the door. But then I saw a silhouette approaching. "There's two of them," I said to the dispatcher. I spun about and lunged for the front door. Just before I reached the doorknob, a hand touched my shoulder.

Terror squeezed a scream out of me. I fumbled for the doorknob and tried to wrench it open, but the man reached around and held it shut. "Shush," he whispered in my ear.

I spun about and slammed my knee into his groin, then smacked him in the eye with the heel of my hand. I let my phone fall to the ground and backed up enough to have swinging room. I was about to smash the side of his head with my baseball bat, but he let out a yelp and took a step back.

"Jesus," he said. "Are you nuts?"

I kept the bat at the ready, but my assailant didn't seem to be much of a threat anymore, doubled over and holding his private parts with one hand while rubbing his cheekbone with the other.

Hair fell into his face. I strained in the darkness to identify him. "Marcus?"

"What the hell did you do that for?" he gasped.

I looked down between his work boots and saw the trampled remnants of a bouquet of flowers. What was he going to kill me with, tulips?

Marcus stayed bent over, placing a hand on each thigh. "I just wanted to make sure you were okay," he panted. "I didn't mean to scare you."

I struggled to right my breathing and gain control of the fear that had consumed me like a shark at mealtime. Then I remembered the intruder at my bedroom window. "Were you in my backyard?"

He straightened and pushed his hands deep in his pockets, probably wanting to make sure everything was still attached. "No. I just got here."

My front door opened, and a man dressed in black with a ski mask covering his face stood looking at us. His eyes and mouth glowed, the moonlight making them seem almost radiant. They looked familiar, yet I couldn't place the tall, slim figure. I adjusted my hold on the bat, debating what body part I should hit to disable him yet leave him alive for questioning.

"Don't move," I said. "Police are on their way."

"Then we better hurry." He laughed, and I flashed back to Dorfman's courtroom and then his visit to my office, and I knew I was dealing with creepy probationer Michael Crowne. Repositioning my hold on the bat, I decided to go for his knees.

"I told you you'd be next," he said, raising a handgun at me. "Put the bat down. Let's go."

I could see Marcus in my peripheral vision. My hero just stood there.

I swallowed the egg of fear that rose in my throat. "I'm not going anywhere with you, Mr. Crowne."

"Oh, you are," he said. "Dead or alive. It's your choice. Now drop the bat."

"No."

He sighed. "You're trying my patience, Casey."

I debated my next move. If I swung at him, he could fire the gun before I even made contact. If I went with him, my fate would be entirely in his hands. We had to settle this here.

Thoughts whirled through my mind like a cyclone as I braced for the gunshot. Was it all going to end for me in front of my house? Would I never know what happened to Hope and Joy? Would Betz and his brothers and sisters on the force be able to find them?

But then Marcus turned on the man and deftly grabbed Crowne's arm and twisted it, so the gun pointed to the front walk.

Both men fell to the ground, struggling and rolling around in an attempt to gain control over the gun. I rushed over to the mess of tangled limbs, raised the bat, and whacked the back of...Oh shit, I hit Marcus. He grunted, letting up on Crowne long enough for him to disengage and stagger to his feet. He stood over Marcus, pulling his foot back to deliver a kick to his side.

Now, my target was clear. I swung the bat as hard as I could, connecting with Crowne's back. I heard a crack and was unsure if it was the bat or his spine fracturing.

Crowne dropped to his knees between me and Marcus. Marcus rolled out of the way and came up on his knees, recovering the gun and pointing it at Crowne.

"Whose side are you on?" Crowne panted to Marcus.

Marcus slowly got to his feet. "You're not going to shoot her. Understand?"

I was about to race to Marcus' side. Felon or not, he saved me. He was on my side. But his next words had me frozen to the spot.

"We have to keep her alive until we find out what she did with the video."

"Then help me with her," Crowne said. "And stop pointing that thing at me. It might go off."

"It might." Marcus grinned at the man and then at me. "Put the bat down, Casey. My back hurts like a son of a bitch."

"Whose side <u>are</u> you on?" I asked. Confusion fogged my brain, and I thought I'd vomit from my sudden jolt of adrenaline.

Marcus looked at me and lowered the gun. He took three steps forward, stopping inches from me, his face dangerously close to mine. He had to feel me swallow hard. "It's complicated," he said softly.

I had no room to swing the bat. I took a step back, but Crowne was behind me. He wrapped his arms around my torso, immobilizing me, forcing me to drop the bat, which landed on my foot.

The sound of screeching tires announced the arrival of a dark-colored van. Crowne pulled me backward toward the vehicle while I kicked at him the best I could. Marcus stuffed the gun in the waistband of his jeans and headed back into my house.

I screamed, flailing about with all the energy I could muster. I managed to get in a few good kicks before two other men, dressed like Crowne, got out of the van, and helped hold me down.

There was more ripping of tape as they loaded me into the back and pushed me onto the floor. A piece of duct tape slapped over my mouth as the door to the van slid shut.

I lay on the floor with four masked men crouched around me, all staring at me like they'd found some creature on the side of the road they were trying to identify. The driver started the engine and pulled away from the curb.

There were no seats in the back of the van, and I used the room to flail and kick at the men. Someone sat on my legs while two others grabbed my arms. I heard more tape rip. And then Marcus leaned over me, holding a piece of tape above my face.

"Sorry," he said. "But this is something I just gotta do." He lowered the tape over my eyes, plunging me into darkness.

Crowne gave a barking laugh. "Guess what I see in my rearview mirror, Ms. Carson? A police cruiser just pulled up in front of your house. Too bad for him, he's a day late and a PO short."

Chapter Thirty-Two

Blinded, I felt every bump and dip in the road as we traveled along. My ankles were bound together. Hands grabbed me and violently rolled me onto my stomach. My arms were jerked behind my back. As they reached for my wrists, I remembered the huge ex-cop who had taught a self-defense class I took a few years back. He demonstrated holding his wrists in such a position that once the tape was wrapped around, he had enough leverage to snap it by quickly twisting his arms. Although impressed with the move, I'd never had the occasion to test his theory. Now was as good a time as any.

I held my arms in the best position I could under the circumstances and lay still. They wrapped the tape a little higher than they would have, had I not gone to that training. This was not the time to fight; surely there would be a better opportunity to try to escape than now, with several goons hovering over me.

"So, what are you going to do?" Marcus said. "Kidnap the entire family?"

"If we have to," a raspy voice answered. "You got a better idea?"

"Where we taking her?" Marcus asked.

"You ask a lot of questions," another man said.

We traveled on in silence. I felt nauseous from both fear and from rolling around in the back of the van like a loose sack of potatoes. My head pounded, and my arms had fallen asleep. But mostly, I felt betrayed. How could I have had feelings for a man who was even partially responsible for my current plight? He was immersed in this mess, and I'd let him get to me just because he was hotter than a lit grill.

Betz would think I was a fool. Instead of helping Hope and Joy, I'd just added to the victim count. And now I feared Kate and her kids would be in danger, too. Maybe even my father. Those thoughts were unbearable. I had to do something, but I was tied up like a wild animal.

The van barreled along twisting roads. I couldn't imagine where we were since the Phoenix metro area was laid out on a grid system, and it was impossible to go more than a quarter of a mile without hitting a traffic light. Unless we were on the freeway and already out of town. Traffic sounds were diminishing. The desert was the perfect place to dump a body. Tears stung my eyes.

About half an hour into the ride, we slowed, then made a sharp right turn that sent me rolling into the wall, before coming to a stop. I really wanted out of this van. I was hot and cramped, and my entire right side was numb. But fear of what came next had me wishing we would drive forever.

I heard grunts and rustling of fabric as people exited the van. An object slid into my hand as a person climbed over me. I fingered it and discovered it was a small pocketknife. One of them was trying to help me. Marcus? I swear there was medication for people like him.

The door slammed. I lay still, holding my breath so I could listen to my surroundings and figure out if I was alone. The only sounds were muffled voices from outside.

I fought to sit up, rolled onto my back, and used my stomach muscles to bring myself upright. Everything hurt. The struggle with my kidnappers happened so fast, I didn't even realize I was getting banged up. I already had some cuts and bruises from before. The last few days had been rough.

I managed to scoot back until I leaned against the van wall. I took a few seconds to catch my breath. I knew they would come back for me. My options were few. With both my hands and feet tied and being blindfolded, fighting back was out of the question. Unless I could find a way to use the knife.

Before I could formulate a plan, the door opened. The front seat groaned from weight settling onto it. And then we were underway again. From the sound of it, I guessed the rest of the men had stayed behind.

I fought gravity to stay upright as we drove over hills and dropped through gullies. Wherever we were, we were getting farther away from the city.

The only thing outside of metro Phoenix was desert. In the desert, bodies tended to rot into something unrecognizable long before they were found. If they were found.

I inched my way from the wall and snapped the pocketknife open. It was impossible to cut the tape; I didn't bend that way. Trying the duct tape maneuver from my self-defense class was a bit more successful as I managed to stretch it out a bit. But the binding didn't snap off as it had for the muscular instructor.

The van stopped, and I fell sideways, whacking my forehead against the floor. Snapping the knife shut, I concealed it in my fisted hand.

"This is as good a spot as any," a voice said.

A few seconds later the side door slid open, and I was pulled by my ankles toward the door.

I fell to the ground with a thud that rattled my teeth. The man rolled me over with his boot. A hand pulled on the tape that covered my eyes. With a hard yank, it, along with half my eyebrows, came off. I blinked. It was dark, except for light coming from the van's headlights that gave me a view of cacti in the distance. My guess was right on. We were in the desert. Just me and him.

As he loomed over me, I couldn't help but flinch.

Michael Crowne licked his lips and gave me a rotten-toothed grin. "Well, hello, Darlin'. Didn't think we'd meet again so soon, did you?"

He pulled a Bowie knife from the sheath on his belt and in one swift motion, sliced the tape between my ankles. Grabbing my arm, he yanked me to my feet. "Walk, Bitch."

He shoved me forward, and I stumbled, my legs still numb. We walked past bushes and cacti that reached for me like long-nailed fingers, scraping my legs through the fabric of my jeans. When we got to a small clearing, he pushed me, so I stood on a stage created by the van's headlights.

I tried to talk, but with the tape across my mouth, I could only mumble.

Crowne laughed. "What's the matter, cat got your tongue?" He slapped his thigh like he'd just said the funniest thing in the history of funny.

I thought about running. He had that damn knife in his hand, and I was unsure if Marcus had kept the gun or if it was back in Crowne's possession. Crowne would have to get close to use the knife.

I clutched the pocketknife I'd been given but didn't see how it would be useful with my hands tied behind my back.

Crowne paced before me. "I got a few problems with you, Bitch. First, you messed up my buddy Ramirez real bad. That man saved my life when we were in the joint together. Now he's got a hole in his head cause of you."

"Second," he said. "You have something that belongs to us."

I wanted to tell him I had no idea what he was talking about. That he had the wrong person. But then I remembered the thumb drive Hope had sent me. I hadn't been able to open the document, so I had no idea what was on it or if it held the video they were looking for. But I wasn't going to share that with this meth head.

"And lastly," he said, stopping in front of me and holding up the knife. "You are a bitch. And it's going to be a pleasure to kill you."

The darkness wasn't welcoming, but it was better than standing still and waiting to be stabbed to death. I darted sideways, stepped out of the circle of light, and bounded into the night.

"Damn bitch," Crowne howled.

I plunged forward, hoping for the best since I couldn't see more than a foot in front of me. I made it about fifty feet before my sneaker caught on a rock, and I went down face first. I really missed my arms.

I lay still, hoping the noise of my fall hadn't alerted Crowne to my whereabouts. Air made its way to the corner of my mouth. The tape was loose. It must have gotten caught on something during my fall. I used my tongue to push it off my lips, getting it to the point that it dangled from the opposite corner of my mouth. I took a few deep breaths, enjoying the fraction of freedom my uncovered mouth provided.

A beam of light lit the brush to my left. Crowne had a flashlight. Dammit.

I sat up and fought to pull my feet under me. I'd made it to a crouch position before he illuminated me from about fifteen feet away.

"Stop playing games, Bitch. Do you really think you can escape?"

"At least tell me what this is all about." I struggled to my feet.

He laughed. "It's about you, putting your nose where it doesn't belong, just like Hope."

"And Joy?"

"Collateral damage."

"Is Hope still alive?" I asked. "Or did you take her to the desert too?"

He walked toward me. "She's alive. She still has value. But you, you're in the way. You're expendable."

"And Joy?"

"How bad do you want to know?"

"What have you got to lose by telling me? You're going to kill me, right?" At least I could die knowing they had a chance to survive this mess.

"You got a point," he said. "Except for one little detail. I've had fun playing with you. Scaring you shitless and all. But you're starting to annoy me. And it's late. I don't want to be out in the desert all night. I got better things to do."

I had to keep him talking. If I had time, a brilliant plan for escape, at least one better than running off into the darkness, might come to me. "What does Hope have that Diablo wants?"

"A video."

"And you think I have it?"

"Some people do, but I think if you did, you would have gone to the cops. Therefore, you are no longer useful."

"Not true," I said, thinking on my feet. "I was afraid it would implicate Hope, so I held onto it. But if I go missing or turn up dead, my attorney has been instructed to turn it over to the police."

He paused, then took a step toward me. "You don't have shit."

"It's a thumb drive," I said.

Crowne hesitated long enough for me to know he was considering the possibility that I was telling the truth.

"Bring me to whoever's in charge, and I'll get the drive for you."

He looked me up and down. "Let's say you're telling the truth about your lawyer and all. That might buy you a few hours. Doesn't mean you still don't have to pay for what you did to Ramirez and just being a bitch in general."

He advanced on me, and I stumbled back. Colliding with a bush, I bounced off it and landed on my ass on a jagged rock. Pain shot up through the roof of my mouth. As soon as I came back to my senses, I pushed the tape between my wrists down on the sharp point of the rock. It started to tear.

Crowne was smiling down at me with his meth-mouth grin. "Thanks for getting in the position." He tucked the flashlight under his arm, put the knife in its sheath, and reached for the fly of his pants.

Oh God, he intended to rape me. Not happening. I pushed down harder on the tape. It gave way just as Crowne leaned over me. I opened the pocketknife, reached around, and stabbed it into his thigh.

He yelped and leaned back far enough for me to squirm backward out of his reach. Getting to my feet, I sprinted toward the light of the van, hoping the keys were in it.

Then I heard the sweetest sound. A helicopter. But how would they find me? I was just a dot in the darkness. How did they even know to look for me? They were probably just passing overhead to some accident scene, and I had no way to get their attention.

I pushed myself to go faster, catching my feet on rocks and stumbling forward, but stopping short of falling. Crowne's ragged breath came from behind me. He was dropping back a bit, the light from his flashlight getting dimmer as more distance grew between us. My runs were paying off.

As I reached the van, I fumbled for the handle, but heard the beep that came from the remote just before I realized he'd locked the doors. Crowne, standing not ten feet behind me, laughed between heavy breaths. "I'm one step ahead of you, Darlin.'"

A cone of light shone down from the sky. If I could get in front of the headlights, they would see me. Would Crowne be stupid enough to kill me with an audience?

As I stumbled into the lighted area, Crowne followed me. Despite the noise and wind created by the helicopter, he yelled, "I'm gonna finish this!"

He grabbed me by the arm. I raised my knee and jammed it into his groin while I slashed him across the torso with the pocketknife. His body stiffened momentarily, and he dropped to his knees. The move put me off balance, and I went down as well, the knife slipping from my hand. I tried to roll away from him, but a cactus blocked me. The needles ripped into my thigh, and I let out a cry.

"Mother fucker," Crowne panted. He grabbed me by the shoulders and climbed on top of me, pinning me to the ground.

"That's good," he hissed. "You're turning me on."

I wanted to vomit. My only hope was that both his hands were on me, which meant he wasn't armed.

His hands went to my throat, and I realized he didn't need a weapon. He had me. Even with the helicopter so close, he had me.

He leaned his body weight onto his hands, and I couldn't get a breath. Pressure mounted behind my eyes, and I became lightheaded, losing focus on his hateful, twisted face. I tried to pry his fingers back, but his grip was tight. I bucked like a mechanical bull, but he didn't let up. The energy to fight was draining from me.

The whirl of the helicopter blades became distant. Bursts of white lights, like Christmas twinkle lights, exploded across my fluttering eyelids.

I hardly cared if I died at that moment; the darkness and fatigue were so welcoming as my body began to shut down. But I wasn't done. Hope and Joy needed me. I felt a pull between them and my mother. I tried to kick my way to the surface, but my actions were futile. I was drowning, sure as I would, in a deep, unforgiving ocean.

Chapter Thirty-Three

As death was about to claim me, the pressure released. Was it over? Was this what the end felt like?

But instead of drifting further away, my head started to clear.

I took one giant, painful gulp of air. And then another. As my senses returned, so did my fear. I coughed, and every inch of my body seized.

"Ma'am," a voice said. Hands gently shook my shoulders. "Are you all right?"

I opened my eyes and focused on the compassionate face of a young deputy. He helped me sit up.

"The paramedics are on their way," he said. "Can you talk?"

My throat burned. I cleared it the best I could and coughed. "What happened to Crowne?" my voice was hoarse.

"We got him, Ma'am. He's not going to hurt you anymore."

"But how did you find me?"

"We got an anonymous tip," he said. "Someone told us the general direction you were headed, and we spotted the van with the helicopter."

Who would have tipped off the cops? Was it the same person who armed me with the pocketknife? Could it have been Marcus, or was that just wishful thinking?

I started to pull off the tape that hung on my wrists, but the deputy stopped me. "Let me get a quick picture of how you were restrained," he said.

I held still while the officer snapped a few photos with his phone. Then, he gently helped me remove the tape. My arms and shoulders burned from being tied up for so long. I looked around as I rubbed my wrists. I counted three police SUVs parked behind Crowne's van. The helicopter still hovered above, illuminating the area.

"He's in custody?" I asked, making sure I had heard him right.

"Yes, Ma'am. He's no longer a threat to you."

"There's a thumb drive," I said to the cop. "It's inserted on my laptop on my dining room table. Please send an officer to get it."

"In good time, Ma'am. Want to get you to the ER first."

"No," I insisted. "It's important. It's what I almost got killed over."

"Okay," he said. "I'll send somebody. What's your address?"

I gave it to him, and he relayed the information over the radio.

Only then did I breathe a sigh of relief.

Dressed in a paper gown that kept falling off my shoulders, I sat on a gurney in Phoenix General's emergency room. My body parts competed for first place in a pain contest. I alternately pressed the gauze the nurse had placed over the nicks in my forearm and my thighs. Aside from a lot of bruises, fingerprints on my neck, and dozens of scrapes, I hadn't fared too badly. That assessment, however, didn't include the nervous breakdown I felt coming on.

The nurse had asked if I wanted to call anyone, and I told her to call Betz. It turned out he was already on his way. I had to wonder if he had some kind of secret radar that alerted him whenever I was in trouble. Lately, it must have been going off constantly.

I grimaced while the nurse cleaned and dressed my wounds. "Do you want to talk to our social worker?" she asked. "These experiences can be emotionally devastating."

I swallowed the lump in my throat. "No thanks. I'm fine."

She didn't look convinced. "You sure?"

I nodded, trying to will the tears that were brimming in my eyes to subside. The last thing I needed was to be a blubbering idiot when Betz arrived.

"Why don't I call her anyway?" she said. "In case you change your mind."

I blew my nose and dabbed tears from my eyes. "Not necessary, I'm fine."

She looked doubtful but gave my hand a pat and left the room. I sighed and leaned back against the inclined mattress. Hope was alive. At least I'd gotten that much information from Crowne. But what about Joy? If I were expendable, wouldn't she be too? And Kate and my father? Were they safe?

I reached for the phone on the bedside table, wincing in pain that simple movement caused, and dialed Kate's number.

"Thank God," she said in a shaky voice. "When Kevin went to pick you up and saw you being shoved into a van, I thought I'd never see you again. Are you okay?"

"Did Kevin call the police?"

"Of course. A cop showed up just after the van drove away, and he waved them down. They tried to follow the van but lost it a few blocks away. You could have been taken anywhere. We've been frantic. Are you okay?"

So, Kevin sent the helicopter? Knocked off my theory that Marcus was somehow on my side. But how did they know to follow me into the desert? "I'm all right." I swallowed the cry that threatened to escape.

"What hospital are you at?" she asked. "I'm coming to see you."

"No. I need you to take the kids and go to San Diego like you planned, but you have to leave right away. They may come after you and the kids."

"Casey, you're scaring me."

"I'm sorry, but you should be scared. I mean it, take the kids, and go. Oh, and Dad. Take Dad."

"Kevin went to get him as soon as the cops were done with him, so don't worry about Dad, he's with us. But they caught the man. Isn't he in custody?"

I looked up as Betz parted the curtains around my bed and eased inside. He came to my bedside and pulled me into his arms. It hurt, but I didn't care. I rested my head on his shoulder and continued my conversation with Kate. "There are others involved. It's far from over."

"Will this guy be able to lead the police to Hope and Joy?" she asked.

"Let's hope so," I said. Although I couldn't picture Crowne rolling over on Diablo. It wouldn't be good for his health. "Look, Betz just walked in. Will you do as I asked?"

"Only if you come with us."

"I can't," I said. "I'll be okay. I'm with Betz."

"All right." She sounded skeptical. "But I want you to call me in the morning. I want to know you're okay."

"I promise," I said. "And Kate? I love you."

Her breath caught. "You haven't said that to me since you were five."

And the dam broke. Tears splashed down my face.

"I love you, too," she said.

I handed Betz the receiver, and he hung up the phone. He sat on the edge of the bed and took my face in his hands, wiping my tears away with his thumbs. "I thought I lost you."

I nodded. I couldn't speak.

"The doctor said you can go home. He said you'd be sore for a while, but there is no major damage."

I nodded some more.

"We have a lot to talk about, don't we?"

I wasn't sure what he meant. Was he talking about what happened to me or the fact that he was the only person I wanted to see right now?

"Your clothes are a disaster, and they're evidence," he said. "I talked the nurse into getting you a pair of scrubs, so you've got something to wear. I'll see if she's gotten them yet." He stood and walked toward the curtain but looked back over his shoulder. He sighed and rubbed the back of his neck before stepping outside.

I sat back and exhaled heavily. I wanted Betz to take me somewhere so we could talk. I felt raw and exposed and wanted to share every exhausting emotion I felt. I had given the sheriff's investigator all the grizzly details, but with Betz, I didn't have to keep it professional. He knew me well enough to understand how this all affected me. I couldn't think of anyone else who got me like he did except my mother.

He returned seconds later and handed me folded blue scrub pants and matching top. Laying them on the bed, he stepped outside the curtain. Wincing with each movement, I got out of bed and carefully pulled the scrubs on. The shirt was a few sizes too big, and the V-neck dipped dangerously low. I tried to shift it back so most of the neckline bared my back, but when I bent to slip on my dirt-covered running shoes, it fell forward again.

"Okay to come in?" Betz called from the other side of the curtain.

I straightened, fixed my shirt, and said, "Sure."

He entered and stuffed his hands in his pockets. "A deputy stopped by. Patrol went to your house. There was no thumb drive in your laptop. They looked all around but couldn't find anything."

"Shit," I said. "I saw Marcus go back into the house. It's probably in the hands of Diablo. But I'm pretty sure Crowne didn't know they had it, or he wouldn't have kept asking me for it. Is he really Diablo?"

"Seems he's doing what he can to get in. Probably thought killing you would ensure him a spot. That doesn't mean they have any intention of letting him in or that he would be privy to what they're up to. In any event, he's not talking."

"And Marcus?"

"Hasn't been around long enough to be a member either, is my guess. Could be a pledge."

The nurse handed me the discharge paperwork, a prescription for painkillers, and instructions to call my primary care physician for a follow-up. I followed Betz out the door. "Can we stop by my place?" I asked. "I want to look for the thumb drive. Maybe the deputy missed it."

"Okay," Betz said. "But then we both gotta get some food and sleep. You're staying at my house tonight."

This time, I didn't argue.

We stopped by my house and sat in the car, the engine running. "You up for this?" Betz asked.

He looked at my hands, fists clenched so tight my fingers were white. I opened them, loosened my jaw, and tried to relax. I never thought I'd see my house again. I'd been snatched from this very place. It would never be the same. Never safe. If someone wanted to get you, they could.

"I'm fine." Opening the door, I slid off my seatbelt, eased off the seat, and stood. The pain was getting stronger. I thought of the painkillers the nurse had given me and vowed not to take them. Even with Betz by my side, I needed to stay alert.

We walked slowly up the walkway to my front door. Betz bent and picked up the baseball bat I'd used to defend myself. It might have been enough had Crowne not had a gun. Thankfully, Marcus seemed to have kept the firearm, or Crowne could have easily finished me off in the desert before help had arrived.

I found my phone under a bush. The screen was smashed and looked like a spider web. It still worked, but it was hard to read the display.

The front door was locked. I moved a flowerpot that housed a dead plant and picked up the last spare key I'd stashed when I'd moved in. I opened the door, and we stepped inside.

My computer sat on the dining room table. But, just as the deputy said, there was no thumb drive in the slot where I'd left it. As I'd told Betz, Marcus had run back inside the house before the van took me away. Crowne had been inside, too, but from our conversation in the desert, I was pretty sure he didn't have it. I was surprised if Marcus had it that he hadn't mentioned it to Crowne.

Something wasn't quite right about that interaction, but my brain was too fuzzy to sort it out.

Just to be sure I hadn't missed anything, I squatted down and checked the floor around the table. My knees almost buckled from the pain, and I yelped.

"Here," Betz said, helping me to a standing position. "Let me look." He moved my bag and the mail that was on the floor. Got on his hands and knees and searched every which way. "It's not here," he said. "Looks like they got what they wanted."

Could anything else possibly go wrong?

I took a moment to change into shorts and a T-shirt, grabbed my toothbrush, and put it in my purse. I locked my door out of habit. Windows and doors did not stop Diablo.

By the time we pulled into Betz's neighborhood, my eyelids drooped. We'd sold the house we'd owned together, and Betz had bought this one after the divorce. All the homes were beige stucco with red tile roofs. He pulled into the driveway of a well-maintained two-story with a huge palm tree and lush grass in the front yard. The garage door lifted, revealing his sister's Prius next to where he parked. I'd forgotten she was staying with him while she and her partner worked things out.

He must have taken my stare at the car as a question. "She says she and Camille are having issues, but it's more likely that she's keeping an eye on me. Been like that ever since she stood in for my parents after they died. In any case, I owe her."

I felt the sting of his words. The only reason Betz would need someone to watch out for him was because he was lonely and working too much. Both my fault.

We exited the car and went inside.

He led me through a laundry room and into a huge brightly lit kitchen that had highly polished marble countertops and stainless-steel appliances. He dimmed the overhead light, soothing my tired eyes.

Jasmine appeared at the bottom of the staircase. Her hair was mussed, and she wore shorts and a tank top. "Everything okay?" she asked, looking me up and down.

I nodded. "I'll be fine."

"Thank God they caught the bastard," she said. "If you don't need me, I'm going back to bed. You'll be safe here."

I smiled at her, then watched her retreat up the stairs.

"You hungry?" he asked. "I haven't eaten since this morning, and I'm starving."

My stomach rumbled at the mention of food. "I could eat."

He pulled some deli meat, cheese, mustard, and two bottles of reduced-carb beer from the refrigerator. Then he took a loaf of low-carb bread from a basket on the counter and popped the tops of both bottles. Sliding one across the granite toward me, he said, "Jasmine does all the shopping. It's better than Styrofoam, but I eat out as much as I can."

I took a sip of beer and grimaced. "I guess you get used to it."

"When?"

I was too tired to laugh.

He made our sandwiches, taking small sips of beer that tasted like turpentine, or at least what I imagined turpentine would taste like. When he finished, he placed my plate in front of me, and we ate standing up, the counter island between us.

I'd finished my sandwich and as much beer as I could stomach before he spoke. "You want to tell me what happened tonight?"

I went through the story, starting with my Internet search on Marcus and ending with the young deputy calling me "Ma'am." Betz kept quiet, his mouth set tight as he took notes on his iPad. When I was done, I let out a long yawn. The microwave clock read two-fifteen. I was so tired; I could have slept standing up.

"So, this Marcus guy got to you?" he said.

"After all I told you, that's what you're concerned about? That I got duped by a criminal?" And I hadn't even told him about our make-out session.

"He doesn't sound like your type."

"Don't worry. Now that I know the truth about him, he's not." I didn't tell him about my suspicions that Marcus had tried to help me by slipping me a pocketknife and calling in my abduction. I was afraid it would sound like I was making excuses for him. I half-wondered if that was exactly what I was doing. It was easier than believing he was a total jerk.

"Even before," Betz said. His look said he thought he knew me better than that.

"What do you care who I date?' I said, my defenses rising. "We're divorced, remember?"

"Oh, so I'm supposed to stop caring about you," he said. "I'm supposed to let you get yourself killed?"

"Yeah," I said, instantly regretting my lame comeback. It was easier than admitting I almost fell for a guy who helped kidnap me. "I'm sorry; you know I get grumpy when I'm tired."

He sighed. "Let me show you where the guestroom is."

I followed him down a bare hallway that screamed bachelor. No photos.

"When you went to the restaurant where Joy and her date had dinner last night," I said. "Did you find anything?"

"They paid in cash. We still don't know who she was with. We're looking at the video from that night, but so far, we've got no ID on the guy." He stopped before a dark room, reached in, and flipped the light switch. A lamp on a bedside table bathed the room in an inviting glow. His grandmother's sleigh bed, nightstand, dresser, and roll-top desk I had hated to part with when we'd divorced, filled the room. I felt a little homesick remembering setting up house with Betz. Those years were some of the best years in my life. Maybe a little hovering wasn't the worst thing in the world. Or maybe I was just tired.

"The bathroom is one door down. Towels are in the cabinet over the toilet. You need anything else?"

I shook my head.

"I've got a great security system, and I doubt they'd figure out you're here, so you should be safe."

"Thank you."

"Good night then." He closed the door gently behind him, and I fell face-first on the bed.

Chapter Thirty-Four

I slept like the dead. One of those heavy sleeps that pulls you in so deeply, it's a struggle to emerge, and you still feel like crap. I hunkered down long after sunlight spilled into the room. Even after I heard dishes clanking in the kitchen. I felt drugged, and sleep seemed like a safe place. Not like I had a job to go to.

When I finally forced my eyes open, it was almost ten. I dangled my legs off the side of the bed. Every muscle throbbed, and I almost curled back under the covers. But hiding wouldn't get me any closer to bringing Hope and Joy home.

A croak came out of my mouth when I tried to clear my throat. I sighed and forced myself to stand up.

Still dressed in my T-shirt and shorts, I padded into the bathroom, where I spent a good three minutes gaping at my image in the mirror. Crowne's fingerprints marked my neck. One eye had turned black and blue, and I had a cut on my forehead that left me with a slight resemblance to Harry Potter. I brushed my teeth, splashed water on my face, and finger-combed my hair the best I could and felt somewhat improved— from hideous to downright scary. Oh well, it was the best I could do.

I wandered down the hallway to the kitchen, where Jasmine sat at the counter with her laptop and a cup of tea. She looked at me and sighed.

"Morning," I said, trying to act like it was normal that I was a guest in her brother's home.

"There's hot water in the kettle and decaf tea bags on the counter if you'd like. There's no coffee in the house."

"I don't suppose you have Diet Coke?"

"You still drinking that poison?"

I nodded.

Jasmine went to the sink and rinsed out her cup before loading it in the dishwasher. "It's pretty much tea or water. Help yourself."

"Is Betz here?"

"No. And he said to sit tight until he gets back. You should be safe here." She turned and leaned against the counter, arms crossed over her chest. Dressed in a white button-down shirt and black pants with a holstered gun on her hip, she could have passed for FBI.

"Well," I said, feeling as awkward as a lumberjack at high tea.

"We need to talk," Jasmine said. "I don't know how to say this nicely, so I'm just going to say it."

I held onto the counter to brace myself for what was coming.

"Do you know how hard Barry fell for you? What your divorce did to him?"

I stuttered. "I think he understood why we ended things."

"That's because he's too proud to tell you otherwise. Maybe it's my fault, but despite knowing how he feels about you, I couldn't tell him to stay out of this case. Probably because he wouldn't listen to me anyway, and the last thing I need, is to discipline my brother for being insubordinate. But he's getting sucked in again, and I don't want to see him get hurt."

My mouth fell open, and I snapped it shut. "I don't want that either."

"At first, I gave him time to grieve the end of his marriage. But two years went by, and he never even had a date. I've been trying to get him to move on for the last year. I set him up with every single woman I know. But they're never good enough for him. I suggested Internet dating, but he has no interest."

I didn't know how to respond. I wanted what was best for Betz, sure, and I knew that I had no claim to him, but I felt a stab of jealousy thinking about him dating other women just the same.

"Do you date?" Jasmine asked. "I know you were going to marry, but you didn't go through with it."

Betz must have told her about Vincent. I thought about Marcus and the one time we went out to dinner. Before I learned the truth about him, I had hoped it would turn into something more. Sometimes, I questioned my decision to end things with Betz, but I really hadn't entertained the idea of us getting back together. I felt like divorce was one of those permanent decisions. Funny, I didn't feel that way about marriage. Maybe I should go to therapy when this is over.

"Our split was hard on me, too," I said. "My next relationship was a miserable attempt to move on. Thankfully, I came to my senses before getting married."

"I'm just protecting my brother," Jasmine said.

"I understand that. But I'm not leading him on. Betz and I are friends. I know a lot of divorced people hate each other, but it wasn't like that with us. We genuinely like each other."

"I think it's more than like on his part. What about yours?"

"I'm sorry," I said. "I don't feel comfortable talking to you about this." I felt I was losing my footing, and I was about to fall on my ass. Betz had been my rock this past week. With all that had happened, I hadn't taken the time to examine my feelings. Jasmine hit a nerve. I couldn't deny there was something still there, but I didn't think either of us had the emotional strength to recover if we tried and it failed again. It was safer to leave things the way they were. Right?

"Just be careful with his heart," she said.

I opened my mouth to respond, but realized it was safer to keep it shut.

"Help yourself to anything in the refrigerator." She closed her laptop and stuffed it in a leather case. "I've got to get to work. Do not go out alone."

As she walked away, I wondered how I could have handled the conversation better. Did she think I enjoyed having bad things happen so I could get Betz's attention? Was I sending off signals even I didn't recognize?

Once I heard her drive away, I took a yogurt from the refrigerator and walked over to the house phone. Automatically, I punched in Betz's number. I wanted to see if there were any updates on the case and if they got any information from Crowne. But Jasmine's accusations rang in my ears, so I disconnected before the call could go through and called Kate instead.

"It's after ten," Kate said. "I've been worried sick."

"Sorry," I said. "I slept late."

"Where are you?"

"Betz's place. I'm having a blast. Please tell me you're in San Diego."

"We got in a few hours ago. Dad's already at the bar. You sure you don't want to fly out and join us? You can recuperate by lying on the beach."

Boy, that sounded tempting. "Maybe after I take care of a few things."

"Casey, I'm worried about you."

"I'm okay. It's Joy and Hope I'm worried about. Diablo doesn't mess around. I hope they haven't hurt them."

"I pray for their safety all day, every day," Kate said. "But you don't need to become the next victim. I'm going crazy worrying about you."

"There's no need. I'm staying out of this. The police can handle it from now on." I just didn't feel right being in the next state when so much was unsolved.

"Is Betz with you now?" Kate asked.

"He stepped out for a few minutes." I hoped that was true. "He'll be back soon."

Kate hesitated. "I hate to even tell you this, and I don't even know if it's important, but I learned something when I got my hair cut yesterday. I'd referred Joy to my girl. She said Joy kept talking about this Howard guy she'd met."

"And?"

"I'm only telling you so you can tell Betz and let him look into it. Promise me you won't do anything stupid, Casey."

My heart started to race. "Who, me?"

"Casey."

"I promise. Now, what did you find out?"

"His last name is Donohoe. He lives in those apartments where Aunt Shelly used to live. You know, the ones on Alma School Road."

"Oh, yeah," I said. "Thanks."

"You'll tell Betz and stay out of it." Her tone was firm.

"Of course," I promised before ending the call.

With the sting of Jasmine's talk still fresh, I resisted the urge to call Betz and share the information, but it was good stuff. Howard Donohoe could have been with Joy when she disappeared. He might know something. I paced the hallway.

Okay, so maybe Jasmine had a point. I still had feelings for Betz, and I was leaning on him too much. But Kate's information was important. I rushed to the phone and dialed his cell, but it went right to voicemail. Damn. I tried his office and got voicemail there as well. I left a message and thought about calling a cab, but I had promised everyone I would not go out alone.

I wasn't about to let this information sit while a bunch of overworked cops figured out where it sat on their priority list. I'd catch a bunch of crap for getting involved again, but my cousins deserved my help.

I hated to reach out to my coworkers, especially since I was on leave, but I had no one else to turn to. I called the office and asked the receptionist if Claire was in. She wasn't, but Jerski was at my office for training and asking about me. "Put him on," I said.

"Remember you said you wanted to help?" I said. "Well, I could really use a ride."

Chapter Thirty-Five

Feeling like an intruder in Betz's home, I left a note on the counter and went outside to wait on the curb for Jerski to arrive. He pulled up less than twenty minutes after my call, which was impressive, given the distance he had to cover. He honked the horn on his Smart Car even though I was sitting right in front of him.

I stifled a joke about how many clowns could fit inside as I slid onto the passenger seat. I said, "Thanks for coming."

He glanced at me. "You look awful."

"Yeah, thanks. Just get me out of here."

He started down the street. "Where to?"

I looked at the gun positioned on his hip. I was unsure of his skills, but figured he'd had the training to protect us. "Alma School and Warner," I said.

"So, what happened to you?"

"I don't want to talk about it."

"Well, you don't have to bite my head off."

I mentally rolled my eyes so he wouldn't catch me. "Sorry."

"That was heartfelt."

"I've been kidnapped, tied up, and almost killed. My cousins are in the hands of maniacs. Excuse me if I'm not myself."

He braked for a light. "Oh, you're yourself. Just as friendly as the last time I saw you."

I swallowed my comeback. Maybe I had been a bit cranky lately, but the truth was, I never had patience for people like Jerski. And my patience was especially short right now. I reminded myself that he was doing me a favor and aside from giving him directions, I remained silent for a while.

"Is this work-related?" he asked. "Because I'm on the clock."

"Not exactly." I played with my phone, which had frozen. Apparently, it had suffered more than a cracked screen the night before. I plugged my old car charger into the lighter and connected it. When nothing happened, I turned it off, hoping to reboot it.

"So, what? You want me to take flex time?"

"It won't take long. You offered to help."

"But the last time I helped you, you committed a crime. And you were so sarcastic. Plus, you were better looking before you got all banged up. I thought I might ask you out."

I should have used a ride service, but even Jerski's company was better than no company at all. This was pitiful. I really needed to do something about my lack of friends. "It won't take long. I really appreciate your help."

He sighed. "Okay, but I want to get back to work by noon."

I turned my sorry-looking phone back on, and it came to life. We drove in silence other than my directing him to the apartment complex where Howard was supposed to live. Jerski dropped me at the rental office, and I went inside. I waited while the manager talked to an elderly couple about renting a one-bedroom apartment.

The manager looked at me like I had just escaped from a mental hospital. "Can I help you?" She had over-teased bottle-blonde hair and wore clothes that were a size too small, yet she looked better than me.

"I'm looking for a tenant of yours. Howard Donohoe."

The woman frowned. "I'm sorry, I can't give out tenant information."

I had left my work ID with Alma, but still had my badge. Using it for unofficial business was unethical, but I honestly no longer cared. What good was following the rules when my cousins were in the hands of Diablo? I fished my shield out of my purse and held it out for her. "I'm with Probation."

She looked at me like I had stolen the badge.

"Please," I said. "It's a matter of life and death. Look at me. I got this way because some very nasty men have kidnapped my cousins, and then they came after me. Your tenant may have information that could help save them.

Please, help me." I was on the verge of tears. The elderly couple diverted their gazes and shifted uncomfortably in their seats.

The manager shook her head. "I don't know. I could get in trouble if I told you he was in unit 1154. I don't think I could share that information. Not even if he were on the verge of being evicted for non-payment of rent."

"I understand." I stepped toward the door. "Thank you just the same."

Outside, I ran up to Jerski's car and tapped on the window. "I got it. Let's go."

Jerski grumbled and got out of the car. "Got what?"

Since he was helping me, it was time he was brought up to speed. "Hope's sister has been kidnapped. The guy who lives here might have been the last person to see her." I raced up the sidewalk and studied the apartment map that was posted outside the office. There were twelve buildings, each housing eight units, four on the first floor and four on the second. I'd only visited my aunt a few times when she lived here, so I wasn't all that familiar with the setup. I found the unit on the map and started in that direction.

"This sounds like a police matter," Jerski muttered, lagging behind. "What do we do if this guy's armed?"

"He was Joy's date," I said. "He's not armed." I tried to sound confident. Truth was, I felt like the whole world was armed except for me. "We'll be careful, just the same."

Finding the apartment close to the pool, I knocked on the peach-colored door and waited before knocking some more.

"Doesn't look like he's home," Jerski said. "Let's go."

I tried the doorknob, which twisted easily in my hand. I ignored the fact that this was a bad sign. "I'm going in," I said.

"Oh, no," Jerski said. "Not again. This is breaking and entering. This is criminal."

"I didn't break anything. And I'm just going to peek inside." I nudged the door open with my foot. "You know, make sure everything's okay."

"You got away with this at your cousin's house because you were family, and your ex-husband covered for you. This man has no relation to you, and we're dealing with Chandler PD. You don't have any ex-husbands with

Chandler PD, do you?"

"Shush." I stuck my head inside the apartment. "Hello? Anybody home?"

No one answered, but I did hear something muffled coming from the other room. "I think they said come in," I told Jerski.

"They did not."

"Pretty sure they did. I'm checking."

"Not me," he said. "I'm staying right here, ready to dial 911 and tell them what you're doing. I won't lose my job over this."

What a baby. I eased inside. I could hear *I Love Lucy* playing on the television in the other room.

The blinds on the windows were closed, and the only light came from a fish tank on the kitchen counter, and what little daylight slipped through the blinds. The apartment was decorated like a hotel room, probably rental furniture. And he was about to be evicted. Howard was a real catch.

"Hello?" I called out.

Sound came from the back room. I stepped carefully, trying not to let my flip-flops clap against my feet as I made my way down the hall. A door to my right was open. A small bathroom. Neat. Empty.

A single door at the end of the hall was closed. I stopped before it. Ricky had switched to Spanish and was really letting Lucy have it. And there was another noise, something muffled. Not wanting to leave my fingerprints behind, I wrapped my shirttail around the knob and twisted. Nudging the door slowly open with my foot, I jumped back at the site of naked Howard tied to a chair with something written with a Sharpie on his forehead. I stepped closer to read *You're too late.*

Howard struggled against the rope that bound his arms and legs. By the smell, I guessed he had been there awhile. His eyes just about bugged out of his head as he moaned and tried his best to tell me something through the tape that covered his mouth. Having recently been a victim of duct tape, I felt for him. I grabbed an edge of the tape and ripped it off.

He took a huge breath, and his eyes went back to normal. "Untie me," he said, panting.

I pulled the sheet off the bed and dropped it over his midsection. I'd seen way more than I wanted to.

"Who did this to you?"

"Untie me," he demanded.

"I'm calling the cops." I pulled my cell phone out of my pocket. "They can untie you."

"No!" Howard shrieked. "No cops. Please, just release me, and you can be on your way."

"What do you have against the police?" I asked, phone in hand.

"I may have a warrant for a slight problem with my ex. I don't want to go to jail. I can't stand jail."

I started to dial. "Sorry, I can't obstruct a police investigation."

"Please," he begged.

"What's going on in there?" Jerski yelled from the door.

"I found Howard," I yelled back. "I'm calling the cops."

"Now you call the police," Jerski said, coming down the hallway. When he saw Howard tied up and naked, he turned stark white. "Oh, shit. What happened here?"

"Call the cops," Howard said, "and I won't tell you anything about what happened. I won't even talk about Joy being hauled off by those men."

I snapped my phone shut. "I'm listening."

He jutted out his chin in defiance.

I gave him my best death glare. "Fine. Then we'll leave, and you can wait until someone else finds you." I started toward the door. "Come on, Jer-I mean, Pete."

"No!" Howard cried. "Don't go. I'll tell you. Just please don't call the cops."

I turned back, crossed my arms, and waited.

"Joy and I came back here after dinner. We were, you know, fooling around when three guys dressed in black came barging through the door. They tied me up while one of them sat on Joy. Then they left me like this and dragged her out of here, kicking and screaming. I can't believe my neighbors didn't report it. They complain if I flush the toilet, for Christ's sake."

"Can you describe the men?"

"They wore ski masks. The only thing I can remember was a tattoo on one guy's hand. Letters across the knuckles."

"What letters?"

"Untie me, and I'll tell you."

I sighed. "We've been through this, Howard. I'm done playing games. We're leaving." I turned and started toward the door.

"Diablo," he cried. "It said Diablo."

Chapter Thirty-Six

"Diablo," Jerski repeated while we waited in Howard's living room for the police to arrive. "That's the gang with that psycho who escaped from court. They've been all over the news. They mean business. I don't like being mixed up in anything involving Diablo."

I wanted to tell him he had nothing to worry about, but at this point, I couldn't be sure of anything.

We had called Chandler police, but now I put a call through to Betz, too. I noticed I had missed a few calls as I dialed, but with my screen smashed, I couldn't decipher where they came from. Howard yelled for us to untie him from the bedroom, and I briefly entertained the idea of putting the duct tape back over his mouth. I walked back to the room and pulled the door shut instead, muffling a string of expletives.

"Where the hell are you?" Betz barked. "Can't you listen just once? I know Jasmine told you to stay put. What do you do? You go God knows where, doing God knows what. You got a death wish or something?"

"I found Joy's date," I said, hoping to derail him before he yelled anymore. He sighed. "Where?"

"At his apartment in Chandler. He was tied up with a note written in marker on his forehead. It said, 'You're too late.'" I wasn't sure who it was meant for, but it was chilling just the same. "I left him as we found him since Chandler PD are on their way. I thought you should know, too."

"You didn't question him, did you? This is a police matter."

"Not much."

I visualized Betz was rubbing the back of his neck again. "And?"

"Men dressed in black wearing ski masks. One of them had a Diablo tat."

"Tell me you're not alone."

"I'm with Jer–I mean another PO."

"Put him on the phone."

"Who?"

"The PO," he said wearily.

I winced and handed the phone to Jerski. "He wants to talk to you."

Jerski reluctantly took the phone. "Hello?"

I heard lots of Okays. Then he ended the call and handed my phone back to me.

"What did he say?" I asked.

"To take you back to his place after Chandler is done with us. He told me to keep you there. Said I could sit on you if I have to."

Jeez.

Two uniformed cops arrived shortly after disconnecting from Betz. They untied Howard and let him get dressed. They took our information, treating us with suspicion until the older one spoke to Betz. After that, they treated me like I was insane.

"You can go," the officer said. "Directly back to Detective Betz's house. You got that?"

I couldn't help but roll my eyes. "Got it."

Fifteen minutes later, we pulled into Betz's driveway. I zoned out on the ride home while Jerski sang along to Miley Cyrus. In that time, I decided that after Betz updated me on the investigation, I'd make the five-hour drive to San Diego and join Kate and the rest of the family on the beach. This was a police matter, and only dumb luck had kept me alive thus far.

Together, Jerski and I walked to the door and waited while I rang the doorbell. When no one answered, I called Betz. "We're here, where are you?"

"Ten minutes away," he said. "You better wait for me, and you better not be alone."

I disconnected. "You will be relieved of your duties soon. My other jailer is on his way."

Jerski planted himself on the front stoop.

I doubted Diablo would put together that I was at my ex-husband's house, but I was glad to have company just the same. I sat next to him. "Thanks for staying."

Jerski raised an eyebrow. "Wow. Didn't know that word was in your vocabulary."

"Can't you just say you're welcome?"

He smiled. "You're welcome."

I nodded. "That's better."

A few minutes later, Betz pulled into the driveway. He made his way to us, shaking his head, his expression grim. "You're wearing me out, Case. All this worrying about you, especially when you are hell-bent on doing things your own way."

"I'm here, aren't I?"

He reached out and shook Jerski's hand. "Did you have to sit on her long?"

Jerski gave a nervous laugh. "For a minute, I thought I'd have to. But she wasn't so bad this time."

I got to my feet. "Stop talking about me like I'm not here."

They both looked at me like they didn't know I was there. Give me a break.

Once Jerski left, we went inside. I was prepared to follow him to the kitchen for a low-carb lunch, but he stopped at the hall closet and pulled out a bulletproof vest. "Put this on. You should probably sleep in it until this is over."

I slipped it over my head, and he helped me fasten the side straps so it fit snugly. Once Betz was satisfied the fit was as good as it was going to get, he stood back and sized me up. I tried to smile, but I felt more like collapsing into his arms and having a good cry.

He reached out and tilted my chin up so he could study my scrapes and bruises. I saw his Adam's apple move as he swallowed hard. "God, Casey," he said.

I cleared my throat and stepped back, so we broke contact. Any more of that, and I would burst into tears.

Betz sighed. "You ready?"

I followed him back outside to the Tahoe. "Where are we going?"

"After you were kidnapped, some other detectives did a search of your neighbor's house but didn't really find anything. I wanted to go back and have another look. Who knows, maybe he returned, although I doubt it. I don't know what else to do with you, so you're sticking with me today."

I didn't admit it, but I was grateful. My trip to San Diego could wait a while. At least Betz was armed and skilled in self-defense. We started the drive toward my house.

"I don't know why I'm even wasting my breath," he said. "But why didn't you call me when you got the information about Howard instead of going there yourself?"

Sharing my conversation with Jasmine was not an option. What could Betz say to make the situation any less awkward? Even worse, he might deny that he had any feelings left for me, which wouldn't help since I would wonder if he was being truthful or trying to save face. "I tried to call you," I said. "It went to voicemail. I left a message. And I wasn't alone. Jerski was with me."

He kept his eyes on the road. His knuckles were white from gripping the steering wheel so tightly. "You should have called Jasmine."

Not on your life. A change of subject seemed in order. "Has Crowne given up any info?"

"Nope. He says he doesn't know anything and denies affiliation with Diablo. He's an asshole. His attorney, the one you asked about, told him not to talk to us."

Matthew Peterson. But telling his client not to talk was part of his job.

We rode the rest of the way in silence. I wondered if Marcus had the thumb drive or if he turned it over to Diablo.

An unmarked car with two detectives waited at the end of my street. We nestled next to them, and Betz lowered my window.

"Give us a description of Marcus," he said.

I cleared my throat. "He's about five-ten, thin, brown hair, almost shoulder length." Given my testosterone-filled audience, I left gorgeous out of my description.

"And he lives alone?" a cop from the other car asked.

"Far as I know."

"Alright," Betz said. "Schultz, you take the back of the house. Remy, come with us to the front."

We drove the short distance to my house and parked two doors down. "Stay behind that wall until I give the all-clear," Betz said as we got out of the car.

As I took my hiding spot, Remy pushed the door open. It had already been kicked in when the first search was done, and the lock had been broken. He and Betz, guns drawn, darted inside. I tried to fight the flashbacks of Joel Quinn's suicide; my stomach tight when I pictured Marcus with the same outcome. My heart was in my throat. Despite everything, I didn't want Marcus to get hurt. I hoped if he was home, he wouldn't resist.

Once they cleared the rooms, Betz motioned me over. "Nobody home."

I walked freely through the house. Looking at the couch, I felt myself blush as I recalled what almost happened there a few nights before.

Schultz looked through kitchen cabinets while Remy overturned sofa cushions and looked behind the couch and even under it. There wasn't much to go through. Marcus had barely moved in. A few pairs of Levi's hung in the closet, folded T-shirts and clean underwear and socks lay on a closet shelf. It was like he'd arrived with nothing and went to Target to get a few changes of clothes. He had no dresser. A green duffle bag sat on the floor. Betz laid it on the bed and went through it. He pulled out a worn copy of Catcher in the Rye and ruffled the pages. A photo fell out. Betz looked at it and handed it to me. "This him?"

I took the photo and moved to the window where there was better light. It was Marcus, all right. Marcus and that grin that had weakened my knees. He had his arm around a girl. She stared back at the camera with the same soulful brown eyes that helped make Marcus so appealing. I'd seen the girl before. Twice in fact. The night I paid a visit to Joel Quinn and in the missing persons article on the Internet.

"It's him," I said. "The girl in the photo must be related to him, same last name. Her name is Courtney, and she's missing from New Jersey. I saw her picture on the Internet just before Crowne and Marcus took me." Remembering that made me shudder. "I'm pretty sure I saw her with Diablo a few days ago as well."

"Hmm," Betz said. "She goes missing and is in the company of Diablo. You think Marcus had something to do with her disappearance? That he sacrificed his own family member for the gang?"

I felt sick. "I don't know. I'm not really getting his ties to this whole mess. Neither he nor Crowne seem like Diablo members."

"Pretty sure Crowne thought killing you was his ticket in."

Memories of his hands on my throat caused me to break into a cold sweat.

Schultz and Remy joined us in the bedroom. "Find anything?" Remy asked.

"Not really," Betz said. "You?"

"There's not much in this place. Looks like he wasn't planning to stay long."

"I called the landlord," Schultz said. "Place was rented month to month. Paid for in cash."

Chapter Thirty-Seven

After Remy and Schultz left, Betz slipped the photo of Marcus and Courtney into an evidence bag. "Just how well do you know this guy, Case?"

I studied my shoes. "Not well. He never offered any real information. He was just conveniently around."

"I'm gonna contact New Jersey, find out what they know about him. Now, I just gotta figure out what to do with you."

I was getting used to being an appendage on whichever poor soul had been assigned the chore of watching me for the day, so I let his remark pass and followed him to the door.

In the car, I fished in my bag for the paper I had with Marcus' probation officer's name and number. Finding it, I asked Betz for his phone. "Mine's almost dead. Maybe his PO can give us something useful." It was then I remembered that I left my charger in Jerski's car.

We sat outside my house in the Tahoe while I dialed New Jersey, putting the phone on speaker mode so we could both hear.

"Probation, this is Charlotte," a friendly voice said.

Betz identified himself and said I was with him. "We've got a situation here, and your client, Marcus Sheldon, is involved. I have a few questions about him."

Charlotte cleared her throat. "Go ahead."

"What's he on supervision for?"

"Assault."

"What was that about?" Betz asked.

209

"He clocked a judge."

"A judge?" I asked.

"I don't have the file in front of me, and I have so many cases, I'm afraid I can't recall the particulars, but I know he attacked a judge."

"Did you know he was in Arizona?" Betz asked.

"I did."

"What reason did he give for coming out here?" Betz asked.

"His sister lives there. She has cancer, and he wanted to help out with the kids."

"You verify any of this?" Betz asked.

Charlotte sighed. "No."

"Seems like he lied," Betz said.

I bit my fist to keep from interjecting my thoughts on her shoddy PO work.

"Is he in custody?" Charlotte asked.

"No," Betz said. "But the court has issued a warrant for his arrest."

"For what?" she sounded uneasy.

"Kidnapping, but I'm sure there will be other charges."

"Oh, no," Charlotte said. "I was so hoping he'd do well. I mean... he seemed like such a nice guy, but I guess you never can tell. I'll have to request a warrant for violating his probation here, too. Can you email me a copy of your warrant?"

"Sure," Betz said. He jotted her email address on the paper I handed him.

"Can you send us a copy of his presentence report?" I asked.

"I can do that," Charlotte said.

Once all the email addresses were exchanged, Betz disconnected and slid his phone in his shirt pocket. "I'm dropping you at my house on my way to the office. You're probably safest there."

Oh, no. I wasn't up for another dose of Jasmine. Although I hated to put myself out of the loop, I was slowing Betz down by making him worry about me. And I was tired. "I think I'll go to San Diego instead." I told him about Kate's invitation.

"Sounds like a good idea," Betz said.

I looked out the window at my house. I wondered if I'd ever feel safe there again or if I'd always flashback to Crowne, Marcus, and his thug buddies dragging me to the van. Before I could get too caught up in the memory, Betz said, "Grab your things. I'm not leaving until you're on your way."

I went to the bedroom and threw some clothes into a backpack. As I crouched down to grab my shoes, I spotted the book where I'd tucked Hope's business card among the pages. I picked it up and pulled out the card. The series of numbers written on the back had meant nothing to me when I'd found it in Melissa King's backpack. But now, I thought about the thumb drive and the access code I hadn't been able to crack. Could this be it? God only knew where the thumb drive had landed, but I stuffed the card into my pocket anyway.

Betz loaded my bag in my car while I stuffed a few Diet Cokes, a bottle of water, two granola bars, and a bottle of Advil into a cooler. I grabbed my cell phone and hoped it would hold a charge at least until I made it out of town.

We stood outside the Jeep. Wind whipped our hair and ruffled the palms of the tree in the yard. A storm was coming.

Betz rubbed the back of his neck. "I should probably follow you to the state line. You'd find trouble in the middle of a church service."

"I'll be fine. Just promise to call me the minute you find out anything about Hope and Joy. And knowing when you have Marcus in custody would be nice, too."

"Will do."

The wind swept a piece of hair across my face, and it caught in my mouth. Betz reached out and looped his finger around it, then tucked it behind my ear. "Better hurry. Hopefully, you can stay ahead of the storm. News said it's gonna be a doozy." We both looked skyward at the dark clouds that were rolling in from the east.

I stepped toward him and gave him an awkward hug before climbing into the Jeep.

"Call me when you get there," he said.

"I will." I backed out of the driveway and waved before driving away. I checked the rear-view mirror. He watched after me, looking like a father who had just put his kindergartner on the bus for the first day of school. I wished I would have told him how much I worried about him, too. He was putting his life on the line, and I couldn't do anything to help him.

I maneuvered the Jeep down the road through the small village of Maricopa, a community whose casinos were often frequented by valley residents. It was a well-used shortcut to Interstate Eight. Once I made it to the freeway, I'd be in San Diego five hours later. Five hours from Diablo. I planned to drive straight to the beach, kick off my shoes, and stand in the surf.

As much as I tried to keep my mind on that pleasant image, thoughts of my cousins in the hands of the thugs who had kidnapped them quickly brought me back to my previous panicky state. We knew the players: Diablo, Marcus, Crowne, and Joel Quinn. I still had no idea what Hope's connection was to the situation. I suspected Matthew Peterson had some knowledge, but he had that whole client confidentiality thing going on.

My gas gauge flirted with the warning button, but I figured I had enough fuel to make it to Buckeye, where I'd stop for a bathroom break and a Diet Coke. There was a Walmart there where I could get a car charger for my sorry phone, too. I thought about getting a new phone but didn't want to take the time to set it up. After Buckeye, it would be straight freeway through the desert. A boring ride that would give me lots of time to process what had happened during the last week. I couldn't do much about the situation with Diablo, but I could brainstorm the facts I'd learned about my mother. Those sat as unsettled with me as if I'd just eaten a bad burrito.

I passed the casino doing fifty-five and barely heard my cell phone chirp. I picked it up. A text message. I glanced at it while keeping an eye on the road. "It's time we talked. I have information about your cousin."

Before reading more, I pulled onto the dirt at the side of the road and slammed on the brakes. I read the rest. "Meet me at my office in half an hour. And come alone."

I didn't recognize the number. "Who is this?" I texted back.

I waited, my heart pounding in my chest. About a minute later, my answer came. "M.P."

Matthew Peterson? Why talk to me now? What led to the sudden change of heart? Had he learned what had happened to me in the desert and realized how serious the situation had become? Was he going to break attorney-client privilege because he knew his clients were out of control?

I sat on the side of the road while cars whizzed by. He said to come alone, but if I did, Betz would kill me if Diablo didn't get to me first. And I trusted him no more than I trusted Marcus. "This is a police matter," I said out loud, hoping I could convince myself to stay out of it.

I scrolled through the contacts in my phone and chose Betz's number. I would let him deal with it. That's what any sane person would do. But fate decided otherwise. When I pushed send, the phone only rang once before going dead.

With a deep breath, I pulled a U-turn and headed back to town, where dark, menacing storm clouds darkened the city.

Chapter Thirty-Eight

J agged lightning sizzled in the late-afternoon sky. I watched the road, glancing at the dashboard clock. It was four-thirty, but the approaching storm made it seem much later. I was going seventy-five, hoping I could get to Matthew Peterson's office before the building closed at five so other staff would likely be around. I knew a convenience store stood just down the street from the law offices that still had a pay phone. Some of my phoneless clients used it sometimes. I planned to stop there and call Betz before I met with Peterson. Hopefully, we could confront him together.

I reached the exit at Seventh Street with only ten minutes to spare. Dime-sized raindrops pummeled my windshield and played a tune on the rag-top of my Jeep. It reminded me of the song that plays in B movies just before the psycho grabs the ignorant girl. Good thing I didn't believe in signs and karma and all that bull.

As I drove past the law office, rain came down harder. I pulled into the 7-Eleven parking lot and positioned the Jeep so I could see the front door to Peterson's office. I kept my eyes glued on the office door.

I stepped out of my car and ran to the phone. Instantly, I was drenched. I dialed 911.

As I did, a Hummer pulled up in front of the office. Two burly men climbed out and rushed through the door to the office.

Oh shit. I waited for my call to go through, but nothing happened. I realized there was an out-of-order sign on the phone just as the men came back out of the building, Matthew Peterson among them. He looked around before getting inside the vehicle, and I wondered if he was looking for me.

Was his offer of information a way to get me here so he could turn me over to Diablo? Or were they taking him against his will?

I squinted to get a better look at the driver, who had stayed in the vehicle. It was another large goon who had to be Diablo. But it was the passenger in the front seat who made my heart stop. It was getting dark, and the rain was coming down hard, but a young girl—not Courtney Sheldon.

As the Hummer pulled away from the curb, I panicked. If I went inside and used their phone to call police, I'd lose the Hummer and possibly this golden opportunity to find Hope and Joy.

I debated my choices for a fraction of a second, and then I was back in my Jeep, pulling out several cars behind the Hummer, my heart in my throat.

I trailed them down Seventh Street and ran a red light at McDowell. A cop stopping me might be a good thing.

But I got away with my little traffic violation and kept the Hummer in view as we pulled onto Interstate 10. The Hummer weaved through rush hour traffic to the carpool lane. Legally, I couldn't drive in the HOV lane, but operating within the law had been slowly slipping away from me. I joined the privileged drivers several cars back.

We traveled along at a good thirty miles per hour, which was impressive given the time of day and the weather conditions. My stomach was knotted so tightly, I thought it would rupture. I had no idea what my plan was or if I could pull it off. I hoped they would lead me to my cousins, and I would then be able to alert the police to the Diablo hideout they had thus far been unable to find. But I had no working phone, no real weapons, and as I was coming to realize, no sense.

Optimism came for a few seconds as I blatantly drove past a patrol car. Okay, I thought, come and get me. I'm alone in the carpool lane. I'd give him a description of the Hummer, and another officer would stop them down the road. But the only thing the cop saw as I slipped by was the cuticle he examined on his right thumb. He probably didn't want to get wet. Damn it.

Once we neared the merge with the Superstition Freeway, traffic thinned, and we picked up speed. Thunder rumbled, and angry lightning ripped the sky open. The spray from cars in front of me had my windshield wipers working overtime. I clutched the steering wheel as hard as I clenched my teeth. My jaw was so tight, it ached.

Just past the 60, the Hummer flew across four lanes of traffic and took the Baseline Road exit. I shifted lanes and followed. I must have cut off five or six cars, or at least the sounding of horns made it seem that way.

As I skidded onto Baseline Road, I prayed my not-so-smooth exit hadn't drawn Diablo's attention to me. They turned toward South Phoenix, and I ended up three cars behind them. The Hummer pulled into the parking lot of a large electronics store, and one of the men climbed out and hurried inside while the Hummer idled at the curb. I drove by and saw the driver had a cell phone to his ear. I still couldn't make out the girl.

I drove down lanes, pretending to look for a parking space, all the while keeping sight of the Hummer. Finding a spot with a good vantage point, I turned off my headlights but kept the motor running. I blasted the defrost system, hoping my windows would stop fogging up.

There was a convenience store on the other side of Baseline Road. I thought about darting over there to try to find a phone to call the police, but I couldn't risk losing the Hummer. And I wondered how many pay phones still existed in the valley or if any of them worked.

A beefy guy with a shaved head and super baggy pants that hung so low on his hips his plaid boxers were exposed came toward me, seemingly not bothered by the rain. He approached a beat-up Chevy Malibu parked next to me and pulled the door open.

I unzipped my window and folded it down. "Excuse me," I said. "Do you have a cell phone I could borrow for a minute?"

He looked at me like I'd just suggested he pull his pants up.

"It's an emergency."

He stuck his big head in my window. "You don't look like you're having no emergency."

He looked me up and down. I realized my rain-soaked shirt probably left little to the imagination and crossed my arms over my chest.

"You ain't half bad," he said. "Your old man beat you up?"

"Can I just use your phone?"

216

CHAPTER THIRTY-EIGHT

He didn't respond, just kept looking at my chest.

I grabbed my wallet. "I'll pay you."

He reached in and snatched it from my hand.

"Hey, give that back."

He grinned, showing rotten teeth that no doubt accounted for the breath. He held my wallet up in the air. "Or what?"

Out of the corner of my eye, I saw the Hummer pull away from the curb.

"I don't have time for this." I wrenched the door open, so it struck the guy in the gut. He went wide-eyed as I reached through the window and stuck my finger in his eye. When he brought his hands up to protect himself, I grabbed my wallet, pulled the door closed, and put the Jeep in first gear.

I drove out of the lot feeling way too calm about what I'd just done. I had fought Ramirez and Crowne. Dealing with a punk like him was just another day at the office.

At Baseline, I hesitated, looking east and west for signs of the Hummer. It was getting dark and harder to see. I squinted at the traffic around me, fearing I'd lost them. But then I spotted the monstrous truck heading west. I turned right and followed for about ten miles. We passed strip malls and apartment buildings, then entered a more rural part of South Phoenix where farms and big empty fields still existed. In the middle of nowhere, we turned south and headed toward the mountain. Ah, the boonies. Perfect.

The road went straight to the mountain, then curved at its base. I dropped back so I wouldn't be seen. It was pitch dark now, and the rain continued. Thunder boomed in the distance, and I caught lightning flashes to the west. Maybe the storm was moving on.

I drove another mile or so before coming to a turnoff. There were several curves on unmarked roads, and I quickly became disoriented. Slowing, the Hummer's taillights came on about a quarter mile down an unpaved road, and they pulled into a driveway of a two-story house.

Chapter Thirty-Nine

I t appeared to be the only house on the street. I pulled over far enough that I could watch the house, but not be seen, turned off my lights, and waited. There were sounds of closing car doors, and then there was only rain on my roof and the occasional thunderclap. I pulled further off the road, concealing my Jeep the best I could behind a few bushes.

A few minutes later, four people exited the house and got back in the Hummer. It started up again and drove past me. Even though the Jeep was hidden, I ducked down in my seat as they went by. I had no idea of my location, tucked back in the mountains and on a dirt road. I had seen no street signs, and there were no streetlights. I debated following them versus checking out the house for an address. I didn't have enough gas to pursue them all over town. Although I didn't know if there were more of them in the house, checking it out seemed to be my best bet.

Locking my purse in the center compartment of my Jeep, I pulled my backpack from the backseat and found my running shoes and socks and put them on. This was no place for flip-flops. My duty bag with my work equipment was in the back seat. I gathered my handcuffs and pepper spray and stuffed them in my back pockets. I shoved my keys in my front pocket, took my department-issued Maglite from beside my seat, and started off down the road.

When I got to the house, I used a cactus for cover and surveyed the area, keeping a death grip on the flashlight, thinking it would make a good weapon if needed. Lights were on in the front room of the house. Upstairs, light seeped from behind one curtained window. Everything else was dark.

I risked a sweep of the area with my flashlight. A six-foot barbwire fence surrounded what I guessed was a half-acre lot. The property was overgrown with weeds and rapidly multiplying prickly pear cactus. No neighbors in sight.

I crept up to the window where the light came from, staying low. The blinds were drawn, but a quarter-inch gap ran along the sides. I cocked my head sideways so I could get a good look. A bed with tussled sheets and a tripod. A set up similar to the one at Technerds. No people in view.

Plans to move around to the backyard and check out the back of the house were interrupted when I heard a low growl behind me. I swallowed and slowly turned around.

A Rottweiler stood not six feet back. He had something in his mouth and dropped it before pulling his snout back in a snarl. I was okay with dogs as long as they didn't want to eat me. This one looked hungry.

"Nice puppy," I tried.

I aimed my flashlight at the dog's paws for a second, revealing a hot pink stiletto-heeled shoe. Joy was here. I wanted to hug the dog, but another growl stopped me.

"Rambo," a voice ordered from the side door. "Get in here."

I tried to shoo him away. "Go on, Rambo, go," I whispered.

But Rambo wasn't buying it. He barked.

I held my flashlight like a baseball bat. "Please, Rambo."

The door burst open, and a floodlight illuminated the yard. "What's going on out here?"

Busted, I froze as our eyes met. Marcus.

"Casey." He stopped ten feet in front of me.

He patted the dog on the head and told him to sit. The dog complied.

"Put the flashlight down, Casey."

"Not a chance." I wasn't leaving without Joy.

"I'm not going to hurt you."

"Of course not. You'll just restrain me and let someone else do the dirty work," I said. I was pretty sure he could order Rambo to take me out, but he had no weapon in his hands. "I know Joy's here," I said. "And I'm not leaving without her."

Marcus shrugged. "Fair enough. If I show you where she is, will you leave?"

Like I could trust him. He was a convicted felon on abscond status, and he'd helped kidnap me. I wasn't sure where Courtney Shelden fit into all this, but it was clear he was part of Diablo. I lowered the flashlight, reached in my pocket, and pulled out my pepper spray. Aiming it at Marcus, I sprayed it into his face, hoping he didn't have a glass eye.

But it worked this time. "Jesus," he said. When he doubled over to rub his eyes, I clunked him in the head with the flashlight. He went down on his knees, and I hit him again. His hands went up to protect his head, and I grabbed his wrist and slapped one handcuff on. Before I could grab the other wrist, Rambo lunged at me and knocked me on my ass. But I held onto Marcus and rolled on top of him.

With the handcuff only fastened to one wrist, I had done nothing more than give him a weapon. I had to keep control.

Marcus tried to flip me over, but I grabbed onto his crotch and held on. "Let go of me or you'll never father a child."

"You've got to listen," he said through gritted teeth.

With my free hand, I reached out and got hold of the flashlight. Bringing it up, I gave him one more whack to the head. He lost his grip on me, and I managed to snap the other handcuff on.

Breathless, I sat back on my heels and looked at Marcus, lying on his side, his hands secured behind him. As I prepared to get to my feet, Rambo charged forward, knocked me flat on my back, and forced all the air from my lungs. Okay, I didn't think this through.

Rambo straddled me, dog drool dripped onto my chin. I looked over the dog's shoulder at the house, thinking Joy was inside. I was moments from setting her free, and I was about to be ripped to shreds by a dog.

"Rambo," Marcus called. "Off."

The dog sniffed my hair, then backed up and sat nicely. I took a minute to catch my breath, then rolled to my hands and knees and staggered to my feet.

"Why did you do that?" I asked, looking down at him. "What the hell is your game?"

"No game," he said. "We're on the same side. You just have to give me a minute to explain."

I rolled my eyes. I was getting tired of this crap. "Joy first." I reached down and grabbed his arm, hoisting him to his feet. "Is anybody else inside?"

"No."

"Then walk." I shoved him forward.

We entered through a side door. I pushed Marcus ahead of me and kicked the door shut behind us. I wiped rain and dog drool off my face with my arm and took in our surroundings. The entryway was covered with dark-paneled wood. An empty room was to my left, and the room with the bed and tripod to my right. A narrow staircase lay in front of us.

"Where?" I asked.

"Upstairs," he said.

I gave him a little shove, and we moved up the stairs. At the top was another hallway with several closed doors. Marcus tilted his head toward the one to the left. "She's in there."

"This better not be a trap," I said.

Marcus sighed. "You're going to have to trust me."

"You're funny," I said.

I pushed him past the door and put my ear to it. Muffled sounds. Someone was in there. But was it Joy? If he wanted me dead, I'd already be dead. Rambo was more than up for the job. Like it or not, I had no choice but to hope he was telling me the truth.

I slowly twisted the knob and eased the door open with the butt of my flashlight.

The door groaned as it moved out of the way. Joy lay flat on her back, tied to the same bedpost I'd seen in the photo. A table lamp cast an eerie glow in the room. Something was stuffed in her mouth, so she couldn't speak, but her eyes bulged, and she squirmed when she saw me.

Grabbing Marcus and pulling him into the room with me, I closed the door and pushed him onto a nearby chair. I rushed over to the bed. She seemed to be in decent shape. No bruises or blood. I was so relieved, my eyes filled with tears.

"Joy," I whispered. "I'm going to take the gag out of your mouth, but I need you to keep quiet. I'm not sure if anyone else is here."

She nodded enthusiastically.

"Promise?"

She nodded again.

I reached down and pulled the scarf out of her mouth.

"God!" she shrieked. "Casey, am I glad to see you. Untie me, for goodness sake. All the blood drained out of my arms hours ago."

"Shush," I said. "If there's someone here, they'll hear you."

"Untie me," she insisted.

I went to work on the knots that bound her to the bed. They were so tight, I wasn't having any luck loosening them. "I need a knife," I said. "I'll be right back."

"Hurry," she said. "I gotta pee something fierce."

I started toward the door, then ran back, and hugged her. "Thank God you're all right." Tears splashed down my face, and I wiped them away with the back of my hand.

"Good lord," she said. "We can do this later. I really gotta pee."

"Right." I rushed toward the door, then remembered Marcus, who was sitting on a chair by the door. His eyes were almost swollen shut from the pepper spray. He had his head back against the wall.

"There's a folding knife in my front pocket," he said.

I reached in his left jean pocket and pulled out a folding knife. "You're full of surprises," I said, coming out with the knife.

He shrugged. "You should hurry. They'll be back soon."

"Yeah," Joy said. "Plus, I'm gonna wet my pants."

Marcus opened one eye and took in the miniskirt that had ridden halfway up Joy's ass, revealing what existed of her panties. "Figure of speech," he said.

I kept an eye on Marcus as I hacked away at the thick rope that held Joy to the bedposts.

CHAPTER THIRTY-NINE

"Is Hope in the house?" I asked.

"Not that I know of," Joy said. "I've pretty much been left here like this. It's been torture."

"Marcus?" I asked.

"No," he said. "She's not. You have to listen to me. I'm trying to help you."

I stopped cutting the rope and pushed some hair out of my face. "You helped kidnap me. You left me with Michael Crowne so he could kill me. You're very helpful, I'll give you that. Problem is, you're helping the bad guys."

"Who do you think ran over Ramirez when he chased you across the street? Who did you think slipped you the pocketknife in the van? Who called the police and told them where they could find you before Crowne had the chance to kill you?"

I stared at him. "He almost did kill me."

"I'm sorry. I did the best I could. I couldn't risk blowing my cover."

"Your cover?"

"The ropes," Joy reminded me.

I worked on the ropes, replaying Marcus's words in my head. Was he an undercover cop? I didn't think so. He didn't have the skills of a law enforcement officer. He had street sense. While I worked, Joy wiggled and complained that if she didn't get to the bathroom in five seconds, it would be too late.

Once free, Joy leapt off the bed and ran for the adjoining bathroom.

I turned to Marcus. "What do you mean, cover? You telling me you're a cop?"

"No," he said. "Just a brother trying to find his missing sister. I know Diablo is responsible for taking her and that they plan to force her into prostitution if they haven't already."

I thought about Courtney Shelden. I could tell him I'd seen her, but I wasn't ready to put any trust in him just yet.

Marcus cleared his throat and continued. "I don't know where they're hiding the girls yet. Letting you and Joy go will blow my cover, but I think they're tired of you and might actually kill you the next time they get a chance. The only reason you're still alive is that after Crown failed, they promised Ramirez he could have the honor of taking care of you."

My mouth went dry. Ramirez wouldn't just kill me. He'd make sure I suffered first.

"Have you seen Hope?" Joy asked, coming out of the bathroom.

"I've seen her," he said. "I'm not sure she's involved willingly, but she's with them. They know she tried to send you information that could bring them down, but they haven't hurt her. She has more freedom than the kidnapped girls, but she's not free to leave, I'm pretty sure of that."

"How did they know she sent me something?" I asked.

"She thought she could trust the gang's attorney. Turns out she was wrong."

"Matthew Peterson?" I asked.

"That would be him," Marcus said.

"She did send me a package," I said. "It disappeared the night I was kidnapped. The last person I saw go in my house was you."

He nodded toward his other pocket. "You mean the thumb drive. I pulled it out of your computer when Crowne took you. Problem is, it's password protected."

I reached in his pocket and pulled out the thumb drive. "How much time do we have before Diablo comes back?"

"Not much," Marcus said. "There's a laptop downstairs."

We followed Marcus down the hall to a room with a desk. A laptop lay open on top of it. I settled in front of it and inserted the flash drive. The screen requesting a passcode popped up.

I took Hope's business card out of my back pocket and typed in the numbers written on the back. I swallowed hard in the instant it took the computer to recognize the encryption. Up popped a single file.

Chapter Forty

The file contained two videos. I clicked on the first one, and my mother's face filled the screen. It hit me like a punch to my stomach. I leaned back in my chair.

Joy reached out and patted my shoulder. "It's okay," she said. "I'm here for you."

"Who is that?" Marcus asked.

"Casey's mother," Joy whispered. Like I couldn't hear.

I swallowed hard and leaned in to get a better view.

My mother sat at her desk in the DA's office. She adjusted her phone so she could record herself, but still cut off the top of her head.

She cleared her throat. "It's November 23rd. I'm making this video." She sighed. "In case I'm not around to finish what I've started. My plan is to place this video and the one I shot earlier today on a thumb drive and give it to my supervisor, Ryan Miller, so he can complete the investigation should something happen to me. I've been asked to explore corruption within the court. I have contacted an FBI agent and am about to turn the matter over to him. If I don't make that appointment, I want some documentation to exist. And frankly, it's hard to know who to trust. Someone I care about has been unwittingly mixed up in this mess by falling in love with the wrong man. Now that she knows who he really is, she has promised to help me bring these people to justice, but I hope doing so isn't putting her in danger. If they were to find out she's helping me, they'll surely kill her."

I let out a long breath. She made the video two days before she died. Hope had to be the person who was helping her. And if she was, was she operating undercover to help my mom? If that was the case, she must have been terrified since my mom's death.

My mother hesitated, looking down at her hands. She leaned forward and continued. "My investigation has led me to a public official who is involved in taking bribes. I don't have concrete proof yet, and as you will see in the other video, my evidence is weak at this point, but I'm close. Unfortunately, I may have been found out. If so, they will come after me... I may have to go away for a while so my family isn't dragged into this any more than they already are. Ryan, if you're watching this, please tell my family I love- "

And then my mother looks up, a startled expression on her face. She reaches for her phone, and the screen goes dark.

Marcus, Joy, and I let out a collective breath. It was now clear this whole Diablo thing and my mother's death were connected. Was this proof she didn't kill herself?

"Play the second video," Joy said.

Marcus looked at me. "You okay?"

A bead of sweat broke out across my brow, but I nodded and pushed play.

The next video was shaky and taken from an odd angle but showed three men talking. Their faces weren't in the frame, but there was a Diablo tattoo on one man's arm. Two of the men were dressed in dark pants and black T-shirts; the third wore a suit. A sculpture of a Greek god sat on a pedestal in the background.

A dark-clothed man handed the man in the suit an envelope.

"How are these girls working out?" a voice said.

"They're young," another said. "It's a process. Takes time to get them to understand they work for us and ain't got a choice anymore."

"And they'll like it."

There was laughter all around.

"How many are actually working?"

"In Phoenix? We got about twenty right now. Don't worry. We got more girls coming in all the time. We'll be up to Jersey standards in no time."

The video cut off at that point.

"I'm not sure how useful that is," I said. "We already know Diablo is involved in human trafficking but don't have enough to prove it. The one girl we have won't talk."

"Yeah," Marcus said. "But I know where that was shot. My sister is one of those girls you keep referring to as being trafficked. I just want to find her and bring her home. I'm no threat to you. In fact, I'm sure you're confused based on what I had to do to maintain my cover, but from the moment we met, I fell for you. That was real."

Heat crept up my neck onto my cheeks. Ejecting the thumb drive, I shoved it in my pocket. Standing, I pulled out the handcuff key. "Turn around."

Marcus turned his back to me. I reached forward and unlocked the handcuffs, then stuffed them in my back pocket.

Marcus turned around, rubbing his wrists. "There's a car out back. You ladies need to get out of here before Diablo returns." He started down the hallway. "Just a sec." He stepped into a bedroom, returned a minute later, and continued down the hall.

We followed. "What about you?" I asked as he opened the back door. We all stepped outside. Wind attacked our hair like a giant mixer. We ran to a parked Ford Taurus.

"Keys are in the ignition," Marcus said. "Go."

I noticed his motorcycle parked on the other side of the car. "And where are you going?"

"To finish this," he said. "I've been to that place where the video was shot, and I know the guy in the suit probably lives there. I bet Hope is with him."

I looked into his puffy eyes and saw sincerity. I nudged Joy. "Go on." I gave her a quick hug. "I'm going with Marcus."

"Are you nuts?" she said.

"Probably."

"I thought you didn't trust me," Marcus said.

I mounted the Harley. "I don't."

Before anyone else could speak, the sound of a motor broke the silence, and headlights lit the driveway. The Hummer was back.

Marcus shoved Joy toward the car and slid in front of me on the motorcycle.

Joy rushed to the Taurus, got in, and threw the car into reverse. After turning around, she tore down the driveway, narrowly missing a collision with the Hummer that was pulling in.

Marcus revved the engine and jerked the bike forward. I had to wrap my arms around him to avoid sliding off. Marcus didn't mess with the driveway; he rode through the yard. The Hummer did a doughnut and followed us.

I chanced a look back. The tank-like vehicle bore down on us. I tightened my hold on Marcus. It took me a moment to realize my stomach was pressed against the gun tucked into the waistband of his jeans.

Chapter Forty-One

We made it to the road and pulled behind Joy. The Hummer was on our tail. I couldn't tell what speed we were going, but it was fast enough to pull the skin on my face tighter than Marcus' abs.

I hoped Joy, at least, would get away. Although she hadn't seemed too traumatized when I found her, I had a feeling the whole family denial-cover-it-up-with-sarcasm thing was at work. Something I knew a little bit about. I also knew the realization of what she'd been through would eventually hit her hard.

With Marcus being armed, I thought we had a fair chance of getting into a gun battle if Diablo caught up to us. I had no idea what kind of shot Marcus was and guessed all of Diablo was armed as well. I also had no idea how many members were in the Hummer or if Hope was with them.

Joy had to be flooring the Ford. She created such a mist from flying through puddles, it looked like she was parting the sea.

And that damn Hummer was getting closer by the second. I could feel the vibrations of it barreling down on us. I was afraid it would run us over, squashing us like a squirrel in the road.

When the road came to a T, Joy took a left, Marcus a sharp right that almost had me sailing into the night. I tightened my hold as we went uphill, thinking how easily I could fly off the bike. And how quickly I'd smash my skull since I hadn't had time to put a helmet on.

As we climbed the hill, I could see the road below us and Joy disappearing around a bend. I chanced a quick look back and saw the Hummer fishtailing behind us. They'd taken the bait. Joy would escape. I thanked God and put my face between Marcus' shoulder blades. Then I realized we were the bait.

Marcus accelerated, increasing the distance between us and our pursuers. I relaxed for a moment. But only a moment, for within seconds, the Hummer gained ground. Marcus was doing well keeping the motorcycle upright on the slick streets, but I sensed he was having trouble doing so at such a high speed.

The Hummer didn't seem to have the same problem. They were so close, I could hear the engine.

And then Marcus did the unexpected. He veered off the road and drove through the desert, passing through a narrow opening between two giant boulders. Even if the Hummer could navigate the sharp turn, they'd never fit through the narrow pass. Once through, we zigzagged around cactus and shrubbery. Branches ripped what skin was left on my legs. I braced for the crash that was surely coming, but Marcus slowed and came to a stop. He turned off the bike and headlight, and we sat in darkness. I turned and watched the Hummer on the road below us, its taillights fading into darkness. We lost them.

Marcus looked over his shoulder at me. "You okay?"

I leaned back. I was panting hard and had no doubt added a few cuts to my plethora of scrapes and bruises, but I was alive. I nodded. "What do we do now?"

Marcus climbed off the bike and paced, shaking the rain off his hair like a wet dog. He rubbed his swollen eyes. "I don't know. We can't stay here. They're probably waiting for us down the road, so we can't turn back. I think there's another road at the top of the hill." He pointed at a dark shape before us. "We could push the bike up there and hope they aren't waiting for us."

"And if they are?"

He looked at me. "You should have gone with Joy. I betrayed them, and when they retaliate, it will be ugly."

"You sound like you're giving up."

"I'm just being realistic."

We were quiet for a moment. Neither of us said it, but we both knew what they would do to me wouldn't be pretty either.

I slid off the bike. "So, let's push this monster up the hill. Hope you ate your Wheaties this morning."

He smiled. "You beat the shit out of me. I've felt better."

I looked at my shoes. "Sorry."

"You had every right," he said. "I probably deserved it for not trusting you sooner."

I shrugged. "You were looking out for your sister, I get it."

We each took a side of the bike. Pushing it was like running into a strong wind. We didn't get too far before we had to rest. Luckily, there was a hiking trail between the two cliffs that wasn't too steep, and eventually, we neared the top.

As we reached the crest, I exhaled a sigh of relief. But my feeling was short-lived as we were immediately lit up by a bright light. I shielded my eyes with my cupped hand and made out a truck parked across the road facing us. Two men stood on either side. Both had guns pointed in our direction. "Hands up," one man said.

Of course, the thugs in the Hummer would have called their buddies to take up posts around the area. I let go of the Harley and raised my hands while taking a step back. My feet hit a slick spot and flew out from under me. I tumbled backward, landing in a bush. Scurrying around it, I crouched out of sight.

"Where the hell did she go?" someone said.

"Get back here, Bitch," a voice called. "Or I finish off your boyfriend."

I froze. I couldn't let them kill Marcus. I didn't know if what he had told me was true and I still couldn't get past his felon status, but he did help me and Joy escape. I also knew Diablo wouldn't give up looking for me just because they'd taken care of him. I had nowhere to go. I was in the middle of the desert, and I couldn't hide forever.

"Don't come out," Marcus said. "They'll kill me either way."

Whatever Marcus was, he was risking his life for me. This was a tough one. Come forward and place myself in the hands of Diablo—who was more than a little ticked off at me—or leave Marcus to whatever fate they saw fit.

A gunshot sounded. "I'm getting tired of waiting. Next shot is for lover boy."

I crawled on my stomach until I could see over the top of the hill. The biggest guy stood directly in front of Marcus, the barrel of the gun pressed to his forehead. The other man swung a tire iron. "Hey, Ruben, let me disfigure pretty boy before you waste him."

"Get the hell out of here, Casey," Marcus yelled.

I couldn't let them kill him. I stood up and stepped into the light.

"Get over here," Ruben ordered as the other man aimed a flashlight in my direction.

Before I could move, headlights appeared at the top of the hill. Gravel crunched as a car skidded out of control and slammed sideways into the truck.

"My truck," Ruben yelled.

The car righted itself, then accelerated toward the men. Ruben and Marcus both scrambled to get out of the way, but the car nailed them, and both men landed on the hood. The car skidded to a stop, depositing Ruben at the top of the cliff. Marcus bounced off the side. The window slid down, allowing me to see the driver. Joy. She revved the engine, and Ruben tried to roll out of the way but sent himself over the edge instead. She backed up and hit the other gangster as he scurried away, sending him skidding on his stomach until his face collided with the over-sized truck tire.

"Get in," Joy called.

I took in the scene. The second gangster lay motionless in the dirt at the side of his truck, and Ruben had disappeared over the cliff. I had time. I ran around the car and found Marcus on the ground.

Leaning over him, I shook his shoulders. "Get up." He didn't respond. I put my hand behind his head and felt something sticky. Blood. "Help me with him," I yelled to Joy.

She put the car into park and hurried over to us. "I swear, Casey, if you get us killed over a man, I'll never forgive you."

She took his feet, I scooped my arms under his armpits, and we dragged-carried him to the car and loaded him into the back seat. Ruben's dropped handgun lay in the dirt. I hesitated, flashing back to my mom's video, remembering her fate and how much I hated guns. But there was no other way to level the playing field if I wanted to survive this. I scooped it up and climbed into the car next to Marcus.

"I didn't run over him, did I?" Joy asked.

"You hit him," I said. "I think he whacked his head on a rock or something."

Joy got behind the wheel. "Let's get out of here." She fluffed her hair, put the car into gear, and sped away.

I held Marcus' head in my lap and smoothed his wet hair back. "Wake up," I said. "Don't you dare die on me."

I lowered my face to his, listening for breaths. He turned his head toward mine and kissed me before I could react.

I smacked him on the shoulder. "How long have you been awake?"

He rubbed his head, and I helped him sit up. "Long enough to know you want me."

"I do not!"

"Do too."

"Stop it," Joy said. "And tell me where to go. I have no idea where the hell we are."

"Thank you," I said. "For coming back for us."

"When I saw the Hummer chasing you, I didn't have to be psychic to know it was bad news. I got lost for a little bit, but then I came up this hill and there were those goons with a gun on Marcus. I felt like Thelma. Or Louise. I can never keep those two straight. Anyway, where am I going?"

"To see the man in charge," Marcus said. "Just go straight until you see the lights of downtown."

Chapter Forty-Two

"How's your head?" I asked Marcus as we approached the city.
"I'm a little dizzy," he admitted. "Are there two of Joy?"
God forbid.

"You probably have a concussion," Joy said. "We should take you to a hospital."

"My sister," he said softly. "She's only fifteen. And there are many others. That girl, Beyoncé, you could see how brainwashed she was. They're too terrified to turn in their pimp. I wasn't sure of his involvement, but after seeing that video… Those girls only know Diablo, not who's really running the show."

"But you know?" I said.

"Not his name, but his face, and I know where he lives. Take the 51," Marcus said. "We're going to Paradise Valley."

"We should go to the police," I said. "Let them handle it from here."

"As soon as Diablo lets the ringleader know what happened back there, they will move the girls. This whole thing started back east. There was a judge involved in the Jersey side of things. I went to the police, but they didn't believe me. I confronted him myself, it got heated. I ended up punching him in the face. All I ended up with was a felony conviction and three years of probation.

"They just keep moving the girls when it looks like they might get caught. When I was getting close, they moved them to Phoenix. I came here and tried to work my way in with the gang, thinking I could figure things out from the inside. I never made it to that level of trust. We'll never find the girls if they move them again. We don't have time for cops."

Marcus guided us down the streets of Paradise Valley. "That's the house up there." He pointed to a mansion perched on a steep part of the mountain overlooking sprawling city lights.

"Impressive," I said.

"I've only been inside once," Marcus said. "It's decorated like a palace. Too gaudy for my taste. When I saw the statue in the video, I knew I'd seen it before."

We drove up the winding mountain road and idled at a closed iron gate that prevented us from going any further.

"He has Dobermans," Marcus said. "And an alarm system."

"Do you think the girls are inside?" Joy asked.

"I doubt it," he said. "Guy like this will pull the strings, but he probably won't get dirty. I'm guessing his relationship with Diablo is he helps them out when they get in trouble with the law, and they line his pockets with money from trafficking."

"We should have stopped and called Betz," I said. "He could get a warrant and get us inside."

"We don't have time for a warrant," Marcus said. "Word has to be out that we escaped. Everyone is probably scrambling to cover their tracks. Cops climb all over this, and they will have time to do just that. Any chance of finding my sister is gone."

"And you'll probably be arrested for kidnapping me and stuff," I said.

"Yeah," Marcus said. "That too."

We sat in the Taurus and kept watch on the house. Rain slowed to a drizzle, and we started to dry out.

Marcus rested his head on my shoulder. I had to admit, I didn't mind.

"How are you feeling?" I asked.

"Okay," he said sleepily. "Just tired."

"Well, stay awake," Joy said. "If you have a concussion, sleeping is the worst thing to do."

"I'm just resting my eyes," he said.

"Well, open them," I said. "I have a plan."

"Let's get this straight," Joy said. "You're just going to ring the bell and ask to go inside?"

"Yeah."

"What if he shoots you?" she said.

"He probably doesn't know who I am. Diablo would have thought they could handle me. They wouldn't bother the big boss with someone as insignificant as me."

"So, you hope," Joy said.

"Either of you got a better idea?" I asked.

Silence told me they didn't.

"I'm going with you," Marcus said.

"But he knows you," I said.

"Not really," he said. "I was in the house once, but he barely noticed me. Diablo was there to drop off a payment. I wasn't even introduced to him."

Although I didn't like the odds that he wouldn't recognize Marcus, I also didn't like the thought of going up there alone. I leaned over the front seat and put my hand on Joy's shoulder. "I need you to find a phone and call the police. Marcus, let's go."

I got out of the car and hid Ruben's Glock in the back waistband of my shorts. Marcus slowly got out to join me. We walked toward the gate. Marcus weaved a bit. I took his arm to steady him.

"I know you want me," he said. "But you should control yourself until this is over."

"You're hilarious. You realize you're walking like a drunk?"

"That's because the house is moving."

"Maybe you should sit this one out."

"No way."

We stopped at the gate. "Okay, then. Here we go." I pressed the intercom and smiled at the video camera when the light came on.

A staticky voice greeted us. "Why, Ms. Carson, what a pleasant surprise."

My heart ticked up another notch. So much for being insignificant. A buzzer sounded, and the gate slowly parted. "He knows my name," I whispered to Marcus. And he sounded familiar, though I couldn't pinpoint

236

why.

He nodded. We started up the driveway.

"I'm armed," Marcus said. "Sure hope I can shoot straight."

I thought about the gun tucked in my shorts. Betz had taken me target shooting once, but I was far from comfortable using one. I hoped it didn't come to that.

Two Dobermans sat on either side of the front door. "Not more dogs," I said. "Why do these people all have mean dogs?"

Before we could climb the steps, the door opened, and Judge Dorfman stood in the doorway. He was dressed in his judge's robe and held a tumbler of whiskey in his hand. "Welcome," he said, ushering us inside.

Chapter Forty-Three

I stopped short and grabbed Marcus's arm. "It's Judge Dorfman."

He looked at me and squinted. "You know him?"

"Come on in," Dorfman bellowed before I could answer.

Marcus and I eased past the dogs and went inside. I glanced around the foyer, that was almost as large as my house, with marble floors and a winding staircase. The statue of the Greek god from the video sat on a pedestal. The video had been shot in this room.

Several suitcases sat by the door.

We followed Judge Dorfman through a giant arched doorway into another ornate room. Tidy bookshelves filled three walls. A giant portrait of the judge hung over a gold-plated fireplace. Hope sat on the sofa. She wore a simple black dress, her hair swept up on top of her head in an elegant bun. When she saw us, her hand shot up to a bruise on her face. She looked down then and clasped her hands in her lap.

Elation and dread cascaded through me at the same time. Hope was alive, and other than a bruise, she looked well. But what was she doing with Dorfman? "Hope," I said, taking a step toward her.

But she stopped me with a shake of her head.

"How nice of you to surrender yourselves to us," Dorfman said. "That was quite a mess you made in the desert."

"Joy's on her way to the police," I said. "You might as well tell us where Marcus' sister and the other girls are."

Dorman looked at Marcus and raised an eyebrow. "Your sister? Ah, so that explains what you're doing here. Why you turned on Diablo." He smiled

238

like he was playing a game, and we were the pieces.

Marcus looked like he wanted to rip the grin off Dorfman's face. "Until now, I didn't know your name or your connection to New Jersey. The judge in Jersey, he your buddy?"

"Ted?" Dorfman said. "We went to law school together."

"Well," Marcus said. "I had the pleasure of punching Ted in the face. I'll do worse to you."

Dorfman laughed. "That was you? You were upset because your sister joined our team. That was the story, wasn't it? But nobody believed you. You see, us judges are untouchable. I have to say, it was pretty brazen of you to try and infiltrate Diablo knowing that Ted knew who you were."

"But he didn't know I was involved with Diablo. Probably thought he was too important to get involved in the day-to-day operations. That was a mistake."

Dorfman laughed. "Could have been. If you figured things out. But you're here, and you're no closer to finding your sister, even if you were right on top of her the whole time. Doesn't look like your plan did any good at all."

Marcus slid his hand under his shirt where the gun was.

Maybe it was time for that. But I hoped we could still talk our way out of this. "Look," I said. "It's over. Tell us where the girls are, and we'll tell the police you cooperated."

"Ms. Carson," he said, lowering himself onto a chair next to the fireplace. "You have been quite a handful. Several people are very angry with you. One of them, perhaps the one most angry, happens to be standing right behind you."

The hair on the back of my neck stood up. I turned to Marcus in time to see someone step from the shadows and wrap him in a bear hug. I didn't recognize this thug and wondered why he would be most angry with me. But then Ramirez entered the room. He still wore the eye patch that probably reminded him every second of every day how much he hated me. Anger steamed off him like mist off a swamp. He flexed his hands into fists several times as he came toward me.

"No," Hope said.

But everyone ignored her.

I tried to duck my way out of Ramirez's advance, but I was backed into a corner and had nowhere to go. Before I could get my hand on my gun, he grabbed me by the arm and pulled me against him. Marcus struggled with his guardian, but I knew that with his head injury and the fact that the goon was twice his size, it wasn't a fair fight. He wouldn't be able to help me. He also had a gun, but the way his arms were pinned to his sides, he wouldn't be able to reach it.

We were both screwed.

Ramirez tightened his grip and dragged me from the room. Hope stood up and followed us, pleading with Ramirez to let me go. "Please, don't hurt her," she cried.

But Ramirez didn't stop. "I'm gonna kill you this time, Bitch." His breath was hot in my ear.

I kicked wildly as he pulled me from the room and into the foyer. Hope followed, beating on Ramirez's back with her fists. He let go of me with one hand and backhanded her, sending her to the floor.

I took advantage of his lightened hold to twist out of his grip while slamming my foot into his instep. He managed to keep hold of me, and we toppled over, taking the pedestal with the Greek god with us. It crashed down onto the marble floor, and the head rolled across the floor. The gun slipped out of my waistband and skidded across the tile, coming to rest behind a potted plant. While Ramirez got on all fours, I crawled out of his reach and scooped up the head. With a two-handed grip, I smashed it into the back of Ramirez's skull as he struggled to his feet. He lost his balance but didn't go all the way down, so I did it again and again until he resisted no more.

I was in such a rage, had such tunnel vision, it was as if me and Ramirez were the only two people in the world. But then I started to be aware of my surroundings, of my own ragged breath, of the blood on my hands. Of Hope whimpering in the corner.

I straightened and dropped the head to the floor. It rolled toward the door, the nose stopping it like a kickstand.

Hope slowly got to her feet and took the few steps between us. "Casey," she said, and she pulled me into a crushing hug.

Dorfman stood in the doorway, clapping. "Bravo. You conquered the beast once more. It will actually be a shame to kill you; you are so resourceful. But I'm afraid we're running out of time."

I pulled away from Hope. Dorfman took his drink off the table and took a sip. The thug had Marcus on his knees with his hands clasped on top of his head and a gun pointed at the top of his skull. I couldn't read the look on Marcus' face. Acceptance? No, it couldn't end this way.

"There's no way out of this," I said to Dorfman. "You can't explain away a bunch of dead bodies."

He laughed. "You sound like your mother."

A switch flipped. I dove for the gun I'd lost in the struggle with Ramirez, lifted it up, and twirled about on my knees, so I was facing the judge, the gun aimed at his chest. "My mother found out about you taking bribes," I said. "She was about to turn you over to the feds."

"Then you know what happens to people when they try to cross me," he said.

"You killed my mother?"

Dorfman shook his head. "Me? No, it wasn't me. I didn't have to."

I took a step closer, keeping the gun pointed at his chest.

"You won't shoot me," he said. "You don't have the guts."

My finger found the trigger. "Who then? Who killed my mom? Did you have one of your goons do it for you?"

Dorfman looked to the gangster who held Marcus for help, but he seemed unsure of what to do next.

I aimed at the portrait Dorfman stood next to and fired off a round, narrowly missing the judge, but hitting his likeness in the middle of the forehead. My accuracy surprised me and filled me with an ounce of confidence. "I'm counting to three," I said. "That was one."

Dorman's arrogant smile melted off his face. "Do something," he said to the man holding Marcus at gunpoint.

The man yanked Marcus to his feet and pushed him away while turning his gun on Hope. "Shoot the judge, and I kill your cousin."

"Go ahead," Hope said. "I've got nothing to live for anymore. You took it all away from me. And I certainly don't want to go away with you," she spat at the judge. "I die inside every time you touch me since I figured out that you were involved in my aunt's death."

"Peterson took that on himself," Dorfman said. "He's the one who found out she was investigating us. He's the one who walked into her office and then covered it up to make it look like a suicide."

"But he did it to protect you," Hope said. "Because you told him to do whatever it took."

Adrenaline kept me upright, but inside, I felt myself shutting down. Matthew Peterson killed my mother. Tears splashed down my face, and I readjusted my grip on the gun. "Did she suffer?" I asked.

Dorfman shrugged. "Put down the gun, Ms. Carson, or as much as I loved her, your cousin will die."

Out of the corner of my eye, I watched Marcus reach back and pull his gun out, aim it at the thug, and pull the trigger. The bullet pierced him in the arm, and he slouched back against the wall. I rushed forward and tackled him, and with Marcus' help, we wrestled the gun from his hands. My handcuffs were still in my back pocket. I reached for them and managed to get his enormous arms behind his back and close enough together that I could snap the cuffs in place.

Out of breath, I leaned back on my haunches and met Marcus' eyes.

He staggered to his feet, then turned the gun on the judge. "My sister," he said. "Where is she?"

Before Dorfman could answer, the dogs barked, and the front door banged open. I turned to see Betz and a bunch of uniforms in the doorway. They all had guns drawn.

Marcus ignored them. "Where?" he demanded.

Dorfman gave a nervous laugh. "You won't dare shoot me. Not in front of all these police officers."

"Put the gun down," Betz ordered.

Marcus glanced over his shoulder at the cops with their weapons aimed at him. But they couldn't get a clear shot with Hope and me in the way.

"I'm aiming for your head," Marcus said, turning his attention back to Dorfman. "But I'm a little dizzy. This could take a while. I might hit you in the chest or the arm. You can bleed to death nice and slow."

Hope came closer and took my hand, our bodies shielding Marcus.

I knew if the police could get a clear shot at Marcus, they'd take it. "No!" I yelled. I lowered my gun to the floor while Hope and I stayed put. "Wait."

"Put the gun down, Marcus," Betz ordered. "We'll take over now."

Marcus ignored Betz, cocked his head to the side, and looked at Dorfman. "Tell me where my sister is, or I shoot."

Dorfman paled. "That would be stupid. The officers will shoot you."

Marcus shrugged. "You think I give a shit?"

Betz motioned for me to get out of the way, but I ignored him. No way would I give the police a clear shot at Marcus. I could talk him down.

"This is ridiculous," Dorfman said. He looked past Marcus at the police. "Officers, these people pushed their way into my home. They were trying to rob me. Do something."

"Save it, Dorfman," Betz said. "We know all about the human trafficking ring and your partnership with Diablo."

"Talk," Marcus said.

"Drop the gun, Marcus," Betz repeated.

"I'm not talking without my lawyer," Dorfman said.

"Casey, get the hell out of the way," Betz said.

"Let the police handle it," I said to Marcus, but he ignored me.

"The girls," Marcus said.

"Jesus," Dorfman said. "Officers, you can't let him shoot me. I order you to do something."

"Last chance," Marcus said.

Dorfman's eyes grew wide, and the front of his pants went wet as he peed himself.

"Wait!" Hope cleared her throat. "There's a house they've been using tucked back in South Mountain. I don't know the address, but I know it's way out there. There's a false wall in the basement. Most of the girls are there."

Marcus lowered the gun, and three officers rushed him, taking him to the ground. Two others approached Dorfman. Betz rushed to me, and I dissolved in his arms as I watched Ramirez come to under the watchful eye of the police.

Chapter Forty-Four

After I told Betz Dorfman said Peterson had killed my mother, he immediately issued an APB for him. But last I'd seen him, he'd been with Diablo, and I had a feeling that tracking him down would not be easy.

With the manhunt for Peterson underway, we switched our attention to the kidnapped girls. I had promised Marcus we would find them before the police took him away.

Since I was the only person not in custody who had been to the house in the desert and had the best chance of finding it quickly, Betz let me come along. "What do you think is going to happen to Marcus?" I asked as we approached South Phoenix in the Tahoe. "He was only trying to save his sister."

"I figured that out when I received his presentence report from his PO this afternoon," Betz said. "He's got a lot of things to clear up. Probation violation, kidnapping, and use of a firearm as a prohibited possessor, to name a few. His fate is in the County Attorney's hands now."

"It doesn't seem fair."

Betz raised an eyebrow. "Seriously, after what he did to you, you care what happens to this guy?"

I wasn't ready to go there. "Speaking of my cousins, I guess Joy got a hold of you?"

"She did. She flagged down a patrol officer in town and asked him to call me. I insisted she go to the hospital and get checked out. I hear she's already hitting on the male nurses, so I'd say she's fine."

"And Hope?"

"She's on her way to the station to be questioned. Not sure she's going to be able to escape some sort of charge, maybe aiding and abetting, at least. Seems she profited from the gang's dealings. It will be interesting to hear her story."

"I hope Marcus' sister and the others are at the house, but I sure didn't see any sign of them when I was there. But I never went into the basement. If we find them, I hope they're physically okay. Psychologically, I'd say it's going to take a while."

Betz adjusted his hands on the steering wheel. "Let's find them first."

Twenty minutes later, we passed my Jeep. It was smashed up, and the word bitch was written in yellow spray paint across the side. I guessed Diablo took out some of their frustration on my poor little Wrangler. A not-so-gentle reminder that some of them were still out there, and I now had enemies who would probably stalk me for the rest of my life.

A wave of panic grabbed me. I tried to shake it off and pulled at the neck of the body armor Betz had loaned me. It was suddenly hard to breathe.

"The Jeep can be fixed." Betz reached over and gave my knee a squeeze.

We rolled to a stop at the end of the long driveway, where Rambo waited for us. "This is it," I said.

Betz parked and waited for the SWAT SUV and six patrol vehicles to catch up to us. "Does the dog bite?" Betz asked.

"If Diablo told him to, he might. What happened to the guys Marcus and I encountered at the top of the mountain?"

"Both alive," Betz said. "After Joy told us what happened, some deputies responded to the area and found Ruben Young wedged between a Saguaro cactus and a boulder at the bottom of a cliff. He'll be picking needles out of his ass for the next few days, but the plant broke his fall. His buddy is in traction, but he'll survive. They are looking at some serious prison time, though."

"Just don't let them near Marcus."

"Don't worry. I already alerted the jail to keep everyone away from Marcus. We really need to have a serious talk about this guy, don't we, Case?"

"There's nothing to talk about."

"Liar."

The last unit arrived, and I undid my seatbelt and got out of the car. Betz did the same.

Our conversation made me forget about Rambo until I saw him bounding toward me, and he knocked me to the ground. I was about to scream when his giant tongue licked my face.

"This is the big mean dog you warned us about?" one of the SWAT guys said.

I wiped dog drool off my cheek and took Betz's hand as he pulled me to my feet. Another officer took control of Rambo. "Nice puppy."

SWAT guys crept up the driveway, guns drawn with patrol behind them, and me and Betz brought up the rear. SWAT entered the house first, making sure there were no Diablo holdouts lurking about.

When we received the *all-clear*, I followed Betz into the basement. The electricity was off, but each cop had a flashlight, and we could see just fine. "Start looking for a false wall," Betz said.

We each took a different section. I put my hands against the concrete, thinking I had just been here, just above the missing girls, and I never had a clue.

"Think I found something," Betz said.

We all waited, holding a giant collective breath as Betz pushed on the wall and slid it to the side. He stepped through the opening and shone his flashlight into the space. I stepped in behind him. Six girls sat on uncovered mattresses. They were dirty and disheveled. All of them shielded their eyes from the flashlight beam and scooted against the walls like beaten dogs.

"It's okay," Betz said, crouching down to their level. "You're all going home."

I looked at the girls, studied each exhausted face. "Marcus's sister," I said. "She's not here."

"He took her," one of the girls said.

"Who?" Betz asked.

"That lawyer," the girl said. "He took her out of here about twenty minutes before you arrived."

Chapter Forty-Five

I sat in the front seat of the patrol car with a uniformed officer. Betz had asked her to take me to the station while he and most of the precinct went on a manhunt for Peterson. There was already an APB out, so he only had to update it, adding that he had a hostage. I'd never been so tense. The man who killed my mother was on the loose, and he had Courtney Sheldon. He was desperate. Not only was I worried he'd get away, but I worried for Courtney's safety. For his mental health, it was best that they had Marcus in custody, and he didn't know what was happening.

The storm had kicked up, grounding any helicopters that could have aided in the search.

The cop who drove me concentrated on driving on the flooding country road and didn't talk much. Grateful to have a few moments of peace and quiet, I put my head back and closed my eyes.

I heard the officer scream before I felt the impact. Something massive slammed into the driver's side of the car and sent the vehicle reeling sideways about twenty feet. I braced for impact, slamming my feet into the floorboard, my forearm braced against the passenger door, as the car smashed into a bolder, putting us at a dead stop.

The car shook as the mountain beside us crumbled, rocks and debris rushing over us. A branch smacked my window. The glass strained, then popped, and mud poured into the car. We both shrieked, and I squeezed my eyes shut, thinking we were going to be rushed away in a river of debris.

But then everything stopped. The only sound, rain bouncing off the roof.

I unbuckled my seatbelt and checked the officer. Blood poured from a cut on her forehead. I reached into the glove compartment to find something to press against her wound. "Are you okay?"

"He came out of nowhere," she said, eyes huge and full of panic. "I'm stuck. I can't move my legs."

Her side of the car had crumpled, trapping her.

I was about to grab the radio to call for help when another scream sounded.

"The other car," the officer said. "Go check on them. I'll call this in."

Passing her the mike, I pushed some of the mud that had landed on me to the floor and tried to open my door, but it wouldn't budge. We were pinned against the mountain.

Only one way out. The windshield. But shards of glass made it too dangerous.

I searched the car for something to clear it. The cop's clipboard. Maybe. Using it like a chisel, I broke the glass and chipped away at the remaining pieces. Satisfied I wouldn't sacrifice any more skin, I managed to get up into the window frame and hoisted myself onto the hood of the car. Rain continued to pummel the earth, but I took a minute to catch my breath and then hopped down. The mud was so thick around the car, the moment I hit the ground, my feet went out from under me, and I slid feet first down an embankment.

Between the dark and the pouring rain, I could barely make out the two headlights of the other car about ten feet away from me. They were pointed toward the sky, which couldn't be good.

I stumbled over to the front end, losing my balance several times in the muck. I was practically on top of it when I realized it was backward on the hill and had no traction in the sludge. Behind it was a sudden drop-off. It was hard to make out the bottom in the dark, but it looked to be about fifty feet down. If the car fell, the occupants would not survive the impact.

The terrain was too uneven and steep to walk up, so I got on my hands and knees and crawled to the passenger window. Once I got close enough, I could make out two people in the front seat. But the windows were fogged up, and I couldn't see faces.

The passenger window started moving. The movement made the car slide back a little. Another scream.

"Don't move," I said.

As the window inched down, the occupants came into view. First Courtney Sheldon. Before I even saw him, I knew Matthew Peterson would be in the driver's seat.

"Shit."

"Help me," Courtney said.

"Stay still," I told her. "The car is on a steep incline. If you move too much, it may fall."

Panic colored her face. Peterson seemed groggy. He lulled his head to the side and looked at me. "Maybe this is the way it's supposed to end."

I ignored him. "We've called for help, Courtney. Just hold on."

She nodded, but the tears streaming down her cheek told me how scared she was.

Mud from the hill snaked toward us, and the car slipped back another foot.

Courtney couldn't hold back her sobs now. We were running out of time. "Listen to me," I said. "I'm going to pull the door open, and you're going to jump toward me. Unbuckle your seatbelt."

She carefully did as she was told.

"You won't have time to think," I said. "You'll just have to jump and do it fast. Can you do that?"

She nodded.

"What about me?" Peterson asked. "I can't get my door open."

I ignored him and locked eyes with Courtney. "On three."

I reached forward and grasped the door handle. "One... Two... Three."

I yanked the door open, and she tumbled out beside me. The car moved back a few more inches, rocking as the weight of the vehicle settled on the edge.

"Help me," Peterson called.

I turned to Courtney. "Can you make it to the patrol car? Find out how soon police will be here and see if there's some rope."

Courtney nodded and scampered up the hill.

I moved down toward the open passenger door and looked at the man who had killed my mother. Bile climbed up my throat. "Tell me about my mother's death." The way the hill sloped, another slide would surely put the car over the cliff.

"It was Dorfman..." he said, his breaths coming in short bursts. "Get me out of here."

"But you're the one who pulled the trigger, aren't you?"

"I didn't," he said.

I pushed soaked hair out of my face. I didn't know what to believe. It could have been Dorfman. But no matter, they could both go to hell. "I'm not helping you unless you tell me the truth."

He sighed and inched across the seat toward the open door. The car rocked. He froze.

Courtney returned with a rope and handed it to me. "The police are having trouble getting through... Road's washed out, but they're on their way."

"Toss me the rope," Peterson said.

"The truth," I said.

The car teetered, then settled back in place. Peterson let out a long breath. "I had no choice. She was closing in on us."

Tears stung my eyes. "So, you shot her?"

He put his head back against the seat and closed his eyes. "She left me no choice."

I gulped air. "Did she suffer?"

"No," he said. "It was quick. She had headphones on and didn't hear me coming."

My anger was so intense, I couldn't see straight. It would be so easy. One push, a little shove, really, and the car would slide over the hill, and Peterson would meet his rightful fate. I stood and got close enough to lean against the car. "No!" Peterson yelled. "Please, I don't want to die."

"Neither did my mother. Neither did her boss." It was so easy. All I had to do was apply a little pressure, and I'd have revenge. I had all the power. But it didn't feel good. I didn't want to be what he was.

"Why did you call me to your office? What were you going to tell me?"

"The truth. I didn't want more blood on my hands. Now throw the rope. Please!"

The car wobbled again, and Peterson's eyes widened.

"Then why take Courtney?" I asked. "And if I even think you're lying, I will push the car over the edge."

"Okay, okay. I never meant to hurt her. And I tried to warn you to watch your back."

"You sent me the text message?" I asked.

Peterson nodded.

"But you weren't trying to help me when you asked me to come to your office."

He was blubbering now, and it was difficult to understand him. "Diablo wanted me to trick you into coming. We didn't think you knew I was involved, so we thought you'd come. But when you didn't get to my office fast enough, they thought I'd played them, and they took me to the desert house. Then they got so busy chasing after you, I managed to sneak away. I grabbed one of the girls in case I needed to negotiate. You would have done the same thing if you were in my shoes."

"You're a disgusting excuse for a human being. You will rot in prison. But I won't stoop to your level." I threw him the rope and yanked him to the ground beside me just before the car tipped over the edge.

Police and firefighters emerged over the ridge as Peterson lay in the mud. When I was sure they saw him, I walked away. Justice would have to take care of him. I couldn't be the one to deal him his fate.

Chapter Forty-Six

I stood on the beach in Coronado, waves lapping at my feet. A tear landed on the heavy box containing my mother's ashes I clutched to my chest. Coronado was my mother's favorite place. Throughout my childhood, we'd vacationed in the sleepy beachside town every summer. We all agreed it was a fitting place to lay her to rest.

I turned back and joined my father, my sister, and her family, and together, we walked to the pier, where a boat waited for us. My father rubbed my back on the way.

The captain helped us board the small vessel and we silently took the ride out to sea. When we came to an idle, we stood and walked to the bow of the boat, where we could see San Diego in the distance.

Kevin cleared his throat. "Kate and I had only been dating about six months when your mom invited me to come along on one of your vacations here. She asked me to join her for a walk. She wanted to make sure I was good enough for her daughter. I was honored to have passed the test."

My sister dabbed her eyes with a handkerchief. "She used to build elaborate sandcastles with our kids. She was the coolest grandma. It was her suggestion we get married on this beach. It was a perfect day, even if it did rain. She chased my veil down the beach when a gust of wind took it."

"I still don't know what she saw in me," our father said. "But I never doubted her love."

I opened the box and let her ashes fly. They carried in the wind, then settled in the sea. "We finished the work you started," I said. "You're free, Mom."

Chapter Forty-Seven

J oy and I sat at a visitor's table at the Estrella jail and watched as the door clanged open and Hope emerged wearing black and white jail stripes.

She slid onto the bench and faced us. Although it had only been a week since I saw her at Dorfman's, she looked like she'd lost weight. The bruise under her eye had faded, but the haunted look in her eyes had intensified.

"How you holding up?" Joy asked.

Hope shrugged frail shoulders. "They have me in a cell by myself. The other inmates don't take it well that I'm a PO."

It was only a matter of time before she lost that status. She was on administrative leave for now, but once she was convicted, she'd have to turn in her badge. My admin leave had thankfully been resolved, and I was scheduled to return to work the following day.

"How did you get mixed up in this mess?" Joy asked.

I held up my hand to stop Hope from answering. "Be careful what you say. We could be called to testify."

But Hope ignored me. "Why do we all do stupid things? I thought I was in love."

"With Dorfman?" I tried not to sound judgmental.

She nodded. "It started when I was supervising Harlan Jones. Dorfman called me to his chambers and asked me to drop a petition I'd filed to revoke Jones' probation. I thought it was strange, but he gave me some bullshit story and asked me to lunch. Soon, we were having dinner together. He started showering me with gifts. Helped me with a down payment for a house.

"A few months later, your mother asked me to meet her. She swore me to secrecy, then told me she'd been surveilling Dorfman. Told me he was corrupt. He was taking bribes from Diablo in exchange for getting the gang members out of any legal trouble. She had a video of him but said it wasn't enough since you couldn't see his face. She told me about the thumb drive she'd hidden in a false compartment in her briefcase with the information she'd gathered thus far. I was supposed to help her get a better tape. She thought my cooperation would absolve me of any trouble I might be in for financially benefiting from Dorfman's business, even if I had no idea what he was doing. But when Aunt Carissa died, I was too afraid to go through with it. I was sure they were behind her death. Suicide was just too big a coincidence.

"I wanted to tell you, Casey. Or go to the police, but the more I learned about Diablo, the more afraid I became. I just found out about the human trafficking part. I realized it was more than the judge just doing Diablo favors and that the girls were at risk. I could no longer sit on the sidelines.

"I spent some time with your father. He would usually fall asleep in his recliner, and I would sneak a look through your mom's stuff. When I found the briefcase, I took it home. The thumb drive was where she said it would be. I held onto it.

"I decided to bring you into the loop, Casey, thinking you could help me bring the matter to the police. Unfortunately, I also trusted Matthew Peterson. He seemed to be struggling with his involvement in the whole business, and I thought he felt like I did. But he told them I sent you the thumb drive. At that point, I still had no idea he was your mother's killer."

"He killed her supervisor, too," I said.

Hope hung her head. "He seemed like a decent guy, but I guess I'm not a very good judge of character. Anyway, once Diablo found out I planned to go to the police, they ambushed me when I was doing a home visit on Harlan Jones. They shot Jones with my gun because they didn't trust him to keep his mouth shut, and they've kept me captive ever since."

"What about Melissa King?" I asked.

"I was desperate. I slipped her the passcode to the thumb drive and asked her to deliver it to you."

"Except she never told me about it. I stumbled upon your business card and only later put it together," I said. "How come Melissa could run free, yet some of the girls were kept in the basement?"

Hope wrung her hands. "They were in different stages. The ones they had for a while, like Melissa, had been brainwashed to obey them. They were too scared to turn on their pimps. Too afraid Diablo would go after their family, and they were terrified of being returned to the basement. The other girls were tested out slowly, given more and more freedom as they proved their loyalty. They really messed with those girls' heads."

"And Joel Quinn?" I asked.

"He owed a debt to Diablo. They forced him to work on the website. I guess he either had a conscience, or he couldn't face going to jail." Tears welled in her eyes, and she wiped at them with the back of her hand. "I sometimes wish I could have taken the same way out."

Joy reached forward and patted her hand. "Honey, this is just a test. You never know what strength you have until you are faced with adversity. I never thought I could defend myself. But between Casey and me, we took down four Diablo gang members. I ran two down, and she stabbed two, one in the eye and one in the leg. Us Carson women are strong."

Hope nodded.

"And we wouldn't have figured out any of this if you hadn't reached out to Casey. Those girls are free because of you. The judge is bound to see that your intentions were good." Joy said.

And I hoped she was psychic after all.

Epilogue

The early morning sun had just broken the horizon when Betz pulled his Tahoe into the body shop parking lot and put it into park. "You want me to wait?"

"Naw. The Jeep's all fixed, and my insurance covered most of the repairs. I just have to put my deductible on my Visa and give up eating for a few months so I can pay it off."

I unbuckled my seatbelt and opened the door. "Thanks for the ride."

Betz put his hand on my arm. "You okay, Case?"

"Sure."

"Okay, then. See you around."

I got out of the Tahoe and was almost to the door when I felt a hand on my shoulder. "Wait."

I turned around and Betz pulled me into his arms. "I'm so happy you survived this. I know how close I came to losing you."

I looked at the sky so I wouldn't cry. "You were very helpful."

"Just doing my job."

"Oh." I took a step back.

Betz rubbed the back of his neck and looked at the ground. "No, that's not true. I don't know why I said that. I'm not sure what this relationship we have is, but I worry about you all the time, Case. I still care about you."

Jasmine's words rang in my ears. Was she right? Could we never be more than friends again? I had to admit, even if it was only to myself, I had no answer to that question. Betz seemed to be waiting for me to say something, but I took the chicken-shit way out. "Don't worry about me. My private eye days are over. From now on, it's work, nine to five. Otherwise, I'm sitting my butt on the couch watching TV. I'm going to become a regular couch potato. I'm going to be so lazy; I'll get fat, and hair will grow out of my chin."

Betz laughed. "You really know how to ruin a moment."

I laughed, too. "Just trying to lighten things up. You've been there for me, and I appreciate it. I hope we can keep this friendship...or whatever it is...going."

Betz turned back to his car. "I don't see any way out of it."

I waved and watched until he was out of sight. The looking at the sky thing no longer worked. I wiped my eyes with the back of my hand and went inside.

Jeep like new, I pulled into the parking lot of the Lower Buckeye Jail just before eight. Since it was so early, there were still plenty of spots. I parked in the first one I found and sat for a minute. Betz's words, or his lack of them, sat heavy in my heart. He still cared about me. I couldn't deny there was something there for me as well. Did I even need to see Marcus? But the pull was stronger than reason.

I hurried through the lot to the jail entrance. I was almost to the door where they released prisoners but stopped when I saw Courtney Sheldon and a woman who must have been her mother waiting by the door.

Courtney barely resembled the dirty, scared girl I'd seen in the desert. The resemblance between her and her brother was much more striking now. She was a looker. But she held a sadness in her eyes that was noticeable even from a distance.

I hung back and leaned against the wall.

After a few minutes, the door bounced open, and Marcus walked out. He was dressed in the same jeans and t-shirt I'd last seen him wearing. His shirt was wrinkled, and he had a black eye, but I'd never seen him look better. I held my breath as he walked out, grinning as he pulled his sister into a long embrace. His love for her was like a bright light; I had to look away. When I looked back, his mother had joined the huddle.

Not wanting to intrude, I turned and started back to the parking lot.

At the sound of footsteps, I looked over my shoulder. Marcus jogged up behind me. "Casey."

I turned just in time to be caught in his arms.

"I didn't want to get in the way," I said.

Marcus held me by the shoulders and looked at me squarely; his grin touched his eyes. "You've gotten in the way since the day we met. I wouldn't have it any other way."

A blush burned my face. Damn it, why did he get to me like this? "I just wanted to make sure you were okay."

"I'll show you how okay I am." And he plunged into an all-out kiss.

I lost my breath, then pulled away. "Your family is watching."

"Let them watch."

I dodged his second kiss. "Are you going back to New Jersey?"

He glanced toward his mom and sister and nodded. "That's my ride. I have to deal with my probation. Since the judge I assaulted was Dorfman's partner, and he's been busted for the Jersey end of the trafficking business, my lawyer says they'll dismiss the charges."

"And you won't be a felon anymore."

Marcus smiled. "Since you don't date felons, it's important I clear that up."

"Long distance relationships never work."

"Oh, it won't be long distance. I'm coming back." He kissed me again, and I didn't stop him. This one was so slow, it made my toes curl.

Now that complicated things.

Acknowledgements

I started writing about Casey Carson many, many years ago. But life—a career in law enforcement and raising a daughter—got in the way. Only the name of the protagonist and her profession remain in this version.

There are many who encouraged me and offered critiques and advice on my journey to publication. First off, I'd like to thank my initial writer's group, who saw an early version of this book and helped me nurse my love of writing: Val Neiman, Wanda McLaughlin, Gary Ponzo, Debra White, and Judy Pearson. When that group disbanded, I found other writers whose encouragement has kept me going: the folks at Inked Voices, Daphene Brown, Charlotte Gruber, typo ninja Lucinda Reed, Mary Keliikoa, and Dawn Ius. Good friends Deneen Bertucci and Jennifer Vaughan and my aunt, Carole Willson, have also cheered me on, reading the book before it found a home with Level Best Books.

Special thanks to Harriette Sackler, who believed in this book and signed me with Level Best Books, and to Verena Rose and Shawn Reilly Simmons for helping me elevate it to its best version.

Without the support of my husband, Paul Hummel, my daughter, Brittany Goyette, my son-in-law, Michael Verdun, and my mother, Beverly Schmidt, I never would have seen Casey's adventures in print. You have always had faith in me, even when I didn't have it in myself. I love you all. Thank you for riding this wild wave with me.

About the Author

Cindy Goyette is a former probation officer who had a front-row seat to the somewhat shady side of life. She kept her sanity by finding humor in most situations. A mix of these things helped her create The Probation Case Files Mystery Series. After spending over twenty years in Arizona, Cindy lives in Washington state with her husband and two Cocker Spaniels.

SOCIAL MEDIA HANDLES:
    twitter @cindy_ccgoyette
    Facebook (Cindy Goyette)

AUTHOR WEBSITE:
    ccgoyette.com

Printed in the USA
CPSIA information can be obtained
at www.ICGtesting.com
LVHW040026080424
776712LV00025B/192